The
Butterfly Dreams

The
Butterfly Dreams

Peter Kline & Syril Kline

GREAT OCEAN PUBLISHERS
ARLINGTON, VIRGINIA

Book and cover design by M.M. Esterman
Cover painting: Margaret Park

Cover background image: Galaxy M100, photographed by the
Hubble Space Telescope. This image was created with support to
Space Telescope Science Institute, operated by the Association of
Universities for Research in Astronomy, Inc., from NASA contract
NAS5-26555, and is reproduced with permission from
AURA/STScI.

For further information contact:

> Great Ocean Publishers
> 1823 North Lincoln Street
> Arlington, VA 22207-3746

First Printing

Library of Congress Cataloging-in-Publication Data
Kline,Peter, 1936-
 The butterfly dreams / Peter Kline & Syril Kline.

 Includes bibliographical references (p.).
 ISBN 0-915556-33-2 (pbk. : alk. paper)
 I. Kline, Syril, 1953- . II. Title.
PS3561.L485B8 1998 813'.54--dc21   98-24098

To my father, Irvin Levin, physicist and cantor,
who on long walks taught me that scientific wisdom
commences with awed wonder at God's creations.

ða

To Hunter Pope Mulford, a dedicated educator,
who influenced me by his examples of dedication,
endurance and total commitment to his students.

PART ONE

I dreamed I was a butterfly. Now that I am awake I wonder, am I a man who dreamed he was a butterfly, or am I butterfly dreaming that I am a man?

— Lao Tsu

Disturbance in the Night

The same dream has haunted me for weeks now. Its simple absurdity reels me into a world of frustration I'd give anything to avoid. It has something to do with my work, but it's more than that too because my feelings in the dream are too intense. With devastating frequency, the dream forces me to take a look into an alien, brutal world.

And honestly, I don't care for what I see.

≥

In the dream, I wander through some sort of prison, most likely a mental institution, a warehouse for those considered useless by society. Bodies lie on the floor trampled by others who blindly step on them, impervious to the pain they cause. I struggle to keep my balance, feeling my way along walls of impersonal gray cinder block, stone cold, dark and uncaring.

I carefully avoid stepping on the unfortunate bodies, but they move underfoot as if they feel compelled to be mauled, as if it's their duty to take my abuse. Why do they ask for this agony? No matter. The important thing is for me to stay on my feet and keep my balance, not to stumble and fall and become one of them.

As I wander the halls I look into the cells, peering into the vacant eyes of the caged incumbents. Each step draws me deeper into this maze of human misery and hopelessness.

I do not know these people.

They have no names. They mean nothing to me.

Yet someone cries out to me in muted fear and I must go to her. I'm unsure which way to turn and wonder whether a ghostly phantom or divine revelation awaits me when I find her.

Suddenly I'm in a different place, carried off and stranded on the shore of another dream. I stand in a large sterile laboratory belonging to Cellutron, Inc., a corporation where I'm negotiating to do some consulting work. White-coated scientists examine brightly colored images of DNA enlarged by their micro-computers. The lab looks more like an art gallery than a research center. Avenues of computer monitors dominate the room. The soft conversations of the researchers, syncopated at first, merge into one rhythmic incantation and there is a palpable force behind the work that I don't understand. When I ask what's going on, the scientists don't answer. One of them turns to face me and motions for me to follow.

Almost instantly, a woman appears at my side, pleading with me to stop the research. Confused but determined, I argue that it doesn't make sense to put an end to technology. Societies build what they value. This is who we are.

As we speak, the chanting from the scientists becomes louder. Still the woman persists in her pleading. Her face is a mask of sad urgency. The chanting grows so loud I can no longer make out her words. She speaks, but I can't hear her.

ð

I usually awaken from the dream at about three in the morning, feeling like I've been dragged by a dull gray cord from the farthest reaches of unconsciousness. It leaves me with a strange sensation I don't care for, any more than I like the warm milk I could drink, if I chose to, to get myself back to sleep. I'd gladly make that sacrifice though, if it weren't for the dream. But I'm firmly awake, always at the same hour when I'm most able to be in tune with myself. I climb from bed and take my musings to my computer.

My computer and I are constant traveling companions these days. It's better than a secretary because you don't have to entertain it with gossip and tedious chitchat or take it out to lunch. It's a lot less expensive, except for some occasional downtime, but that's easy to fix.

People are much harder — inscrutable really. Who can you trust these days? But machines are pretty reliable. My computer does what I tell it to do, so our relationship is cool, not the way it usually is with a flesh and blood person.

This morning seems different. A siren pierces the distance with a faint sense of mystery, marking a disturbance in some far-away place. Curiosity overtakes me and I'm compelled to attend to this jarring but now diminishing sound. As I look out the window I feel an unaccountable quiet that makes it difficult to focus on the tasks which lie ahead for me today.

On some level I suppose I welcome these nocturnal interruptions. In the daylight I don't have much chance to think anymore. Everyone I know is caught up in the same futility. It's called work. It pays the mortgage. I'm just another urban warrior in a highly technological clan of hunters and gatherers. We're all rushing to keep up. We thought we were advancing, but truth be known, none of us are. We're backsliding — waterbugs caught in a bathtub struggling against the whirlpool that's dragging us inexorably down the drain.

ક

Something strange is going on outside my window.

I see a flashing light, perhaps from the same police car whose siren split the air a moment ago. I continue working on my journal, vaguely aware that the rotating lights aren't coming from the front of the house, which faces the road, but from the open field in back that stretches out for several acres before it disappears into a tangle of woods. At first the lights seem normal, and I'm too absorbed in my thoughts to register any irregularity out there.

The rotating beams pulsate across the ceiling like searchlights in an array of colors invading my most private thoughts, distracting me from my task, which is to lecture this intimate journal of mine on all subjects of interest to us both. I roll my shoulders and sit up straight, fighting off sleep, vowing to purchase a more ergonomic desk chair when my next check arrives.

Suddenly my eyes fix on the field below my window. I sense a chaotic activity down there, something indescribable yet alluring. Untangling myself from my journal, I go to the bathroom to empty my bladder, hoping to void myself of an encroaching awareness that those lights aren't going to disappear so soon.

With a towel wrapped around me to cover my nakedness, I come out of the bathroom and peer down into the dim remains of night. The glare of the rotating lights originates from a large circular craft settled beyond the garden, probably a helicopter, though I see no rotors and hear no engine. In the shadows near the house, strangers wander through my yard examining various objects with flashlights. They seem puzzled by the stone gargoyles who keep watch on the house.

I wonder if they're detectives at a suspected crime scene gathering evidence relating to events I know nothing about. In a moment of panic I imagine standing before a tribunal accused of some bizarre act I didn't commit. The absurdity of this dominates my thinking. Why do these strange notions drift into my head? I turn towards my computer to finish my work.

Suddenly the room spins under my feet and I feel like I'm falling.

Watchman While I Sleep

Blue light surrounds me.

Other than the nightmarish reality of absolute quiet, there's nothing upsetting here. In fact, it's so relaxing to look around that I get the half-wakeful, paradoxical feeling that what I'm experiencing ought to be idyllic. Nevertheless I'm riddled with anxiety and confusion. I force myself to know where I am. I feel a moral compunction about this — I ought to know where I am.

By all rights, my pulse should be racing but it has actually slowed down. Strange. I can't account for where this feeling of relaxation is coming from, because I'm anything but calm. What is this remarkable place? It seems to be nothing but blue light, not a physical place. Another dream?

I force myself to alertness, observing that I'm awake and lying in some sort of a room; and for a moment lucidity returns, bounded by four walls: a structure that makes sense. I've always enjoyed a well-defined sense of order. It has directed me, stood me in good stead, as Grandfather used to say.

But now my mind is reeling; order and balance have deserted me. I'm afloat in a bottomless room, involuntarily breaking all the laws of physics. I close my eyes to squeeze away the illusion, but the sensation of floating remains. The disjointed room refuses to vanish. No sense of floors joined to walls or walls supporting a ceiling, nothing to hold on to, no points of reference or navigation to guide me. A diffuse blue light emanates from no particular source, and I'm alone. A hollow sensation defines my stomach. I feel ungrounded, as if no reality contains me, no vessel holds me in place.

Instantly my body is drawn to a hard surface, as if attracted by a magnet. I lie like a cadaver supported by a stone slab pressed hard against my back, the only grounding separating me from oblivion. I feel helpless, a victim of an abduction with unfathomable motives.

Protectively I move my hands to my chest and discover that I'm fully clothed in a business suit, as if ready to head off to work. Only a short time ago I was naked except for my towel, alone in the privacy of my bedroom. I don't remember dressing or arriving at this place, wherever it is, and have no idea what time it is either. Logical questions try to drive out the chaotic discrepancies, but it's a losing battle.

ᐧᐧ

I notice the man watching me.

Standing off to my left and slightly behind me, he observes that I'm awake. He looks down at the stone slab where I'm laid out like a dead thing and I try to read his face, searching for a response and knowing that I might not like the one I receive.

Wordlessly, he reaches for my forehead with the palm of his hand as if to discern a fever. I jerk away but he persists and I give in. The warmth of his hand penetrates my skin and I feel suffusing relaxation, a deeply pleasing, wonderful safety. In the light of my circumstances, it doesn't make sense, but logic and reason have forsaken me. Oddly enough, I feel no terror at his uninvited touch, though I usually withdraw from physical contact with other men. Without knowing why, I'm at ease now. Something about this man is calming.

Strange that I've never seen a face like his before, although there is something familiar about it. His agelessly wise face is human, but real people don't look like this. Eyes, nose, mouth, all the requisite features are present, but so is something else. Kindness, sensitivity, compassion — words not frequently used in my world these days, but still, that's what's etched into this face. You see expressions like this only on saints or martyrs in old oil paintings where earthly goodness is idealized beyond believability.

Nobody I know looks like that.

He radiates a light from within, glowing with combined knowledge and mystery. His expression eases my fears and I feel connected to him in a way I don't understand.

He sits beside me on the slab. He is dressed in a loose-fitting jersey and slacks, which give him a more prosaic appearance.

"How are you feeling?" he asks.

"I'm all right, I guess." The timidity in my voice surprises me. Usually, if I'm frightened, no one can tell — I've cultivated considerable *savoir-faire* over time, schooled by years in leadership roles in front of seminar rooms. No one can penetrate my shield — until *now*, it seems.

"I'm glad you're feeling better."

"So am I. But I'm a little disoriented."

"It's no wonder. But don't worry, everything will be all right. Can I get you anything?"

"Yes. An explanation for all of this."

He smiles at my insistence on reason as if to dismiss it as superfluous.

After what seems like a great deal of time, he replies.

"Rest a while. There's plenty of time for explanations, I assure you."

He speaks formally, clearly enunciating words like an accomplished actor with cultivated rich tones. It's English spoken as an intoned art form, light years away from street talk.

"You're Noah Gershom, aren't you?" he asks.

"Yes, I am."

"Interesting last name. Gershom. It means stranger in a strange land, from the Hebrew — *ger shom*."

"I didn't know it had a meaning."

"Everything has a meaning. That shouldn't surprise you, with a name like Noah."

I struggle to understand what he's driving at, perhaps because I'm still dazed by all of this. I can't seem to activate my body to sit or stand or move. I hope I'm not in some sort of instant replay of Noah's Biblical dilemma, sailing against a tidal wave of impending doom. That's a far cry from anything I've ever encountered, even in some of the larger corporate disasters I've had to rescue people from.

"I understand you're a corporate consultant."

"Yes. I work with a number of different companies. I help people adjust to the chaos in their lives."

"There must be a great deal of it."

"Work? Yes. I do very nicely."

"No, I mean chaos. Your people revel in it."

"Well, things aren't as predictable as they used to be. My job is to reconcile people with the inevitable, to make them feel better about the bad things that are happening to them. Get them over their need for security, predictability, a one-way career path."

"Sounds like we're in the same line of work," he smiles.

"How so?"

"I counsel people through great, earth-shattering changes, much as you do. I inspire them to have faith in themselves."

Somehow it doesn't seem like the same thing at all.

"What do you call yourself? I mean, what do you do?" I ask. He thinks this over and smiles.

"Oh! You want to know the name of my job. I'm a prophet."

Well, no one can say that I'm a model of good behavior, or a great visionary or wise prophet or anything like that. I'm just a guy with a certain amount of influence, that's how I think of myself, sort of okay in my own time. I glance skeptically in the man's direction, eyes narrowed, but my expression doesn't appear to move him. I sharpen my inquiry, making it more specific.

"So? What is your name? What do I call you?"

"My name is Isaiah."

I look at him in disbelief.

"Not the real Isaiah!" I'm not sure why I've blurted out such an idiotic remark. After all, even basketball players are named Isaiah. It's a good name, not reserved only for prophets.

"Actually, not yet, but I'm working on it. Prophets aren't born to the task. They're shaped by the world they live in and the need to alert people to disaster. Humanity is still a work in progress."

"Most of the people I know think it's finished."

"Cynicism doesn't make my job any easier."

Despite this remark, he seems unperturbed by my sarcasm, perhaps because he wishes to distance himself from it. Still, there's sincerity in his voice, and I can usually spot that kind of thing right away. You don't hear it much these days, so it stands out when you do. I feel an intense liking for Isaiah, grateful to be in his presence. People don't usually have that effect on me. He has the charismatic quality of Destiny's Chosen, those people singled out by divine providence, pure chance or motivation, to play important roles in human events. I remember reading about the Biblical Isaiah's prophecies; lots of bizarre visions and symbols, mostly about world peace.

"Why don't you try sitting up now?"

This time my muscles cooperate and move me into a seated position.

"Are you better?"

"I guess I'm okay. How *should* I feel? Where am I?"

"You're in transit. Very few of your species have ever traveled this fast."

Your species! No one's ever said that to me before! And what does he mean by "in transit"?

I grow impatient, desperate to know where I am and where I'm going, all the small but important details that govern the lives of — what did he say? — my species. Even though I sense I'm involved in a significant event, something visceral tells me my life is about to be turned upside down and inside out. Chaos again. I usually help others out of it better than I can help myself.

I've made a study of chaos. My work centers around it. Some people can't think until they sort out everything to their liking. But life doesn't work that way, as I've told my clients time and again. Sorting is learning, even if there's no grounding, no basis on which to build significance or discernment. I myself enjoy a little upheaval every now and then, provided it's in its most desirable form, the kind that can easily be managed. A good bout of chaos can be a growing experience, though it took me a long time to understand and appreciate that.

Now I'm not so sure I've mastered the art.

If chaos is a place, I'm stuck in the middle of it. All the laws of order have been suspended here. Time, space, you name it, none of it can be counted on. It's weird, but at the same time, refreshing. For some reason I don't care very much that the law of gravity has been deactivated. What's most absurd is not just that I still don't know how I got here, but that I don't care about knowing these particulars. You'd think I'd be consumed with fear but instead my imagination is ignited one moment only to be extinguished the next, like a match in the wind. I care, I don't care. I'm resolved, I'm puzzled. It's in and out, like a baby's shifting moods.

"We're traveling together," Isaiah tells me. "That's our job right now."

"Our job! But I've got to be at work! I can't travel anywhere now!" I exclaim, remembering my schedule and work commitments. "I have a 10:00 a.m. meeting with the CEO of Cellutron!"

"*Not today,*" he says, mixing severity with kindness.

"Look, Isaiah, I'm a business consultant, I don't have the kind of job where I can just take a day off without explanation. I can't just not show up for work! I have a reputation to uphold."

"They won't miss you, not even for a minute," he says.

Somehow that isn't very reassuring.

"Look, that's my life's work! I sell businesses my time and my brains! My reputation is at stake!"

"You also bear little responsibility for any chaos you leave in the wake of your advice, isn't that correct?"

I swallow hard, not wanting to admit he's right, and search for the best excuse I can think of to cover myself.

"That's what I'm paid to do, to come in, stir everything up and electrify the place. But my clients are the ones who have to make the changes. I can't do it for them." Besides, I silently think, if they're unhappy with my advice they can hire another consultant, and then another after that. It's the consulting food chain, that's all it is. It's nature's way of working through the belly of the business world.

Isaiah is silent.

"Look," I continue, "there's lots of loose cannons rolling around these days, plenty of people to blame when things go wrong. I'm no different from any other consultant. I work hard, present my best advice, and get on with my life. It's all part of the game. CEOs play it too, and quite well, I might add. They come in and shake things up, cutting jobs, laying off workers for short term gains to make themselves look good on paper. That's the way it's done these days. There's not such a thing as real security anymore. I'm not sure they ever was, really; but there was a short time when people felt entitled to jobs and now they know it isn't that simple!"

"You're the kind of person who hides behind rules and regulations, aren't you?" he says. "Slogans and mottoes are your armor."

"I suppose so, yes. What else can you hide behind?"

"You're always a little afraid of other people. You have no particular anchors out there, Noah, just some sparse and superficial relationships you call love affairs, but nothing binding, no deep attachments and commitments. It must be hard for you to find your place in the world."

My extinct marriage and other casual friendships cross my mind. I'm not proud of any of them.

"Look, I've got to be getting home. People will be looking for me," I say abruptly. My slipshod personal life is exposed and violated and I don't want anyone to look closely at it. I try to move, but am suddenly overcome by extreme fatigue. I lie back on the slab, an uneasy sleep inching through my body, fogging up my brain. Isaiah stands by me as if waiting for something. *This is his doing*, I tell myself. *He is causing a deep sleep to fall upon me.*

"No one will miss you," he says softly. "You haven't established deep connections with anyone in this lifetime, male or female."

He doesn't know everything, I tell myself. It's not my fault all the women I've ever known have sensed something missing in me, some piece cut away from my personality. What was it Ellen said at our divorce? *Something essential to human relationships just isn't in you.* I've been told that more than once by several different women, but I'm not sure what's missing. I'm a nice guy, good income, solid career. How could I know what's missing if no one's ever been able to describe it to me?

"You're alone in life," Isaiah says.

"That's not my fault."

"Whose is it, then?"

"I don't know. I haven't had an easy time."

"You've got to take part of the responsibility, though, even if the ways of your society make everyone a stranger in a strange land, a seeker after something unknowable and unfindable. Your whole string of assumptions is skewed."

"But that's not my fault."

"Isn't it? You could have seen yourself as a man who builds rather than abandons, but that kind of thinking is too risky for you. You opted out of the process by not feeling any pleasure in your work, choosing benign detachment over creative dedication. You never looked for the greater connections between what you do and the people you do it for! You've failed to see the reality and wholeness of your own existence with the rest of the world."

I listen, but I can't say I'm taking it all in.

"You see, we're trying an experiment here, and I have every reason to believe it will work," he says.

"Experiment?"

Like a battery running on low, I have only enough strength to relax and listen. I'm getting very sleepy.

"Are you beginning to understand that we brought you here to be part of a very important project?"

"Yes. But I'm not sure what it's about."

"We want to know whether we can eliminate a great deal of misery by taking a short cut in the historical process."

I can't make any sense out of this, and being sleepy, I don't try. It isn't possible to detour through history.

"Do you need to use a bathroom?" he asks, like a parent asking a child before a long car trip.

"No. I took care of that before I left."

Odd. I hadn't known I was going anywhere then.

"What about something to eat?"

"Well, actually, I usually have breakfast about now, at least I think so, since I'm not sure exactly what time it is. No. I'm too shaken up to eat."

"Anything at all that I can get for you?"

"No, I don't think so."

"All right, then. You might want to sleep some more."

"No thanks." I start to sit up, but something other than my own weakness prevents it.

"It's all right to sleep. I'll keep watch."

What a strange thing to say! No one has watched me sleep since I was child. Mom used to before she and Dad died, but after that I was pretty much in charge of myself, even after Grandfather took me in. I wonder if Isaiah considers me a child. He seems so concerned for my comfort.

I close my eyes and sink into a deep, refreshing sleep, this time devoid of dreams.

My Journey

How much time elapses before waking consciousness returns I don't know. I rise slowly from the concrete slab, my feet upheld on the invisible floor by a strange force unknown to me. I rub the sleep from my eyes, determined to discover something about my circumstances and Isaiah.

"Where are we going?"

"On a journey."

"Where to?"

"You'll have to decide that for yourself."

"And how am I supposed to do that? This trip is your idea. You're in control, not me. Look, this wasn't my plan in the first place."

"Actually, it was, and you're more in control than you think. You decided to go on this trip the same way you've decided everything else in your life. You just go with the flow, as your people say. But it's your flow. You created it; though, at present I suspect you have no idea that's true."

Considering I plan everything right down to the schedule of suits I wear, I believe I seldom if ever go with the flow. I hate that expression. In fact, I teach other people how to go with the flow, but I always have to force them to do it. It isn't something I do well at all, but telling other people to do it is another story.

"Look, I'm not a rocket scientist, but we're airborne, aren't we? Are we in some kind of spacecraft?"

"Well, you can call it whatever you like: spacecraft, flying saucer, cruise ship, galactic frigate. The purpose is still the same: to get us from one place to another very fast."

"But it feels like we're just cruising."

"Relative speed," he says. "Surely you've heard of it."

I nod and a shiver runs through me.

"But where are we going?"

"Everywhere. We're going to travel the universe inside and out. It's sort of a Cook's Tour, if I understand the reference."

I believe he does.

The idea that I'd ever travel to a distant planet used to haunt me when I was a kid. The excitement and sheer danger of it were overwhelming and I flirted with space travel as an exotic potential career choice. I think all of us baby boomers did, but I had a love-hate relationship with the idea. Astronauts were the heroes of the sixties, and everyone wanted to grow up and have a piece of moon rock secretly tucked into their sock drawer. Kids dream big things like that when they're young and then they enter the adult world and find nothing but disappointments. I ought to know. Losing both my parents was my first clue. My life's been okay, but I've had my heart bashed in a lot.

"This is one high-tech adventure," I laugh. "It's a variation on a theme, that's for sure."

"You make it sound dramatic, but that's not what's going on here, at least not in the sense you mean. We're not traveling through the galaxy as much as we're traveling through existence itself. The word 'journey' best describes it. It's more internal than external, and you won't be in any danger. You'll be traveling in familiar territory. Trust me."

This doesn't feel right. I've been around enough to know that you can't trust anyone who asks you to trust them, but this time I suppose I have to. Isaiah seems in control of things and besides, there's a certain mystery in all this that's enticing. I can't afford to worry about it. If you worry about everything that might go wrong, you never get anywhere in life. It's taken me a lifetime to come to that. It isn't my natural inclination.

"Perhaps I should introduce you to my colleagues," he says.

"Your colleagues?"

Surprised, I notice that two other people have joined us.

Two Visitors

Neither of these visitors has Isaiah's air of eminence and sophistication, but in fairness, no two earth people are exactly the same either. You have to make allowances. The two are dressed in clothes like Isaiah's and it occurs to me that perhaps it's some kind of uniform. Both seem impatient, as if they've been interrupted at an important task and wish to get back to it.

"These are my colleagues, Enoch and Bena. They'll try to make your visit as instructive and comfortable as possible."

I look the newcomers over. Bena, the woman, meets my gaze with a warm smile that removes all traces of her hurried attitude. I have no doubt of her sincerity. She's good looking, but right now that doesn't matter. Enoch is small and rotund, shorter and stouter than Isaiah but sleek looking none the less. Though he does not speak, his expression suggests a sense of humor, something I don't sense in Isaiah. Enoch nods in my direction.

"We know this journey is an unusual one but I want you to be aware of your capable guides. Enoch and Bena will do an excellent job of escorting you on this voyage," Isaiah says.

"Like guardian angels?" I ask, unsure of why I would be thinking such a thing.

"Like guardian angels." Bena smiles reassuringly. Even Enoch, with his straightforward and serious demeanor manages a grin and a gentlemanly bow. Obligingly, they turn and disappear.

I look for the door they used to exit and see none.

On some level, I'm disconcerted by this implausible disappearance. I'm not sure why I'm buying into all this, but I suppose I'm undergoing a suspension of disbelief, which is quite unusual for me. I'm an ardent realist, allergic to departures from reality. Puzzled but still taking everything in, I accept Bena and Enoch's exit as a routine part of the storytelling. After all, I'm in no position to challenge such dematerializations and ethereal comings and goings. My mind authorizes these distortions as it does in my dreams and after a moment it seems completely natural for Bena and Enoch to have moved about on thin air. I have no inclination to question their behavior any further.

"Are you all right?" Isaiah asks me.

"Yes. A little tired, though."

I lie back on my slab, staring up at the place where a ceiling should be.

"What do you think of my colleagues?"

"They're nice, I guess. Are they a lot like you?"

"If you mean similar in personality, no. Everyone's different. We have as wide an assortment of personalities among us as you have in the best and worst of your society. But there is a difference. We've learned to live our best natures and expel our worst ones. Our social structure is purposely designed so that everyone is able to exemplify the best that's in them. After all, that's the proper function of society: to support and not dominate, to be a system that forms a background for human action, not some tangled mumbo-jumbo of laws, prejudices, intractabilities and barriers. There's nothing in our society to antagonize and invoke the worst in people. Human nature does not vary from one place to another, but our understanding of it is totally different from yours. Almost everything you call human nature isn't human nature at all. It's just a logical consequence of the dehumanizing way you consistently treat each other."

This makes me bristle. I'm in no mood to be blamed for the collective bad behavior of my earthly contemporaries. I, Noah Gershom, am better than that.

He senses I don't like it and shifts the focus back to our two recent visitors.

"You'll like Bena. She's a student of balance, a specialist in the distinctions between talent, understanding, knowledge, intuition and wisdom. And Enoch is what you might call a technologist. He monitors and measures the components of all the universal systems. We're all different, and yet very much the same."

"Well, okay. You've explained what they are, perhaps you can tell me about yourself," I say, satisfied that he's decided to forget attacking me and the rest of humankind, at least for now. I can't do anything about the way my society functions. I'm not responsible for the evils of the world.

He should be smart enough to know that.

The One

"As I told you before, my specialty is prophecy," Isaiah says, "although I have spent a good deal of time in the antiquated study of human history. Prophecy and history are very much the same."

"How could that be? Prophecy is about the future and history is about the past."

"Only in an earth-centered point of view. Everything is part of The One. Everyone who has ever lived and everyone who is *going* to live."

There's no end to the curve balls this man can throw! I'm not willing to describe him as compassionate anymore. Irritating — that would be more like it.

"Well, perhaps to you there's no difference," I say, "the way people like you measure time."

"My people don't measure time, Noah. We simply exist in it. And whatever you think The One is, I can guarantee it's not what you think."

"And what do I think?"

His smile taunts me, as if he expects me to be able to answer this question. I haven't got a clue, but I'm getting increasingly annoyed with these conundrums and enigmas. I just want to go home and do my job, that's all.

Still, I don't want to leave him with the impression that I'm nothing but a fool. That's not my style, I'm too smart for that. When I get thrown a curve ball I usually figure out how to hit a home run out of the ballpark. I give Isaiah's question some thought even though I feel at a marked disadvantage in answering it. My response requires careful consideration.

First off, how could I know what I don't know? And even more important, how could there be no difference between prophecy and history and between everyone who has ever lived and everyone who is ever *going* to live? The difference should be obvious to anyone, a fundamental consequence of the tragedy that sooner or later enshrouds us all. Death is the one reality no philosopher has ever been able to argue away, at least not to my satisfaction. Being alive and being dead are monumentally different things. People are born, they live and they die. That's it. My parents died and left me alone when I was a kid. That's how it is: black and white, no gray areas, very basic, no arguments, none that work anyway at helping you get your loved ones back.

History itself defines vast differences between those people who've lived at one time and those in another. This is so obvious no explanation is required.

And yet here I am thinking about it for the first time in my life as if it makes sense to question it. What's happening to me? Have they injected some drug into my brain or is this some mild form of hypnosis? I'm not afraid; but my reactions are so unlike me, I'm confused.

Isaiah watches the quiet evolution of my thoughts.

"Are you talking about reincarnation?" I ask, extending a tentative toe into philosophical waters I'd rather not step into.

"You can call it that, if you choose. What's really happening is that some part of all people exists in the eternal state. We're always part of The One, regardless of our form. Most of Earth's religions know this."

"You won't find reincarnation in Christianity," I remind him.

"No," he says. "It was edited out, but it was a part of all the eastern religions, including Judaism. The Bond of Eternal Life is a very strong belief. You see, time and place are physical aspects of your universe. The soul itself is metaphysical and ethereal and much harder to fathom. It's part of the realm of energy, not matter, and the world of energy is something you materialists barely have a glimmer of understanding about."

I never thought of myself as having a soul. When my parents died I gave up having faith in anything. Mom and Dad and everyone in the world were biological creatures. My parents were necessary for my existence. I mourned them when they died, and something in me died with them.

To this day I bear the scars of that separation.

An Issue Impossible to Settle

"**I** see. So you're telling me reincarnation is a fact of life, and that we've all lived many times before and will again, and that people in the future are pretty much the same as those who've lived in the past, accounting for human nature and all that?"

"Something like that."

"But wouldn't the times people live in cause them to be different?"

"Not exactly. It's not quite that simple."

"Oh? How is it, then?" I experience another twinge of exasperation. I'm trying to play Isaiah's game and keep my mind open, but it's a struggle.

"I don't think you can understand it now," he says.

"Oh? Do you think I'll ever be able to?"

"Probably not."

"Do *you* understand it?

"No, not completely," he sighs. "Some principles are easier to understand while others require huge leaps of faith, similar to the one you made when you undertook this journey in the first place. What some people call reincarnation is as distant from the truth as your notion that when one dies, all consciousness is lost forever.

Both ideas are bizarrely incorrect, the consequences of limited ego-maniacal thinking. What might be correct cannot be understood by creatures at our level of understanding, any more than a cat can understand a mathematical equation. We're simply not adapted to dealing with the innermost secrets of the universe. We're not at that level, not even remotely."

"Not even you?"

"I'm not that different from you except through my experiences. For instance, I've never worked in the corporate world."

I decide not to go further in this direction and let go of the question. If neither of us can understand it, there's no use discussing it, is there? Thank God for that.

So far, all I know is that some people are trying an experiment with me but they don't seem sure of what they're trying to prove. In fact, they don't seem sure of anything. Maybe that's why I can't get any answers out of this guy.

Instead, there are a whole lot of questions.

News of the Experiment

"When can I go home?"

"Say the word and you'll be back at the time you left without any memory of what's happened here. You won't even suspect anything. Is that what you want?"

I shrug my shoulders. I'm very close to taking him up on his offer. I have things to do back home and leaving this place makes sense. I don't care about history or the future or this experimental cosmic clean-up he's proposing. The world's in too much of a mess to clean itself up anyway. Opting out is tempting. Staying could be dangerous, and if I can forget this whole experience, I can go back to my life without interruption. I like my life; parts of it anyway. Going home sounds like a great idea.

But I'd be missing something, undoubtedly a once in a lifetime opportunity. Staying could be important. After all, it isn't every day you meet a prophet named Isaiah.

"What would happen if I go back now? Any special consequences?"

"I don't suppose so, not immediate ones, anyway, not specifically directed at you. On the other hand, if we can make this experiment work, we might be able to eliminate an enormous amount of suffering. Does that idea appeal to you?"

Thinking it over, I wonder if I really do owe anything to anyone on my planet. What has the human race ever done for me? Besides, I'm not sure it's my job to straighten things out for other people, even though I get paid to do that in corporations. That's a heavy load in itself, but carrying the weight of the entire world on my shoulders, that's a different story. I'm not sure I'm equal to the task.

"Of course you are," he says aloud. "That's why we chose you and you chose us."

"Let me see if I understand this," I say. "If I go along with your experiment, I might be able to do some good for the world?"

"Yes."

I can't help laughing at this.

"Funny you should choose me for such a mission! If you leave out my professional contribution to the Fortune 500 companies, I haven't done much good except increase profits. The most I've ever done to benefit humanity is contribute old clothes to the Salvation Army. It's ludicrous to pick me, you're grossly overestimating my good will. There are millions of people much more philanthropic than I!"

"But you play a part no one else can play, Noah, just because of who you are."

My personal feelings don't seem to matter anymore. I set aside all resistance to this conversation and the whole experiment I was drafted for without my consent. He says I chose it but I don't recall signing off on anything.

"Okay," I say in my best negotiating voice. "What if I work with you on the condition that if I'm not completely satisfied I can leave?"

"You can make that decision at any point in the experiment.

If you decide you don't want to participate, we'll return you to your bedroom and the whole incident will never have occurred. Not many experiments are as foolproof as this, to lend themselves to such easy cancellation."

It seems strange, but I don't have any objections. It seems simple enough: if their experiment works, I'll be some kind of a hero. If it doesn't, I can go home, no questions asked. Which isn't exactly true.

There have been far too many questions so far.

Pushing Back Against Time

Just then it occurs to me that all along in this conversation we've been playing tricks with time.

While Isaiah and I talk, things are happening around us, but I don't feel a clock ticking on the wall of my awareness. I'm used to answering to that clock. I live according to calendar schedules and appointment books. Now moments hang in mid-air like drops of water suspended from a faucet.

Impossible! Everyone knows time's a one way street, a single arrow which can never fly backwards once it's been fired. You simply can't go back; even thinking about it is a childish absurdity. Interfering with the past would force the present to be different and alter the universe entirely. It would be a paradox, quite impossible, let alone undesirable and ridiculous, like having someone come in and rearrange your living room furniture without your permission.

Besides, what's happening in the world shouldn't be tampered with. It's history in the making and that's that. Monkeying with time just isn't done. That's a hard and fast rule of the physical universe, and I, for one, have learned to live with it. I'd like to keep it that way.

How much global history or future would I obliterate if I were to return to my bed now or at any other time? If I unfolded time and twisted it back to suit my convenience, everything I'm experiencing now would never have happened. By that action my encounter with Isaiah would be rendered a non-occurrence. But if I went back could I fix my mistakes and win back lost contracts and clients, resurrect my parents from the dead, prevent my bitter divorce from Ellen?

Do I really want to turn back time?

ᘛ

When I was nine, my parents died on impact in a head-on collision in our family car. I sat up that night, soaked in tears and scared to death, trying to think back time, to push it in the other direction and stop the world at the point where Mom and Dad could have avoided the oncoming truck. I worked hard to think back the very moment when they kissed me goodnight, trying to stop them from going out, to avoid the accident altogether. If they'd stayed home it wouldn't have happened.

That was the last time I saw them.

What a naive kid, to think that if I worked hard enough I could force time backwards and make things happen differently. At the age of nine I knew that *one little point in time* had changed my life forever. If I could only reshape that one instant, that one chance, if I could only start the whole process over, do one little thing to make it all different . . . .

Everyone said I was too young to stand by my parents' graveside. I was barred from the funeral because Grandfather wanted it that way. At the time I thought it was because he wasn't sure I could handle it, but now I think it would have hurt him as much as it hurt me. I dealt with the trauma of the funeral and the accident by playing them in my imagination over and over again, though I never told anyone. I'm sure it was harsher in my mind than it actually was. I stayed in my room and cried. There was nothing else for a kid to do.

As I grew up I'm ashamed to say that my parents' faces eventually faded from my memory. I promised myself I'd never trade my emotions for the love of parents, beautiful women or anything that had a heartbeat. Cold in the grave, that's where life stops. Stuck at a point in time, like a butterfly trapped in a glass paperweight.

That's how it ends, for sure.

"You said it would be possible to go backwards in time," I ask. "Do you know something the rest of us don't?"

"Before we go into that I'd like you to observe a beautiful sight."

As a Bridegroom Loves His Bride

"Okay, if that's what's on the agenda," I smile, standing up and moving freely for the first time since arriving here.

Immediately I feel an intense flow of energy surging through me, a driving force I haven't experienced since my mid-twenties when I finished graduate school and felt I could take on the world. I've never felt healthier than I do right now. My chronic back pain is gone, as well as the smaller middle-aged aches my body seems to have accumulated over the years.

"What you see will bring perspective to our discussion," Isaiah says while ushering me forward.

"That's good. I'm interested in what you have to say, but I admit I'm skeptical. Who wouldn't be?"

"It's quite understandable in the context of your life. Take a look and tell me what you see."

We stand in a misty room with no remarkable features, except that it's awash in blue light. Isaiah points to a large open door I hadn't noticed before. Its sudden appearance surprises me. With deliberate steps and a cautious mind I follow him through it and we find ourselves standing in a gallery of paintings.

"What do you think?" he asks.

"Of the paintings, you mean? Well, they're nice, but to tell you the truth, I'm a bit unschooled in art. I don't really understand it."

"That's a pity. As I understand it," Isaiah says, "art is a visual representation of thoughts and feelings. These great masterpieces are in their original forms: Raphael, Monet, Vermeer, Renoir, Picasso, some of the great artistic geniuses of your culture. There are many others, of course. This is just a small traveling exhibit."

I reach out to touch Vermeer's *Woman Holding a Balance* and my hand passes through it.

"Sorry. I forgot to tell you these works of art aren't really here."

"Oh? So where are they? Do they only *seem* to be here?"

"In a manner of speaking. This is only one of the many virtual art galleries we carry with us so we can enjoy the comforts of home. We carry our cultural experiences with us, as if we're hermit crabs in our shells. We live in one for a while until we enlarge our experiences and grow further. At any rate, this art is mostly recognizable to you, even if you say you don't know or understand it. It's part of your culture, whether you're aware of it or not. You've still internalized its symbolic meaning. That's why we have it on display. It's part of our late historical collection."

"Art — don't leave home without it," I joke.

"We never do," Isaiah says seriously. "As you can see, we have the ability to call up any environment we want, when and where we want it. Nature herself is never violated in the process. The structures of your time have been replaced by electronic images that can be shaped into any substance and form we want. We can redecorate our environments as often as we like when it suits us. It's simpler than collecting material objects. All you do is visualize it to make it happen, just like the paintings you see before you."

At the blink of an eye, the gallery disappears.

Once again we are in a small enclosure of seamless mist, with a window suspended in mid-air. Because of where it is, I know that until a moment ago it must have been the door to the art gallery. But now it looks out on a night sky.

"Look at this lovely sight," Isaiah says, gesturing towards it. "You'll find it more glorious than those paintings."

I gaze out the window, beholding a truly miraculous spectacle, one I never before dreamed of seeing with my own eyes.

Earth, nestled blue and white against the blackness of the universe, greets my gaze with a brilliance far more impressive and moving than any photograph of it I've ever seen. It shines with an inner light, not glazed but majestic, vibrating, thriving with energy. A profound feeling of reverence rises in me, the most intense bonding with this planet I've ever felt, even when I walked its surface.

I had no idea of the magnitude of its beauty when it lay beneath my feet.

My home, my Grandfather's house, the garden of my childhood, the nesting place of my existence lies before me summed up in a distant orb, concealing mountains, lakes, rivers, trees and intimate treasures, the greatest of all miracles.

"The Earth! I never imagined I'd ever see this sight!"

"Have you forgotten your childhood dreams, Noah? Once you wanted to sail the galaxy and wander the universe. It's not a crime that you didn't until now. In your time, most people never will see anything like this; but if they did, it would transform their lives forever. Surely this is the most beautiful planet in all the galaxies, the bright jewel of God's creation, and we love it as a bridegroom loves his bride."

For a reason I don't understand, tears well up inside me. Filled with an intense sadness and desire for reunion with my homeland, I long for my people and something or someone I can't identify. I've had this feeling of longing once before, some time ago.

I'd given it up for dead.

The most intense love I've ever known floods my heart as I look down on Earth. I'm sure I'm the only one giving our planet this much thought. Why do I feel such tenderness towards this hunk of rock simmering in war and hate, festering in poverty and disease? Tenderness isn't part of the daily rat race. Do people have to be removed from something in order to feel closer to it?

In the storm of my inner thoughts, I sense a subtle voice, a presence, a quiet echo long forgotten in my separation from Earth. The words are familiar, but I can't distinguish the voice.

Someone on Earth longs for my return.

I know this, but don't know how I know. This fleeting insight leaves me no clue of face or name so all I can do is dismiss it.

I detect a look of sadness on Isaiah's face, as if he is disappointed. Perhaps I've failed part of the experiment.

"Who are the enlightened souls who look upon Earth as a bridegroom loves his bride?" I ask.

"The entire human race, Noah."

I explode in derisive laughter. "Not the human race I know!"

"No," he says. "They're all dead and gone. What you're looking at is not the Earth you live on. It's Earth more than a thousand years from your time, Noah. Earth in the year 3015."

"My God!"

I'm trembling with terror. My whole world is gone! I'd guessed that we were cheating time on this journey, but now the full impact of my abduction becomes clear to me. Everyone I've ever known is dead and has been dead for more than a thousand years! I'm alone in the universe, amputated from my environment, a guinea pig in some experiment. Surely the human race has ended and Earth is inhabited by a different breed of creature, superior to us, but not like us.

"Don't take it so hard," Isaiah says.

"How can you say that? Everything I've known is over."

"Not exactly, Noah. You'll be returned to your own time before you know it. This way you'll have a chance to see your world as it will be more than a thousand years in the future. You'll come to understand what it will take to make things less painful for your fellow humans. That, after all, is one of the intentions of this experiment."

"That's not the point, not at all," I tell him. "Why did you do this to me?" I feel kidnapped into this experiment, like an animal, a lab rat, separated from my home and everything I know.

"Why are you forcing me into this bitter isolation?" My emotions are too strong to control. I break down and cry. I can't stop myself.

Going Beyond History

Isaiah makes no move to answer. Instead he lowers himself to the floor and bows his head in meditation.

As strange as it seems, the disarming quality of this act dissolves my anguish and makes me feel that everything's all right.

It's strange. There's a subtle grandeur in Isaiah's reverent gesture. It affords me a glimpse of something, just a touch, that I've always suspected was possible, but never quite experienced before. It's a fleeting, yet at the same time substantial impression, like watching a single autumn leaf nestling into the air for its descent, a moment of quietude caught with the corner of one's eye. Only a moment ago I was caught up in anxiety and desperation, even more terrifyingly isolating than when my parents died. Yet now I feel calm.

I sit cross legged on the floor facing Isaiah, ready to resume my conversation with him, this time with more dignity. I have just experienced the ultimate human loneliness, the essential knowing that at the moment of death there is no one who can be there except yourself, alone in your fate, severed from everyone and everything. The final moment of isolation lies at the root of all consciousness, of all life.

I look up into a smiling face. This Isaiah offers as consolation, as if such a miracle could be possible. In patient silence I wait until he resumes speaking.

"I'm sorry to have upset you," he says, raising his eyes and looking deeply into mine. His tone, not the words, offers redemption.

"I jumped to conclusions. It's just that everyone I once knew in my life is gone."

"Let me reassure you," Isaiah says. "The people you've known have not come to an end. Only *history* is gone."

"How can that be? How can history be *gone*?"

In my mind's eye I see a few survivors of a nuclear holocaust hiding in caves, estranged from one another, gravely attempting to keep something of themselves alive. I wonder whether I myself could hold onto any remnant of a desire to live, under those conditions.

"The tormented history of the human species which you call civilization is gasping its last breath," Isaiah tells me. "Humanity, long separated from its own soul, will re-emerge from the devastation of twenty thousand years of oppression. Together you and your contemporaries will begin the process of creating a new way of being, more gratifying than anything your world has known before."

"But I don't understand," I say. "What do you mean, history is coming to an end? What about human accomplishment, and all the great cultural achievements?"

"What exactly do you think history *is*?" Isaiah asks.

I think about this for a moment, and all that comes to mind is a definition Mrs. Hammersmith taught me in junior high school. Simple enough, I had supposed at the time. "History is everything that ever happened."

"Then history consists primarily of events in distant galaxies?"

"No, of course not."

"Why don't you give me some examples of historical events?" he asks.

For some reason, it takes me a while to nail down a few.

"The discovery of America, the defeat of the Spanish Armada, the Revolutionary War, the Civil War —"

"That's military history, isn't it?" says Isaiah. "Is that the kind of history you're interested in?"

"Not really," I reply, though most of the history I remember is about armed battles and political struggles. It occurs to me that the story of our planet consists of war dominating the imaginations of the authors of history books.

"How about the history of culture? The Renaissance, the Age

of Reason, the New England Transcendentalists —"

"Ah," he replies, "the history of fashionable ideas."

"Why not call them *great* ideas? What's wrong with that?"

"What constitutes greatness, my friend?"

"Whatever people *think* is great, I suppose."

"Don't take this the wrong way, but it sounds as if you don't have a very clear idea about what history is," says Isaiah.

"Well then, why don't you just tell me what it is instead of quizzing me on the subject?"

"It sounds as if you believe that history is a collection of events leading up to a person's own time, shaping the way they live their lives — as if the whole point of the struggles of the past has been to produce a culture exactly in one form which everyone can experience. No one is interested in a history of events that could not apply to them. That's why, if you live in the United States you don't necessarily study the history of Peru. It doesn't directly apply to your life, and people want to know only those things which do."

"I suppose so."

"And, of course," he continues, "interpretations of history are likely to change. What at one time is taken for historical fact is quite likely to be viewed in a different light and perhaps even edited out of history altogether at some other time."

"I guess you're right."

"But suppose people were to take total responsibility for themselves. What if nothing special could be credited with making them what they are? Suppose the most important events in their lives were purely personal in their own minds, or in families or communities. Suppose all the disruptive things that happen in the world, such as wars, oppression or fashionable trends were to cease and every community became responsible for its own evolution? Imagine participating in a continuing global dialogue where everything is of such value that no particular event can be singled out as history."

"Say more."

"If you were to examine events in tightly organized cultures over periods of centuries, you would find very little recorded history. Of course, there are instruments of culture: legends, epic poems, works of art. But history would record only the peaceful lives of the group as they moved from day to day in ways that were important to them. How much time would you spend studying the detailed family history of someone who happens to work on the floor above you in the company you're consulting for?"

"None. Not unless it was directly important in some project. Are you telling me that community takes the place of history, then?"

"In a healthy society, there's very little history and a great deal of community. There are no wars, so there's no military history. There are few major upheavals because society has stabilized itself into satisfying relationships and opportunities for all people, so there's no cultural history. There are no superficial trends to capture and bind human attention, because people can pick and choose from a variety of different cultural influences, all of them of great value. Under such conditions, everyone is distinctly individual and at the same time profoundly human. People can relate to one another in significant ways. No form of communication is pushed aside at the expense of others. Value and importance are not legislated but spontaneously generated, shared openly where sharing is important. There are no great heroes elevated above others, because everyone is heroic. There are no criminals because the community has eliminated crime and the corrupting influences that invite it. And so there is no longer history — only a deeply satisfying and enriching way of life for everyone."

Dreams, the Soul and Society

"But surely there must be important technological advances!"

"There are some, yes," says Isaiah. "But technology is of no great significance in such a society. It is secondary, part of the background. Take the society I come from. Our souls are important to us, and we spend our lives cultivating experiences of intense personal value for ourselves. Our lives are lived as works of art, and they are so very treasured and cherished that there is no way to select out those who are more valuable than others."

I think about my neighbor Ted Dorfman, always washing his car, polishing the chrome, correcting little dinks, glossing every nick and scratch sustained in the supermarket parking lot. Does Ted care for his soul the way he cares for his car, cleaning it up before taking it out for a spin every now and then?

And my ex-wife Ellen, transfusing Neiman-Marcus and Cartier's with plastic money almost daily, as if owning things will somehow make her more valuable than most of the people she knows.

"Tell me," says Isaiah, a quizzical smile on his face, "when you think of the Eighteenth Century, what do you think of?"

"The great age of rationalism. The birth of political liberty. John Stuart Mill. Adam Smith. George Washington. Thomas Jefferson."

"Would you like to know who is remembered from that century in our time?"

"Sure."

"The Senoi."

"Who?"

"The Senoi people. We think they were the most effective culture the world in your time had ever known. They existed almost up to your time, but they were in their heyday in the Eighteenth Century. Yet I dare say their culture is unknown to you."

"You're correct," I reply. "Tell me about them."

"Their civilization was based on dream interpretation. At the beginning of every day the adults told each other their dreams, and acted on whatever wisdom could be derived from them. Then they spent time with the younger members of their families, listening to them and instructing them on their dreams."

"I have vivid dreams," I whisper. "Very disturbing ones. They recur, but I don't know what that means."

Isaiah smiles as if he has an answer.

"Dreams are the connecting point between the world of the spirit, where we come from, and the worlds we explore as visitors. The world of everyday reality is purely a fabric of our imaginations. It is what we call the dreams, not the so-called realities that are fundamental."

I object strenuously to this point of view.

Because of my work, I know that the latest neurological research discounts dreams as having no particular meaning. It pokes holes in the mystique that powered Freudian psychology for nearly a century. That's why I'm frustrated with my own recurring dreams, my brain cells idling in neutral when I'm not awake. Somehow they've gotten into a well-worn circuit that I can't shake. I mention this to Isaiah.

"Ah," he says with a cryptic smile, "there it is again, that rationalistic mentality that has held humanity's spirits in chains for centuries. It's difficult for us in our time to imagine it, but there it is. To us, you're a curiosity. Of course the neurologists never took the trouble to explain the source of one salient fact that was demonstrated in your time and many times since."

"What's that?"

"A certain percentage of dreams refer to actual events."

"I suppose so," I say. "But surely there can be no mystery in that. It doesn't make them meaningful, merely randomly reflective of our experiences."

"Not from the point of view of *my* time," says Isaiah, "but from yours, there should be some mystery for you to consider. Research carried out earlier in your century, in the 1930's I believe, revealed that of all dreams referring to reality, more or less half are based on events that occurred prior to the dream."

"Oh? And what about the rest?"

"Those refer to events occurring *after* the dream. In other words, approximately fifty percent of those dreams are what you'd call precognitive."

"But that's impossible!"

"Of course, from your so-called scientific point of view, that's how it would seem," Isaiah says. "Dream research repeatedly documented something which, from your perspective, was quite clearly impossible. As far as we've been able to learn, no one made any attempt to reconcile what was known about dreams with the way events unfolded themselves in time."

Isaiah doesn't have much trouble making himself clear. After all, here I am, flying around at the speed of light in a time one thousand years in my future. He might be making all this up, but he's got me convinced that he has some technologies distinctly outside of my awareness and experience. So I'm not disposed to argue anything.

Instead, I seize an opportunity that might make life easier for me. "I have very disturbing dreams. I don't seem able to stop them."

"Tell me about them."

"I wander through some sort of prison searching for someone but I don't know who I'm supposed to find. I look into people's eyes and step over squirming bodies but I never escape the prison or find the person who needs me. The gut wrenching agony of the people — that's the worst part, because I can smell and touch it."

"I thought so. And you have this dream repeatedly?"

"Yes. Almost every night."

"And it doesn't mean anything to you?"

"No. It's too hard to think about, much less analyze."

"Well, you'll continue having it until you do. Once you've figured out what it's trying to tell you, it will stop. This dream is only a part of your personality speaking in vague metaphors, but it's an important part, trying to get your attention by any means possible. Terror seems to work with you. That's why you have nightmares."

"I see."

I've always known this. I suppose I was only protecting myself from the dream, clinging to the idea that it was just background noise so I wouldn't take it seriously.

"So what do you think you're trying to tell yourself?"

"Well, maybe that there's someone missing from my life — someone very important."

"Is that true?"

"I don't know. I have a successful career, I'm doing well. I'm highly regarded."

"So?"

"Isn't that the point?"

"Is that what your dream is saying?"

"No."

"So? What's the point?"

"It seems that in some sense I don't have the kind of companionship I need in my life."

"Does anyone of your species have that?"

"Interesting question. Some people do, I suppose."

"Is something incomplete about your relationships?"

"The dream seems to be saying that."

"What's the point of life?" Isaiah asks.

"Maybe there's no point. 'He who dies with the most toys wins,'" I cynically remark. "I saw that on a tee shirt once."

"What does it mean to you?"

"The object of capitalism is to consume all you can. You're a success if you make a lot of money, if you own a lot of stuff, like boats and summer homes and sports cars and diamonds. Stuff."

"Isn't that pretty simplistic?"

He's right. I feel silly. But I'll be damned if *I* know what the real point is.

For a moment I pause and think of the people who make it to the top of the human heap, stop, look around and say to themselves, "There must be more to life than this." And then they start taking Prozac.

I feel ashamed.

"How come it took you to help me see this?"

Isaiah looks puzzled.

"That's what none of us can understand about your time," he says. "To us it seems so genuinely *feeble minded*, if you'll excuse the bigoted expression."

As he says this, I find that it seems that way to me, too. And yet I feel strangely offended by the remark, as if he had done harm to someone I care about. The ambivalence doesn't make any sense.

"Think about it," Isaiah continues. "You folks put an awful lot of time and energy into what you call 'making it' — whatever that means — into climbing the ladder of success to get to the power at the top. You take all of that really seriously, as if it were the most important thing in the world. But what you don't take seriously is the condition of your immortal souls.

"Of course, most of you don't think you have souls, or you deny that others have them. You maintain that the soul is fiction and that you're just a bundle of nerve connections in the brain, like a complex telecommunications system. You pretend to know all about consciousness when you haven't the faintest clue about what it is or where it comes from. To those of us who live more than a thousand years after you, you seem even more primitive than most of the peoples you think of as being savages in your present time. Nearly all the Native American cultures had far more sophisticated views of life than all but a tiny fraction of your people have. You beg every important question there is and spend your lives worrying about things that really don't matter. And the strange thing is, that almost no one in your time speaks out against this runaway insanity in any meaningful way."

"Well, I certainly don't agree with that," I counter. "Everyone and his brother complains about virtually every aspect of our civilization. There are books about books about books on every problem in our world, from abortion to ecology to the litigious society, to politics — there's an infinite library of books about how bad life is."

"I said *meaningful.*"

"You think none of those books are meaningful?"

"Certainly not in our time," Isaiah says. "That's my point. If your so-called thinkers really thought meaningfully about any of those things, they'd see that the solutions are fairly simple. They wouldn't waste their time anatomizing mistakes, they'd just do things differently and be done with it. It's not hard. Take my word for it. In your time, society was trying to work out its systems, but nobody seemed to have much idea how to go about it. You were like children trying to figure out how to work some complex piece of equipment that was quite beyond you. That's why we're doing this experiment."

Finally, a clue! Now perhaps I'll understand about this experiment he keeps referring to.

"We think, Noah, that if you have a chance to observe the way we live and go back to your own time and use the insights of your observations, you'll be able to clear up an awful lot of problems our ancestors had to live through."

"So you've got everything figured out and we haven't?"

He nods.

"This is your chance to make things right. Remember, history is the record of humanity's more serious mistakes. Once there are no more serious mistakes, there is no more history."

"Was the Constitution of the United States a mistake?"

"No, but it was a corrective for a huge collection of social and political errors: poverty, discrimination, inequity. If there hadn't been so many mistakes, no Constitution would have been necessary. The Senoi didn't need one. They used community principles to guarantee their freedoms. They had no crime for hundreds of years and always got along well with each other, living ideal, fulfilled lives. You made a Constitution which certainly improved things, but your lives still remained unfulfilled and troubled. As a result you spent a great deal of your time fighting with each other about what the Constitution meant."

At this I capitulate. I'll settle for the fact that history is a record of mistakes. No one has come forward with a better idea, as far as I know. After all, why all the talk about learning the lessons of history or else having to repeat them, if that weren't precisely what history is all about?

Still, having no history makes me nervous.

Hope for the Future

After a few moments of contemplation, the implications of the discussion sink in.

As they do, I am awestruck. What a wonderful way to live, without neurosis or crime or warfare, continuously delighted in the flowing stream of events that surround us every day.

I wish it were possible!

The standard Twentieth Century visions of doom and gloom for Earth are completely off track. A Utopian society of pure joy awaits us in the future, a society which lacks civilization only because it has evolved beyond it. At least that's what I've put together from the clues Isaiah has given me.

Then I think about the impressions of the human race I get while watching TV.

"You say this positive future is coming in my time? I don't think you know what you're dealing with. The human race isn't ready for such a way of life," I say.

"Perhaps not," Isaiah replies, too thoughtfully for my taste.

If there's going to be a happy future, I don't want to just sit here and talk about it, I want to get with the program! Just do it!

But, if history is a record of mistakes, it's not clear which ones are set in stone and which ones might be subject to revision. It might be possible to alter history, even after it has occurred, but that's something I can't fathom at all.

Isaiah looks at me with a penetrating gaze.

"If it's true that your contemporaries are unready for such a state of affairs, human suffering will be much greater than it needs to be. That is, it *will* be, unless you can lend a hand, Noah, in a slightly more decisive fashion than we had originally thought."

"What sort of a hand would you want me to lend?"

Isaiah sighs and shifts into a more comfortable position.

"It's an interesting question, but not one for me to answer. You'll have to answer it from your own experience. My job is to act as an interpreter, not work out all the details for you."

I've heard that line before; I've used it myself, in my work, whenever I want to opt out of a sticky situation. Is this what he's been trying to do all along? Is this whole business about the fact that Isaiah is trying to get me to think differently but isn't willing to take responsibility for the results? Now that the shoe is on the other foot, I don't much care for this way of effecting change.

"I can summarize the essence of what's happened," Isaiah continues. "Any interpreter worth his salt should at least do that." He shoots me a glance that tells me he's called me on my act, and I settle down to listen.

"Start out this way: the science of your time was built on a set of false premises, which in turn provided a false foundation for the behavior which structured your civilization."

"A set of false premises?"

Isaiah nods.

"Imagine yourself to be one of the most brilliant human beings ever to walk your planet, the Greek philosopher of physics, Democritus."

The Atomic Mistake

Isaiah rises to his feet while I sit on the floor looking up at him in the respectful way a student watches a teacher.

"In your imagination, I'd like you to take on the mind and spirit of Democritus, and in this being, welcome into your nostrils the aroma of freshly baking bread. What conveys the smell of bread to your senses?"

Studying his face, I sense the image of Democritus stirring in his imagination. His voice softens, becoming a little wistful, as if he hopes I'm getting the point of what he's driving at. His tone is hypnotic, so I close my eyes while listening, to get the full effect, which is not quite like anything I've ever felt. I am moved — not emotionally, but physically moved — carried away into the minds and spirits of the people he describes, as the intensity of his tone urges me into their feelings and thoughts. In response to his suggestions, strange images surge through my fantasy.

"Assuming the perspective of this great intellect, Democritus, notice that you're in someone's kitchen. Savor how it feels to allow the delicious fragrance of the bread to enter your nostrils and leave traces of itself with lingering appeal: the attractive anticipations of a taste you so easily recognize. Your brilliant mind seizes the notion that it would have taken some special conveyance to waft this fragrance into your senses. What mechanism causes this to occur? Something has wandered in the air from the bread to your nose and into your spirit. What can this be? The answer you invent is profoundly intuitive and accurately perceptive of the deeper workings of nature. By its sheer weight of persuasion it will imprison the human mind for the next two and a half millennia.

"Something in the air — but what is it?

"Atoms! you say to yourself, defining the mysterious, invisible mechanisms that transport the fragrance of bread to your senses. You define them as the tiniest particles that make up the material world surrounding you, so tiny that they cannot be divided further. In essence these are merely miniature versions of the things you see, like bricks in a building — microscopic to be sure, but present nonetheless. You envision tiny particles of matter filling space, indivisible, comprising all things and stuffing them with substance, making them whole, full, weighty, capable of all the struggles implied in the condition of being. These tiny particles come in a multitude of shapes, sizes and textures, and from such differences among them, the vast array of material substances, even light, are constructed. In the beginning, you reason that these tiny bits of matter floated in a sea of chaos; but over time they became arranged, creating the patterns out of which the world was formed and has subsequently taken shape in all its manifold differences."

From the infinitely small to the wondrously large —

"And so the aroma of baking bread has given rise in your mind to a theory of nature. Atoms: a metaphorical theory so successful it will drive away all other contenders for more than two thousand years, freezing the human imagination in the prison of a sea of matter, blinding it to the corresponding essence of nature, which no philosopher of your eminence had the wit or wisdom to define. From this experience you have formulated complex notions of the universe made up of atoms and void. For you, atoms became the most essential feature of material existence."

As Isaiah ceases speaking, the smell of warm bread begins to fade. I open my eyes and see him standing across the room from me, his posture slightly dejected. He must be imagining some sacrilege, taking personal offense at what Democritus had wrought so long ago in someone's Mediterranean kitchen.

As I watch, his pose reassumes its erect stature. Once again he strides about the room, inviting me to close my eyes and bask in the comforting atmosphere of these thought-commanding visions. His voice softens again, causing my eyelids to grow heavy, as I anticipate further images, hoping to smell the bread again.

"Consider this," he continues. "While inhaling the bouquet of bread in the context of more generalized thought, Democritus ignores aspects of this staple that for centuries have sparked other kinds of impulses in other cultures. Among his countrymen, the Eleusinian Mysteries celebrated the relationship between life, death and rebirth and the sacred role of the harvest of corn and grain in assuring the continuity of life, as well as its sustenance.

"For the Hebrews, the baking of bread is a collaboration between God and His people. At each meal the bread receives blessing; praise for its creation goes to God, not to the mortal hands of the baker. Spirituality and skill together contribute to the finished product. The baking of bread is the culmination of a great and noble ceremonial progression. From the planting of wheat to the growing and harvesting, to the loosening and sorting of grains from chaff, it is a cycle symbolic of life itself. The Almighty provided food to those who had the knowledge to cultivate and transform it.

"Imagine that you are a baker of bread, midway in the hierarchy, dependent on the seemingly unconscious forces of nature to collaborate with the Infinitely Conscious God. You, mortal baker, can shape the loaf and bake it on the fire, but you can never be the sole reason for the bread's existence. You know that the gift of its life is in the kernels of grain which originate in the generosity of the Infinite Open-Handed God, whose name, so great as to be unutterable, means 'having always been and always to be.' Enduring. The great creative originator and ultimate transmuter of the universe is a partner in the baking of bread."

At this point, Isaiah quickens his speech, as if he is reaching out to grasp and rejoice in a mystery. An attitude of urgency vibrates in his voice.

Manna

"Imagine escaping into a barren desert with no promise of food, facing certain starvation. It's an ultimate act of faith impossible without the aid of the Almighty. And just when survival seems impossible, manna falls from heaven to feed you as it did the Hebrews in the desert after the Exodus from Egypt. Manna is symbolic sustenance, *not* bread, *not* made by mortal hands, provided for those with the faith to harvest it. How committed to choosing God one must be to have that kind of faith, that the Open-Handed God will send manna, a direct and personal provision of sustenance, with no mortal hands applied to its making. It means that sustenance is there for you always — open your eyes and see it; it will fall like rain and you need only gather it. It will taste exactly as each person likes."

Who has faith like that in our time? I wonder.

"In your time, Noah, people have forgotten this faith. They think there are no longer any miracles. Your sages, even your great religious leaders, turn up their noses at miracles, declaring them 'unscientific' while all around you the miracle of nature spins out its infinite web of expanding life. Without the assistance of the Almighty, nothing could have been born."

He turns to me with an accusing expression on his face. "Noah, even in your time science was able to prove that the world could not have existed except by the mind and spiritual hands of the Creator."

I'm not pleased with this remark. Science has proved no such thing. What is he trying to pull?

"Do you believe in miracles?" he asks.

"Of course not. They're just metaphors. The manna from

heaven, the parting of the Red Sea, the Exodus itself. These are legends, misinterpreted natural acts that might have occurred in some form, but in thousands of years have been generalized into something divine. Divinity itself is a metaphor. We are creations of chance, the freak accident of a blind, chaotic swirl in the ocean's slime. It certainly was an unlikely event, and you can call it a miracle if you want. But we're here because certain natural laws generated us. The notion of God, thanks to the wisdom of science, has become more sophisticated than it was for the ancient Hebrews, who knew nothing of the Law of Gravity, Relativity Theory, or any of the other physical rules that make up the universe. Blind chance is the great creator. We must accept and live with it. Sure, we don't like it and it's a blow to our egos, but we must accept it. People are forever trying to see themselves as more noble, more at the center of things than they really are and science is objective enough to help us back off from that foolishness. That's what's gospel for me, and I know that when we've finally accepted the wisdom of science and abide by it without useless fear and harmful superstition, we can obtain the insights we need to survive."

"Do you believe in miracles?" he asks again, making plain that he wants an answer. Quietly I tell him no.

"On what grounds? On what grounds do you reject miracles?"

"On scientific grounds! You've had a thousand years to deepen your understanding of such things. Surely there's no longer any remaining trace of the superstition that was so prevalent in my time."

"Ah, my friend, how wrong you are! Did it never occur to you that what you took for science only complicated the confusion of your time? Did you never notice that scientists glossed over the very issues they found most difficult to explain?"

"Such as?"

"Many scientists declared that consciousness is an accidental product of a universe of chance."

"Well, what else could any thinking person believe?"

"Any thinking person would have to conclude the opposite, because in your time it was also known that consciousness is necessary for the construction of any particle of material reality. It was known that without consciousness, not one of those things you deified as the building blocks of this chance-universe could possibly have existed. Your scientists understood that an electron is nothing more and nothing less than a probability, that it cannot become an actuality until examined by some mind. The very existence of matter itself was known to be a partnership between a perceiving mind and indeterminate probability. It was known that matter contains no solid substance, but purely and simply mind stuff.

"Your scientists knew this, but they did not follow it to its inevitable conclusion. Most of them were unable to see that the universe itself is a seemingly endless complex of conscious thought.

"Only this conscious thought can give birth to anything. Just as every cell in your body is conscious in its own way, so the people who lived in your time were in the process of putting together the framework that would move the Gaia consciousness to a new level of awareness. You created for the Earth a congealed brain which could articulate its thoughts and plan for its future. You, the very scientists who denied the consciousness of the universe and laughed at its miracles, were part of the miracle that God used to create the world you are now going to visit, a world that is itself conscious and produced by the collective thought of every person alive in it."

This notion is so absurd that I can't even fathom it. Miracles. Dark superstition carried a thousand years into the future. It's enough to make me feel total despair about the human condition. But it's not new to me, really. From time to time I've heard predictions that the future would be a regression, a decay into an earlier state of human society, perhaps imprisoned in the chains forged by superstition. After all, in the past there have been long periods of decline, of loss of most of the values that were present in earlier times. Why shouldn't this happen in the future as well?

What is there for the human race to look forward to, then? At this moment I feel only scorn for Isaiah. What kind of world does he want me to believe in? What is he summoning me to accomplish? I don't like what he's telling me. I want clear statements, clear answers, a definition of reality that I can understand and be comfortable with. I don't want to know that the future that lies a thousand years ahead is merely another long dark age of superstitious departure from the truths of practical reality.

"Are you really asking me to take seriously the notion that edible food dropped from heaven when the Hebrews asked for it?"

"I am."

"Actual edible food actually dropped from an actual heaven?"

"Yes."

"Then Jonah was actually swallowed by a whale?"

"No, that was a metaphor."

"And the world was created in seven days?"

"Six actually, with one day of rest. Some people think that's a metaphor too."

"Well then, how do I separate the miracles from the metaphors?"

"Miracles occur when faith is profoundly at issue, if and only if a next step must be taken. In the complexity of time, the future draws out what it needs from the past. It does so by creating laws that shape events. Sometimes, when a particular event is needed, it will form that event much as an impregnated mother forms a child in her womb. Those events which are needed to take things to a new level are the miracles, and they occur just as they are spoken of in certain traditions that were handed down to your people and believed both by those considered naive, as well as by your most brilliant sages. The average people of your time lacked the courage and wisdom to believe in miracles. That's the pity. When is the last time you heard anyone talk about manna or abiding sustenance?" he asks.

"Never," I reply.

"Yet it's the essential holiness of life, not measured by political or social yardsticks, but by faith in something greater than yourself, always protecting, always shielding you. In the service of your world's materialistic purposes, you have squandered life everywhere — you have proliferated Death.

"Now allow yourself to see in your mind's eye the meaning of the higher gift, the manna showering from heaven a distinctive bounty of life that each individual can know and prize uniquely. It is the greatest of all mysteries, the capacity of each person to know his or her own God-consciousness."

Isaiah pauses, his voice filled with sadness at the mistakes of history, of humanity's wrong turns from which we've tried to recover. Once again I've slipped into the suspension of disbelief, and rich fantasy that this episode invites. Suddenly I feel guilty for the ineptitude of my own time, as well as for my momentary lapse of trust. I decide to follow Isaiah through this discourse. I'm curious to see where it will lead and what it does for him.

"When the Hebrews hastened out of Egypt, they were forced to leave so quickly that the art of bread making had to be sacrificed. Matzo, unleavened bread, became a symbol of freedom, and it was blessed with gratitude in addition to the blessing over bread, acknowledgment again of the powerful collaboration between God and the Hebrews, between the spiritual and the physical.

"The Christians took bread in another context, symbolic of the body of God. Communion represents ingesting the body of God through the partaking of bread, assimilating, in a miraculous way, the power of God within oneself as an affirmation that we are all inclusive of some part of the Godhead."

So compelling are his words that for a passing moment I feel as if I'm linked directly with the Godhead. What has become of the rationality and skepticism that protected me so? I know it's madness, but I've given my consent to these sublime and unfamiliar feelings by being here. I'm truly of two minds, one linking me to my time, the other taking me on this amazing journey in which I find I can accept everything this man says.

"Islam, Buddhism, Hinduism, the Native American religions: all the spiritual quests of the world recognize bread as a gift of life, like manna, each of them savoring it in their own unique way.

"And to this day, even in your own time, Noah, the best bread makers know they must bake as an act of meditation, persuading their bread to rise into its most excellent and fulfilling form, as part of a sacred ritual: the preparation of food, sustenance for the body and the spirit."

The Universe As Mind

I raise my eyes to meet Isaiah's earnest gaze, feeling as if I've just enjoyed the refreshment of a long sleep, even though we've been deep in conversation for some time. Caught up in the wonder of his fascinating images, I've put my skepticism aside.

We sit in silence for a few moments, looking away from each other, engaged in our own thoughts. Evidently he has had something compelling to tell me, something fundamental; and the truth is, I feel a bit bewildered, no longer knowing whether to argue or agree with him.

"Those atoms of Democritus, which he invented in his imagination, are all very well in themselves," Isaiah says, "but they're devoid of the wisdom of allusiveness needed to enrich an idea in its simplest form. Nothing is as simple as he made it."

"What is this wisdom of allusiveness, then?"

"The awareness that goes beyond the notion that matter is created by bundling little bits of things together. That's false. It ignores the involvement of energy, so much so that at that microscopic level anything we would think of as matter is absent. The mysterious nature of matter surrounds and imbues itself with enlivening energy, flowing in and out in a constant stream, connecting it with everything else in the universe. Energy, the kind known to your mystics but not studied by your scientists, can be simultaneously present everywhere. Harmonic relationships organize it into structures and into life, the anchoring place for Mind. Atoms are only mathematical points of demarcation in the great Hymn of Nature. Each is linked throughout the universe with others, and ultimately with everything. All are manifestations of some precise awareness, some particular pointillistic insight in the Eternal Mind. Without the energetic power that surrounds and defines each atom, channeled directly from the Infinite Wisdom of the Creative Force, the atoms themselves would lie lifeless in empty space, unconnected and incapable of procreation."

I can't exactly follow everything Isaiah's saying, but I think I understand his overall meaning. For everything tangible, there is a metaphysical energy that pulsates through its core. Everything has meaning, nothing is ordinary, nothing must be taken merely at face value. But even as I turn these thoughts over in my mind, I realize how far I am from really accepting them.

Isaiah understands much that is beyond me, yet his vision is strangely coherent. It seems illogical on the face of it, but when he points the finger and begins to dissect my beliefs, I find that none of my answers can withstand his analysis. Perhaps I should not fight, but follow where he leads. After all, he's putting a great deal of time and energy into this. He must care about me very much.

"Go on," I say, "Tell me more."

"Very well, then, where were we?" He seems to have become momentarily lost in his own inner webwork of thoughts and associations. He runs his fingers through his hair and looks off into space. Suddenly I feel awkward sitting across from him and I get up and pace. As I do, his flow of ideas resumes.

"Oh yes. Think back again about Democritus. See how he simplifies his sensation of the smell of bread into an abstraction. In doing so, he removes all that is holy and sacred, egotistically assuming that our sensory impressions alone should determine the nature of reality. The Eleusinian Mysteries no longer have a place in the scheme of things. This is a turning point in the history of thought. From Democritus' time to yours, scientific prejudice leans solidly in favor of matter, and it's hard to think of the world as anything but substance. The mystical gifts of the Creator gradually fade into the background, losing touch with human realities. There's a secular attitude fragmenting your culture's awareness of any significance in the daily business at hand."

I'm not so sure about this.

"There are lots of organized religions on Earth; do you mean to tell me they aren't spiritually inclined? You might say we render unto Caesar the things that are Caesar's but that does not mean we do not render unto God — "

Isaiah throws up his hand to interrupt me.

"In a contest between God and Caesar, Caesar always wins —"

"No!"

"— because he has more substantial weapons, given the perspective from which people in your time look at things!"

Once again I'm silent, unprepared to argue such matters. No, we humans can't be as seduced by material things as all that.

Can we?

"Perhaps you can see now that a great crevice ran between the science of your time and the perceptions of religious thinkers, a schism which could be attributed to something called reductionism. Unfortunately, since Democritus' insight was fundamentally incomplete, his concept fostered a skewed impression of the world in all who followed him. Science itself was founded on the rock of objectivity implied by atomic structure, which seemed so real and obvious that no one challenged it.

"The assumption of reductionism is correct, of course, but it is insufficient," Isaiah smiles. "Like listening to half of a telephone conversation. The reductionists didn't see — couldn't see — that the universe is built from the top down, just as much as it's built from the bottom up. They could see the action of the bricklayers, but the role of the architect was totally beyond them. They were unaware of the Laws of Resonance, so they looked only at material things, not at relationships."

"Of course they looked at relationships!" I interrupt, indignantly. "What do you think chemistry is about? What do you think electronic circuits consist of?"

"Those relationships are generated by material entities," he replies calmly, undisturbed by my protests.

"Not material! Electronics is energy, not matter, and chemistry has energy in it as well. No, distinctly not material."

"The relationships, though, are generated by material things. Electricity requires the material component of a circuit of wires. The mixture of two or more acids is material as well, even though it combines and releases energy. No, what I am talking about is relationships among the non-material energy fields themselves."

"How can you have energy fields that don't involve anything material?"

"Have you ever heard the term Love?"

"Of course," I say, squaring my shoulders. Does he think I'm dead or something?

"Is love generated out of material things?"

"Sure it is," I reply. "Love is a product of hormonal secretions in the human body. Everyone knows that."

"Maybe everyone in your time knows that," he says, "but not everyone in our time, which, you might want to recall, comes a thousand years after yours."

"Your society has regressed then."

"Perhaps we have," he replies, turning on that enigmatic grin.

He seems a little ashamed of himself for having pulled rank on me when he should have been guiding me along the path of wisdom. I like the feeling of power I get from pushing him into a tone that takes on a hint of defensiveness. If I can back him into a corner when he's over a thousand years ahead of me, well, that's something.

Immediately he removes the rigidity from his tone, leaving me disappointed.

"Now, don't get me wrong, it's true that in a certain sense we have regressed, but that's not necessarily a bad thing. We've returned to the roots of our being in a way that your contemporaries simply can't imagine."

"Well, I'm confused," I admit. "I need to hear more of what you have to say about relationships."

Cultures and Relationships

"First," Isaiah says, "I'd like you to think about a defining characteristic of your culture."

He has an irritating way of digressing from the question at

hand, as I've noticed several times. But I'm getting used to this circuitous dialogue. Isaiah paces, expressing his evident irritation with the conditions under which I've lived during my life as a human.

"How would you describe the kinds of relationships your culture elicited from the people you knew?"

It's a tough question. I think it over, trying to find a convenient way to sum it up.

"Most people hunger for relationships," I say. "But I don't think we understand how they work. Too many people feel isolated and alienated from each other and from society. It's even true that many of us feel we're wasting our lives looking for the perfect person, and living with blinders on most of the time. There may be no such person anyway, but you don't know until it's too late."

I let this sink in before trying to summarize my own experience. The truth is, it's not something I think about much unless I'm depressed or provoked into a conversation like this one.

"I try not to think about relationships very much," I say quietly.

"I know. This subject is quite a strain for you, isn't it?"

"Not really."

I don't want to let him have that one and he smiles as if he knows it.

"You're not fully processing these thoughts yet," he says, a certain unnerving condescension in his voice. "You haven't considered all the implications. When you do, you'll need a great deal more sleep and your mind will need to spend more time thinking about your relationships and your society and what they mean to you."

"I'll take that on faith."

"Do that."

As if to mark this change in the conversation, I move to the window and once more examine the distant planet of my birth, whose glassy image has become larger. Are we coming in for a landing?

"For the most part," Isaiah says, "the people in your culture spent their time acquiring and making things. The secret of your economy was bigger and better technology, more success at manufacturing, more ability to inspire others to want to buy and consume material objects . . ."

"That's not true," I break in, annoyed at his past tense reference to my time period and planet. Only a brief while ago I walked on Earth, was a part of it, was connected to it. I insist on using the present tense to refer to my world as it spins innocently in the window behind me. He's the one who forced me here.

"We're aware that we're moving from goods and services to information as our main economic product."

"That's not the point," says Isaiah. "The Information Age was nothing better than an excuse for doing a more comprehensive job of selling things. But nevertheless, you stumbled in the right direction in spite of yourselves. The networking of communications born of the Information Age eventually pushed humanity away from its obsession with material objects. After that, the onset of the great catastrophes pushed you even farther from it. But in your time that obsession was carried to the point where you treated human beings as if they, too, were objects. Even the President of the United States was a product, packaged and marketed like breakfast cereal or dog food. And you related to the planet itself as a purely material object to be exhaustively exploited, threatening its entire system of balance.

"But thanks to the enormous transformation virtual reality brought about, the human race was able to generate a great many material things at will, enormously decreasing their value so people began to focus their attention on things that were much more important."

"I still don't see what you're driving at."

"I told you. Love," he says.

"Oh, I get it. You're trying to dismiss my time period by saying that it lacked basic love? Love is an individual matter. Either people experience it or they don't. It can't be legislated, and it certainly can't become an automatic part of an entire culture! Anyway, I can't see where it would come from. Right now as we speak, the amount of misery, torment, viciousness and squalid immorality is increasing. Half the world is a playground for death, plague, despotic oppression and political violence. The other half is busily engaged in doing everything possible to make the poor poorer so the rich can get obscenely wealthy with no benefit to society at all. It isn't nice out there. Don't you think we all know that? What are your intentions for me, anyway? Are you under some delusion that I could actually do something about all this?"

"Well, that's up to you, of course," says Isaiah, treating my question as if it were something other than rhetorical. "Think about it. As you yourself said, society is breaking up. You are drowning in divorces, horrifying wars, rampant crime and drugs, poverty over more than half the world, famine, disease, terrorism — all the disruptions resulting from a failure to think about relationships. Despite that, the writing was on the wall with neon lights and sirens but you never got the point. As a culture it didn't dawn on you that in order to make everything work, you might first have to attend to what was going on within yourselves."

"Inner work, you mean? The inner child? We tried that stuff but it didn't fly. You can't get away with that kind of bullshit in a corporate environment. My generation's focus has changed from a commitment to tuning in and dropping out to balance sheets and bottom lines. There's nothing anyone can do about that. Either you get with the program or you have to find some kind of a niche in a society that has no concern for you at all."

Contempt for Isaiah's oversimplifications grows in me. I've been there, I've embraced Love Power, placed flowers down the barrels of National Guard rifles. I did all that. Love, Love, Love, but it didn't make society any better. It was only a silly distraction from the true nature of the human condition, which is to enforce the Territorial Imperative, to give to those who have, and hold down those who have not. There's always a war going on somewhere and I can't be concerned with the whole world. I have to build a career. I've got my own life and there's no more room underground. It's packed with cynical, disempowered, mute deserters; radicals in their youth who have become raving fiscal conservatives, attacking the values they supported a generation ago as if they too were in another world.

Still, I know Isaiah speaks the truth. I've spent most of my life inuring myself to the consequences of it. Something has been missing in my quest for love, in seeking it for myself and for the world. I don't like having his insight shoved down my throat; but still, it's the truth.

"Your generation needed to learn to make every marriage last," he says, "and you had no interest in such a thing. You needed to build an agenda that would make every parent-child relationship nurturing, every work experience fulfilling, every community fully functioning, every rehabilitation a total success. You needed to build the best educational system possible instead of hanging on to old, worn out traditions that kept education frozen hundreds of years behind its time. You had the opportunity to educate every child and adult in the world to a high level of intellect. There were methods available to you that would have accomplished that. But you saw no reason to pursue them. You did not see that education was important to your survival. The trouble was, you didn't really believe it could make any difference, because within yourselves you believed people were stupid. You had become so infatuated with the soon-to-be outmoded system of the market economy that you lost sight of what really creates wealth, and in the pursuit of the all-important bottom line, you failed to do the most fundamental things that would have improved your economy. You chose to believe that people who couldn't make it were simply bad and inadequate, and that survival of the fittest, a radical misinterpretation of the evolutionary process, was an appropriate way to think about a supposedly enlightened society with democratic principles.

"You, the people who made up the United States of America in the Twentieth Century, chose to blow every advantage that by mid-century you had developed for yourselves in order to bathe in the squalor of individual laissez-faireism in its crudest form. You hadn't the slightest sense of the possibilities you had created that could have built a better world, and you did everything you could to push your world towards extinction."

A cloud of violent anger has settled over his face. He looks at me thoughtfully, as if sensing that on some level I agree with him. To some extent I do. I'm not going to fight this anymore.

"The damage done in your time paralyzed the world for half a century and pushed it near the point of extinction, when virtually every advanced life form would have been killed off, except for the cockroaches. Fortunately, by the middle of the century after yours, healing forces gathered enough momentum to stop the reign of terror you brought upon yourselves. Not before a number of natural catastrophes, though, but fortunately they weren't enough to wipe us all out."

The Foundation of My Commitment

"So what do you want me to do exactly?" I ask.

"When you leave us, take back those elements of our society that you can understand and offer them to the people in your time. We believe that if your contemporaries had had more access to information about their possibilities, they might have made different choices and avoided great misery. Even in our own time we still suffer some of the scars left by the abominable decisions made while your people were alive, Noah. If we can transform the spirit that you ended your century with, we believe the results could have a positive impact on what's possible for us, even today."

Is he serious? Does he really believe one person could have such an influence? I am panic-stricken! Isaiah has something ambitious planned for me, something more complicated than anything I've ever undertaken. A heavy burden hangs on my shoulders as I contemplate a responsibility I can't imagine fulfilling.

I test the limits of my weightiness. I ignore Isaiah's words and walk off in one direction without turning back. As I do, the walls recede, and it seems as if the room moves with me. Isaiah remains in view, looking quizzically at me with an enigmatic smile on his face. He seems to be following me too, sliding along on the floor though he hasn't moved except to follow my actions with his penetrating gaze.

After walking for a while, I turn back and realize I'm looking down at Isaiah. By standing while he is sitting I've taken a position above him, even though I know it's a futile gesture.

"You're going to tell me something I'm not sure I want to know."

"Then why bring it up?" he says.

I reply that his answer might relieve my burden.

He smiles in that nerve-wracking way of his.

"I won't tell you anything you don't want to know. I've already said that your participation in this experiment is voluntary. You can return any time you please as if it had never happened. All traces will be wiped from your memory. Are you ready to return, then?"

Without hesitation I answer.

"Return me! I want out! I don't want any part of this depressing confrontation! You came into my life unannounced and jerked me out of bed, from my quiet sleep . . ." Then I remember my bouts of insomnia.

"It wasn't from your bed. You were writing at your computer. What were you writing about?"

"Private thoughts."

"About what?"

"About the futility of life."

"And—?"

"The injustice of that."

"Go on."

"And if only I could —"

"What? If only you could what?"

"Get close to someone. Just one person."

"So, then, you were feeling imprisoned in Hell. The Hell that is yourself without the perspective of another person."

"That's right."

"Well, if you stay with us, Noah, you'll find a way to cure yourself of that Hell. You were thinking Hell was other people though, weren't you?"

"I was thinking, well, damn other people!"

"The only people who were close to you were your parents. Do you feel that way about them?"

"Yes. No. Well, maybe. I suppose I did. Yes."

"Why?"

"Because they abandoned me. They stole the closeness I'd had with them."

"No, you took that from yourself."

He's right. But I was so young when they died.

"What we're asking you to do, Noah, is to go into the Hell of the totally isolated self and rescue the person inside. It won't be easy. It will strain your endurance, but when you're done, you will have atoned for the crime you committed."

"What crime?"

"You beat an innocent woman to death."

"I did not!"

"You did. You don't remember it."

"I could never do such a thing! I couldn't act violently towards anyone. It's not in me."

"Maybe not now. You'll see."

"What terrible things do I have in me?"

"If you stay, you'll see them. Do you want to go back?"

"No!"

What will I see? Isaiah must be making all this up. I'm not that sort of person. If I were, of course, no one could love me. But Isaiah seems to love me. Why? Perhaps he understands something about love, or about me, that I need to find out. Or, perhaps it's just . . .

"Because you're human," Isaiah says, reading my thoughts. "It is the only qualification one needs to be loved. We are all One and the Same. We must love each other purely for being humans."

I listen to this and bask in it, though I can't fully comprehend his way of thinking.

He's right. I don't want to go back to what I was before. I lived that way for a long time, but I've changed just enough never to go back. Even without any memory of what's happened here, some part of me would never be able to stand it. I'd never be happy, never at peace.

"You've existed for all eternity and always will," Isaiah says. "You'll have to make your peace with the tragedies in your life. There's no escape."

Strangely, the idea calms me. I'm ready to go on now.

"Tell me more about this experiment. I want to cooperate and help if can, but I have to tell you, I feel manipulated. You're jerking me around like a puppet on a string."

Isaiah faces me at eye level.

"Oh, that's impossible. You've chosen everything in your life. You're living out the dream you created long ago for yourself."

"That can't be!" I protest, thinking about my dead parents, my alcoholic grandfather, my unhappy marriage to Ellen, my difficulties in school, on the job, in society. "I'd never have chosen to take on all this crap!"

"On some level you did," Isaiah says quietly. "We seldom make choices unequivocally."

"What does that mean?"

"Some part of us is always discontented with the choices we've made, and we wonder what things might have been like if we'd made them differently. That's particularly true if your life is based on fundamentally dishonest judgments about its meaning."

I back away from him like an injured animal shielding its wounds, taking refuge in the sight of Earth from the window. We don't seem any closer to it, even after all this time. What's going on? I imagine myself walking down a long mirrored hallway which reflects another version of me on either side. Mirror after mirror repeats into infinity. Could I realize more than one choice in my life's design? Could I really move forward and backward in time and have things come out differently without disrupting the master plan of the universe?

Suddenly I turn to Isaiah, squarely facing him. For the first time I feel as if there's far more to me than I've ever acknowledged. The things that I once believed were important are not so crucial anymore, while other things that I imagined were insignificant have taken on extreme importance. For the first time in my life I accept what I'm feeling instead of pushing it away. Whatever I feel, I'm going to accept as part of me, to be acknowledged and welcomed. It used to be that unwelcome feelings disconnected from me and became my enemy. I'm not going to do that to myself anymore. I've had enough isolation, tormented with the demons of my unacknowledged fears.

"Tell me what you have to say."

"You don't want to go back, then?"

"No. I'm committed. This is it. Tell me what you want me to do. Tell me what my mission is."

"I can't," he says. "You have to figure it out yourself. All I can do is help you get some perspective on the thinking and behavior of your time so you can move things along."

My stomach is churning, but I feel determined. I've accepted the challenge and its consequences.

"Let's get on with it, then."

The Disaster of Civilization

He assesses me critically for a moment; then, seeming to see the strength I'm beginning to build, he clears his throat and continues: "What's at stake here is the way human beings must reattune themselves to the cosmos. Your contemporaries have largely lost touch with their humanity, and that's the source of the great discontent, fragmentation and general misery of your time."

"Just what is this 'humanity' thing they've lost touch with?"

Again, a faraway look comes into his eyes.

"For millions of years, we were hunter-gatherers," he says. "We lived seamlessly in nature, collecting her fruits each day, knowing that her bounty was inexhaustible, but that we needed to work hard enough to meet her half way. We didn't know how to think of ourselves apart from her, we were intimately connected to her and to one another. We knew ourselves through each other, through the world around us, as a child when she talks of herself in the third person sees herself as the entire universe. In those distant times, we heard in our minds messages that guided our daily activities. They spoke to us in units of thought that eventually became sign language and then spoken language, as we took great wisdom into our heads and shared it with each other. There were stories, epic poems, dances, drama and song — all tracing our species back to its origins in the mists of time and the love of the gods, who were the idealized selves of the many people that lived within us.

"The messages kept us together, bound us tightly in our families and tribes. We didn't have to learn what is right and wrong, we knew no difference between good and evil, because there was no difference. It was all merged in the expression of the Mother Of Us All, the natural force that pulsed through our bodies like a heartbeat and shaped the realm that surrounded us in the form of seasons and cycles of day and night."

He pauses, looking suddenly depressed.

"But then, Noah, the great catastrophe occurred."

"The great catastrophe?"

"It was the time of the floods that encompassed the entire globe. It was brought on as one of the Great Destroyers in the solar system careened into the Atlantic Ocean. For a long time most of the Earth was submerged by flood waters. We knew what it was to lose our families and friends and to have to begin again. Those that survived mourned the loss of families and tribes, and a racial memory developed that was transformed into a search for something to protect us. We began to know good from evil. Our attunement with the gods, or at-one-ment, was what we called good. Whatever separated us from them was evil. We labored day and night to assure good and to exorcise evil from ourselves. We discovered the arts of cultivation, and we invented agriculture, learning the details of seasonal cycles. We observed and noted the patterns in the stars. Our lifelong struggles were inscribed there, and we studied them to predict how we must protect ourselves. We invented prophecy and religion."

He pauses and smiles self consciously.

"That is where I come in. Prophecy."

"What do you mean by prophecy?"

"In your time you call it vision. It's knowing what creates the future, and it's based on seeing into the future through our connection with the light."

"What light?"

"The light that feeds our life and binds the entire universe into a single creative burst, the creative act that makes our future even as it makes our past. The future and past grow simultaneously in both directions from the central core of creation, elaborating each other, making love to one another. I know it's hard for you to understand this in the context of the myth of matter, but it's deeply etched into your soul as the marriage of memory and desire."

"It's beautiful, very poetic," I say. I am becoming skeptical of my skepticism, wondering if in my logical and scientific pursuit of understanding I have not missed some essential unseen ingredient. "What in particular makes you think that people are alienated from their own humanity?"

"Civilization was a very logical affair," says Isaiah. "It was our species' attempt to impose order on a universe that we felt betrayed us. It was the farewell to the notion that for thousands of years all things were expressions of eternal goodness. Then we invented judgment, law and condemnation. We imposed on ourselves the myth of our own sinfulness because we couldn't believe the gods made war on us capriciously. Out of our desire to appease the gods, we engineered the logical processes that would help us understand who they were and how they worked, so that we could appease them and protect ourselves from further catastrophe."

"It sounds like it all grew entirely out of fear."

"Exactly, Noah. That is why the protection we designed for ourselves became the catastrophe itself, an extension of the disaster of the flood, for it permanently imbedded a sense of loss, enslavement and the myth of scarcity to further divide us. No longer did we live in harmony with nature — the flood had taught us the folly of that. We viewed nature as an antagonist and sought to vanquish her, which alienated us from our own natures. We set aside nurturing, replacing it with domination and control. Violence replaced tenderness. Rationalism replaced intuition. We saw only detail, but lost the sense of totality. We focused on self-interest rather than on the interests of the community, dividing and conquering one another, and the universe as well.

"That's why we gravitated to the myth of atomic structure instead of the myth of the oneness of all things. We saw the universe as isolated fragments of things instead of as One Gigantic Idea, resonating within itself, producing infinite variation. We learned how to justify everything according to our selfish desires, rather than the eternal verities of nature."

"Are you condemning logic, thought and rationality?" I ask, incredulous.

"No," he says. "By no means would I condemn those qualities. In our time we've learned to see beyond the simple description of civilization as our species' greatest catastrophe, a defense against the flood. We've learned that a catastrophe is a call to action, a leap to the next level of development. This emergence of civilization built the full consciousness of the human race, articulated its structure, gave our species its destiny, which was to become the brain and nervous system of this planet. The instinctive forces of evolution invented stability and order, creating the garden in which the lion and the lamb could lie down peacefully together. God constructed the conversation, the dance of intellect, the art of continuous creation, the elaboration of beauty reflected in the mirror, the harmony of vine and fig tree. It was our transition to the Great Homecoming which your time couldn't imagine, but in which our time has learned to live. In order to find itself, it had to invent logic."

"It sounds as if the spirit were inventing the means to deny its own existence," I say.

"Admirably put," he responds.

"Why would it want to do that?"

"In the realm of free will," Isaiah says, "it has to be possible for the children of the Creator to deny that One exists. If they are compelled to acknowledge One, they have no free will. So things had to turn out this way."

"An extremely round about way for the Creator to prove a point," I say, wrinkling my brow at the logic of putting oneself out of business.

"The ways of God are unfathomable to us humans," says Isaiah.

I know that.

"Then why try to fathom them?" I ask.

"The search for understanding that is beyond our reach takes us to higher levels of insight," he says.

I have no answer for that.

Lost In Time

I am beginning to feel a little tired by now. I have no idea how long it's been since I passed out in my bedroom and began this far-fetched journey.

I get up and walk around, feeling the need to stretch my legs. Going up and down a few steps would be great exercise, but there aren't any stairs. As I walk, I carefully note the way the edge of space always recedes before me. This is intriguing.

Everything is bathed in blue light, which reminds me of my computer screen. For the first time since I arrived, I long to log into my journal again. Funny how I've put it out of my mind.

As I walk along and space precedes me, I realize I could walk for many miles in a straight line. Even though it seems we are in a very small place, that space is designed to regenerate as much of itself as one might need. I can walk a great distance in any one direction, and yet, with a few steps, return to Isaiah and talk to him. I try to imagine how this might work, determined that I won't ask him about it. It seems like it's time for me to work a few things out for myself.

Perhaps the floor is like a treadmill. As I walk, it rotates beneath my feet, giving me a sense of infinite opportunity; you don't usually get this feeling on a treadmill.

At any rate, it is quite remarkable that the floor can arrange itself this way in any direction. Still, more than a thousand years into the future is surely enough time to perfect a relatively simple effect like this.

I remember the wonderful art gallery Isaiah showed me soon

after I first arrived here. I wonder how the space I am in is constructed and whether, apart from the two assistants I was briefly introduced to, we are the only ones here.

A lot has happened, but how much time has passed?

"Where are we in time?" I ask Isaiah.

"No one can really say," he replies, walking towards me. "When we're traveling at great speeds across vast distances, our time ceases to be absolutely measurable in relation to anyone else's time. Of course, now that we're moving in the direction of a landing, we're very much closer to Earth at the time you're about to visit it. We're still traveling fast enough, though, so that a precise measurement is impossible."

"But if we're traveling so fast at such a great distance, why do I look out the window and see no sign that we're any closer to the Earth? It feels like we ought to have reached it by now."

"What you see out the window is still many light years away," he responds. "It's a focused image of Earth, projected for our benefit to keep us on course, but it's not a direct view. If it were, you'd have been right; we should have landed long ago, based on what you saw."

"When you travel anywhere you're always looking at the image of your destination?" I inquire.

He nods. "Actually, that's a very old invention, quite close to your time. The development of programmed unmanned vehicles that could fix a destination and travel to it by the best possible route occurred quite close to your time. In fact, I think it may already have been invented by the time we picked you up."

In the Sistine Chapel

He grins broadly and, as if reading my earlier thoughts, blinks the art gallery into view. This time I find myself standing inside the Sistine Chapel, looking up at the ceiling, just as I did on my visit to Rome about two years ago. I focus on God's creation of Adam, and feel the scene coming to meet me, as if I were on an elevator moving towards it.

How does the device know I am looking at it?

But I find an answer. It's sensitive enough to read the fine movements of my eyes and respond to them obligingly. Not bad! Still, in a thousand years of advancing technology, easily to be expected.

I regard the great painting of the Last Judgment directly in front of me, and am once again firmly on the marble floor of the chapel, with all the accouterments of worship around me.

This painting was tampered with after Michelangelo painted it, I remember. He painted all the figures naked and a later artist covered them with disfiguring folds of inappropriately colored clothing . . .

As the thought enters my mind, the painting shifts, displaying the nude figures Michelangelo originally painted. I am floored! This has to be the way it was meant to look! But what caused the painting to change so I can see it in its original form? Is the art gallery aware of my thoughts by reading my mind, capable of showing me whatever I wish to see at the moment I wish to see it? I can't invent my own solution to this technological problem.

I feel a sudden discontinuity between what I am experiencing and what Isaiah and I have been talking about.

"Move the paintings away, would you please?" I ask him.

He makes no motion to do so, but at my words, the Sistine Chapel disappears and we are once again surrounded with that same relaxing blue light.

"Doesn't a device like this get in the way of building a proper relationship to nature?" I ask.

Isaiah laughs with apparent pleasure, as if he thinks I am on the right track for once.

"As long as we humans lived in a primeval state, there was no need for virtual reality. But once we were cast out of the Garden of Eden with the advent of civilization, once we were thrust into a direct confrontation with unclear and ambiguous Nature, the phenomena we began to experience in relation to the environment became very complex indeed. Virtual reality has enabled us to see those larger or smaller features of nature that are essential for us to understand and get along with her. It allows us to see long term trends, or evaluate how a tiny disturbance in some part of the environment can generate huge consequences in another."

"Like mind reading?"

"Sort of," says Isaiah. "Virtual reality represents the content of both left brain and right brain. It enables us to shift our perspective, sometimes coming in close to our field of vision, allowing us to see minute details, and sometimes receding back so we can get the scope and vision of the entire view we're looking at. Only as we've learned to see these interrelationships have we learned to respect Nature and build the kind of environment for ourselves that we need if we are to survive as a species on our planet."

"And in my time," I say, "we're just figuring out how to use this tool which you think of as part of the natural environment because it's been with you for so long."

"It's truly an extension of our human intelligence," he nods. "In a sense it was ordained from the beginning that we should develop and use it just the way we now do. That's why our extremely complex brains were evolved in the first place, so we could play our proper role in the ongoing process of creation."

Why We Create Our Losses

"So then, you really think that the process of evolution is purposeful?"

"Yes and no," he says.

"But how can it be both at once?" I ask.

"It's a creative process. If you've ever written a poem or a story or painted a picture or created a tune in your head, you'll know what I mean. The process seems to flow. But as you allow it to flow, you shape it subtly. Sometimes you stop it altogether and work on it. You have a general sense of where you're going, but the process itself takes over much of the time, and creates for you.

"That's very much the way the universe creates itself. It just flows most of the time, but at crucial points, thinking takes over. It's not the kind of thinking you and I do, not at all; but it is a kind of thinking, and it shapes things and directs them. It comes from a conscious awareness of the position and movement of every subatomic particle that makes up the trillions of galaxies. It is that extraordinary multiple awareness that we call omniscience, which can give meaning and shape to the tiniest events whenever that is needed. And what we call omnipotence is the ability of that omniscience to affect a change at any point when it seems appropriate to do so. It is that process that people pray to when they seek miracles."

"But many times people pray and their prayers are not answered," I say. "Many times good people have bad things happen to them. Many times things happen that are repulsive even to think about."

"Yes, that is true, from a worldly perspective," says Isaiah.

"But you must remember that consciousness itself is evolving and that it needs these tragic events, these 'bad things,' as you call them, to shape the ongoing life that a particular phase or fragment of the consciousness is developing. Consciousness moves, in its evolution, from the ultimate simplicity of an awareness of pure being to a multi-layered repertoire of a wide range of behaviors, value judgments, experiences and ideas that may take millions of years to build. It evolves as surely as the physical bodies that hold it evolve.

"Looking back over our lives most of us can see the sense of much that happened which we didn't like at the time. Sometimes we can't, though, which means that the meaning of the event which we deplore is something we cannot access within the context of our current lifetime. In general, though, we find that the universe will give us much that we need, but not necessarily what we want, and usually not when we want it."

"I've never been able to understand why my parents were taken from me," I say. "I feel even now that their deaths deprived me of a basic need. I needed them then."

"Think of it this way. One of the reasons you were picked for this experiment was that the very loss of your parents forced you to develop a certain sense of responsibility and a certain skepticism about the rightness of things that has closed you off in many respects in the past, but can open you up in the future to be perceptive and aware of many things other people who did not suffer such a loss cannot be aware of. The very loss of the symbols of security in your life makes you more vulnerable to, and therefore more aware of, the larger insecurities of your time."

"It certainly hasn't made me happy."

"But what makes you think happiness is the point?" he says. "You did not go to earth to achieve happiness, you had that already. You went to it to achieve a new development in your consciousness."

"What nonsense."

"Not at all. The ability to experience joy exactly mirrors the ability to experience grief. Positive emotions have their mirror in negative ones. When you have suffered, you have developed the capacity for greater joys. That collective experience which you've had in life you can carry with you through all eternity. You come to earth to increase your capacity for such sensitivities, so you can experience greater joy in the long run."

"I don't find that explanation very satisfying," I say.

"Let me put it differently, then," replies Isaiah. "Each little fragment of our lives contains the whole of the universe, so whatever you experience always has meaning in terms of its totality. You are always in direct contact with the Mind of God, and through the Mind of God you're also in contact with everyone and everything else in the universe. The nature of this contact is marshaled through the Laws of Resonance, so you will be attracted to those people and events most in harmony with your current state of being. As that condition of being changes, so will the people and events you are drawn to. By changing your condition, you have the potential of becoming intimately related to anything anywhere in the universe."

"But the universe is so incredibly immense . . ."

"Indeed so," he says, anticipating my question. "But you also have an unlimited amount of time to explore all possible relationships. In order that this unlimited time not overwhelm you, you have an unlimited number of conscious states you can enter into. Though your sense of self will always be present, your memory of your previous consciousnesses will fade. Only when you become more advanced in the quality of your consciousness will you be able to remember and contact other states of consciousness outside of the one you've adopted for your current state of being."

"And that's what's believed to be true in your time?" I ask.

"Yes," replies Isaiah, "but don't be so impatient about it. One of the gravest of your problems," he continues, "was that you obsessed so much about time. As the philosopher Eric Hoffer said of your contemporaries, 'We are taught not to waste time and brought up to waste our lives.' Because you didn't understand how time is played out, you couldn't use it to govern your lives well. Unlike you and your contemporaries, many of the so-called primitive peoples who were driven out by the catastrophe you call civilization, very well understood time and how it played out."

Doing Without Atoms

Time? Is there such a thing as time anymore, out here in space between two widely separated periods in human experience? I certainly can't feel it from where I am sitting.

Isaiah continues, "You don't understand much of anything happening in your own time, the time you've selected for the stage of evolution important to your soul."

"I have no way of understanding it," I say, feeling more helpless than a newborn infant. "You keep reminding me of that."

"I know, but it's my job to help you find a way to do so."

Suddenly I feel sick to my stomach. Isaiah expects me to change everything about myself. I am in no way qualified for the task he has planned for me. I feel committed to it and at the same time totally inadequate.

I want to sit down, but don't see a place where I can. I start to sink down, with the intention of sitting on the floor; but from out of nowhere a platform materializes beneath me, allowing me to gently ease myself into a sitting position. Isaiah too sits down facing me on another, mirrored version of this conveniently placed piece of cosmic furniture.

"How did that work?" I ask feebly, dimly trapped in my new awareness, a jumble of Never-Never Land impressions.

"It surprises you, doesn't it?" says Isaiah, smiling in his friendly but nevertheless irritating way.

"Yes," I say, "if you insist on using so mild a word to label my confusion, it surprises me. If you're going to call this virtual furniture, it's something that doesn't exist yet for me, and I don't understand it at all."

Isaiah laughs heartily.

"The sight of a television set would have surprised your ancestors," he reminds me. "They'd have wondered how people could appear inside a box and move around in so many different sizes, while changing their scenery so often. It would have seemed bizarrely impossible to them."

"I suppose so," I say, wondering what my ancestors would have thought of commercials.

"There's far less difference between what you've just experienced — the materialization of a bench out of thin air — and the world you're used to, than there is between a color TV broadcast and the average Eighteenth Century person's daily reality. In their time, it was believed that if you were to travel at, say fifty miles an hour, you would suffocate from the rush of air in your face. Their orientation towards technology and the physical realm was almost unrecognizably different from yours."

"But I understand how TV works, and I don't understand how this works," I protest with some irritation, gently patting the platform on which I am sitting.

"No, you don't understand how TV works," says Isaiah. "If you did, you'd be able to extrapolate how it's possible to materialize any object where and when you wish. The ability to focus and broadcast radio waves is only a short step removed from the ability to shape magnetic fields and produce the illusion of objects which perception cannot distinguish from the real thing. Though these objects don't have atomic structure, they're accomplished by the same process atomic structure makes possible: the interface of magnetic fields to produce an illusion of solidity, which, in reality, isn't any more present in things composed of atoms than it is in the object you're now sitting on."

Is it really all that simple?

"As you continue visiting with us, I hope you'll gain a basic understanding of this process, for this aspect of mental interaction with energy has liberated us from the technological drive to destroy the Earth. Consider the enormous advantages we've achieved. By being able to materialize things like furniture, or even whole buildings, simply by pulling together magnetic fields into focused structures, we save the labor of building them, and also the assault on the environment that occurred long ago when people stole building materials from the Earth."

This is really too good to be true. "You mean you can actually create the illusion of atoms out of nothing? You mean that there's no difference between real matter and this made up stuff? I don't see how that's possible."

"It wouldn't be if we had to rely on atoms. But atoms are largely irrelevant to the structures human beings call matter. The surrounding fields which organize the atoms produce all the characteristics of elements that we've come to depend on in our complex retreat from materialism. As I told you, what you're sitting on doesn't have any atoms in it at all. At least, not beyond those that were already within the atmosphere out of which this was instantaneously built."

"I guess I understand that," I say, but still it's hard to believe him. I slap my hand hard against the side of the platform and feel the sharp sting of pain. It feels a bit like marble. A bright pink color suffuses my hand.

"There must be atoms in this thing!" I say, rubbing my stinging hand.

"Oh? What do atoms feel like?"

"Well, I suppose I have no idea," I say, though I know how my hand feels.

"Atoms are one structure for building material objects, but not the only structure. Magnetic fields have just as much power to create impenetrable barriers as atoms do. Even in your time it was commonplace for physicists to build magnetic walls so impenetrable that atoms traveling at high speeds could not crash through them. Simply by lining up the magnetic fields of all atoms already in the atmosphere, we're able to create substances that seem no different from other material substances, but actually have only the tiniest fraction of true matter in their makeup. This is an extremely complex technology, but it's not unrelated to the technology that powers a television set. TV uses magnetic fields in a primitive way to produce the illusion of people talking to one another. Similarly the magnetized iron filings on tape produce the illusion of instruments and human voices engaged in musical performances. It's all done with light and magnetic fields. In your time, though, despite the fact that you had some of the basis for this technology, it would have been prohibitively expensive to use it in this manner, since you would have had to keep electrical current constantly supplied to maintain the object you were creating in proper shape. A power outage could have caused a whole city to disappear if you'd tried to do this sort of thing with the technology you had then. Our technology is, of course, a great deal more sophisticated than that."

"I imagine so," I say. "But how did this thing get here?" I ask, referring to the platform. "It appeared the moment I started to sit down."

"It got here because I willed it," says Isaiah.

Extensions of Ourselves

"You willed it here?"

Isaiah nods. "Today we understand that energy patterns generated by our thinking can be brought under conscious control using thought waves. In your time these were crudely measurable on electroencephalographs. Today, in our time, any human being can be trained to produce thought forms that can be detected by technological systems. In order to produce a platform like this one, I mentally visualize a symbol that's designed to be detected by one of our lasers. We learn a number of different symbols — a whole language, in fact — that we use to communicate with these laser systems, and they materialize the objects we want when we want them. Some of our most usable responses were universal human reactions already, based on subtle eye movements. That's why the system can respond to thought patterns in simple ways."

"A-Amazing —" I stammer.

"This new language of technology has benefited the human species enormously. It has greatly improved our somewhat atrophied ability to visualize; and this has helped us in many other important things, such as techniques of self-discovery and communication."

"I can imagine there might be a way to explain how you got the bench for *you*, but how did you get it for *me*?"

"It's as simple to learn as sign language or typing were in your day. I used the symbols I can project into thought forms to provide you with a bench before you sank onto it."

"Very thoughtful of you," I say, laughing. "Or perhaps it was thoughtful of the technology! Who should I be thanking, anyway?"

"Who gets the thanks when you drive someone around in your car? You? or the car?"

"Yes, I get the point."

"We long ago accepted technology as an extension of ourselves," says Isaiah, "just as, in fact, you do. Don't you get angry at an automobile that cuts in front of you, as if it were the technology, not the driver that is at fault?"

"Not really," I say because I don't want to concede the point; but now that he's made the observation I realize I actually do think that way sometimes.

"Anyway, if it makes you happy, you can thank both of us," Isaiah continues.

"As we have learned to use our technology more effectively, we've brought it to the point where we can reduce its imposition on natural forces to the vanishing point.

"For example, our use of transportation has been enormously reduced compared to what was in your time. We're content to stay in our homes almost all the time, since we can easily surround ourselves with virtual reproductions. As you've already experienced, it's possible to walk for miles in your own front hall and surround yourself with any scenery you might choose. There's very little demand for recreational travel since we can be in an extraordinary number of environments any time we want. People have returned to the ancient custom of spending their lives in a single community, enabling them to build strong, enduring relationships."

Not much intimacy in my world, I reflect. Everyone's running scared of everyone else, at least in my set. You can live out your life in an apartment building and never see, let alone get to know, more than a tiny handful of the people who live there. You can't trust your neighbor because you don't know your neighbor; so how can this state of affairs foster anyone's desire to be their brother's keeper?

"Still, I think I ought to give you a bit more of a chance to see what our technology is actually capable of," Isaiah says, breaking in on my musings.

Encounter with a Witch

Suddenly we are no longer sitting in our hazy blue room. We stand in the middle of a busy street filled with people and horses, in a time and place I vaguely recognize.

An overwhelming smell accosts my senses, so revolting and putrid I gag. Where are we? The smell is pervasive. As I glance up, a ghastly sight fills me with revulsion.

Disembodied heads are lined up on spikes, displayed over the crowd. Blood drips from two of them, but the rest are gore-encrusted, their flesh partially eaten. I realize the street I am standing on is London Bridge! People pass before the sickening review of severed heads on the bridge as if nothing is amiss. Mud-stained children chase one another through the crowd, oblivious to the stench and its source, as if it were routine.

I am in England in what must be the Sixteenth or Seventeenth century.

I barely collect my thoughts when I'm seized and carried off by a newly arrived mob of people, violently wrought-up and running across the bridge. Like a rushing river surging forward, they carry me along, a piece of driftwood on strong current.

I lose sight of Isaiah.

Separated from my tour guide, I am seized with terror, lost in this terrible century among these barbaric people. This is no amusement park entertainment. This is real, the danger palpable to all my senses. My heart is pumping frantically. Panic surges through my body. I am not prepared for this, not in any way. All reason, all feeling is lost in fear. Things could easily get out of hand in a mob like this. Where is Isaiah?

Suddenly my eyes are drawn to the man leading the crowd. His thick neck and hurtling arms are red hot with anger. As I focus my gaze on the back of his head, I feel hypnotized. My sense of being is catapulted right into that head, and I become that man, raging, lusting for blood, bent on destruction. I am in front now, leading the mob in furious pursuit.

A terrified woman, her long black hair streaming behind her, speeds ahead of me.

"Witch!" I cry. "Kill the witch!"

My accusation echoes from the mob behind me.

I realize I do not know her. She throws a terrified glance over her shoulder. Suddenly I'm horrified. I know I'm wrong, that this woman is innocent. I must stop before the mob takes over. A wave of guilt sweeps through me but the rage is stronger. It has a life of its own. Nothing can stop me. I am like two different people in the same body, aware of both, yet unable to communicate between the two. Caught up in this murderous lust, a prisoner of rage and death, I, as much as my victim, am trapped.

The woman trips and falls, and in an instant my body is upon her. I raise my fist to strike. She twists under me and her eyes catch mine. My rage melts into pity. In the act of striking her, I know I'm killing an innocent person. An agonizing love fills me one moment, only to be extinguished the next. And in one terrible movement my hands wring her neck, forcing life suddenly from her.

Her limp body falls. All motion stops. I lie in silence, forced to confront what I have done.

My mind freezes. I pull myself up from the bridge and walk into town, passing the savage faces of the mob.

A worthless and wasted life has just begun.

Somewhere in the back of my consciousness I hear a familiar voice.

I'm seated on the platform facing Isaiah as before, yet in my mind I'm still on London Bridge.

I can't shake myself free of despair. My body is still suffering the after-effects of the panic and exertion.

Tears fill my eyes.

Isaiah waits.

But it wasn't real. The whole thing was an illusion; not one ounce of reality in it anywhere! I can't believe I bought into all that! I was never on London Bridge. Isaiah projected that tragedy for my benefit and I allowed myself to be carried away with it. Ridiculous behavior, feeling so involved in the drama, like a child talking back to a TV set.

Isaiah has a knowing look, as if he sees some change in me.

I question him with my eyes, but he withdraws his concern, letting it fade into triviality.

"See how much we can do with our technology?" he says, pacing the floor to distract me from what has just happened. His voice is calm and unruffled, despite the anguish I feel.

"I was in high-tech fear and rage — and — guilt," I admit, still shaking.

"I know. I was there. I saw you."

"Why didn't you stop me?"

"I'm not allowed to interfere with the plan, no matter how terrible it may seem at any given moment."

"It was a horrifying experience!"

"Sorry, but you chose the setting from the menu of your own consciousness."

"If that came from my own consciousness, then you put it there. You planted that suggestion a little while ago."

"I'm sorry. You're quite mistaken."

A deep question troubles me but I'm afraid to ask it. Isaiah seems unconcerned about my feelings. I don't think I'll ever be the same again.

"You experienced something troubling," he says, sounding like a dime store psychoanalyst.

"That's an understatement! I killed someone!"

"Very unfortunate," he says calmly. "But you needed to do that for some reason, though why isn't clear. In due time, I'm certain you'll find out what it means."

For the first time he notices how badly I'm shaken. The memory of what I've done will torment me forever. And that woman — I killed her!

What was that trace of recognition that passed between her

and that man, or was it me? Whatever it was, I can't think about it!

"Just relax," Isaiah says. "This experience has deeply affected you in a way I didn't anticipate."

I can tell he's lying. He has always known exactly what would happen. It's all part of the experiment.

"There is a way to reduce the trauma," he says. "Follow my finger as I move it in front of your eyes. Don't move your head, just follow with your eyes."

Still a bit numb, I follow his directions. As his finger moves rapidly around in circles, I trace the gyrations of its motion. After thirty seconds, he stops and asks how I feel.

I am surprised to find myself relaxed and relieved from my trauma. Fear and desperation seem distant, more like faded memories than distinct realities.

"Good," he says. "Let's do that again."

Before we're finished, he puts me through five episodes of these eye movements. Then he asks me how I feel. I admit that my frenzied emotions are entirely gone. I am calm again.

"What's that you just did?" I ask. "Is it some sort of hypnosis?"

"The brain has an infinite capacity to adjust," says Isaiah. "This technique was known in your time, but I'd forgotten that someone in your social milieu might not know about it. Emotional demands are commonplace for us, and we use rapid eye movements to re-acclimatize ourselves. Whenever we're thrown off emotionally, we rebalance ourselves using this technique."

By now, London Bridge is far behind me. I am eager to return to our former conversation.

The Trouble With Einstein

"You said you wanted me to come to some kind of basic understanding," I remind him. "You also said I don't understand how television works. Let's deal with the easier of these two questions first. What is it about television I don't understand?"

"You have no understanding of the electromagnetic spectrum — what it is, and how it relates to matter," Isaiah replies. "You should understand it, given the state of knowledge about technology in your time — but you don't."

"Why should I?" I want to know, feeling rather defensive on this point.

"Because it's clearly symbolized and embedded in the most famous equation ever written, the equation on which Einstein based his theory of relativity."

"Show me," I said, becoming downright irritated with my know-it-all mentor. I check my irrational fervor, though, reminding myself that he knows many things I can't know. After all, he is the more advanced being, and anyone living in his time would probably know most of the things he's been telling me. Perhaps, or perhaps not, depending on how well informed they might be. Are there any more at home like him, I wonder? Do people vary greatly in his time too? I have no way of guessing what he might know that would set him apart from others, even in his own time.

"The trouble with Einstein was that he never even remotely understood his own theory," says Isaiah.

"Say that again?"

"Einstein was a dyed in the wool Newtonian who resisted the true meaning of relativity to his dying day. He never exploited the most interesting implications of that famous equation of his."

"Please clue me in on what you're driving at," I demand.

"What I'm driving at is the matter myth, which we've already given some thought to, but let's go into it more deeply now, shall we? I think we're ready. You've had some experiences that should prepare you better for what you're going to see in our world."

I nod, and he continues, "In your time you didn't understand that matter was a myth because you didn't understand half of the most famous equation ever written."

"Which one?"

"$E = mc^2$."

"We knew that equation very well. I myself have followed through the derivation of it that Einstein supplied. I understand why it leads to the conclusions that it does."

"Very well, what does it mean, then?"

"Essentially what it boils down to is that matter and energy are interchangeable."

"Wrong. Sorry, but that's the Newtonian version. It has a certain poor power of its own, I admit. It helped produce the atomic bomb. But that's not the meaning of the equation — not even remotely. You knew the m, but you did not know the E and the c^2."

"All right, then, explain it to me."

"The equation clearly states that matter is energy. You see, if the equation meant what you said it did, it would be written $E = m$."

"Now you're really in trouble with your reasoning," I protest. "I may not be a mathematician, but I am aware that the whole point of the equation is that energy and mass are not equal. A small amount of mass produces a great deal of energy. You have to put something beside the m in the equation in order to get E. That's the point."

"Why?"

"Because E is enormously larger than m."

"What does that mean?"

"What do you mean, what does it mean? You're supposed to know!"

Isaiah smiles.

"Let me repeat the question. What does it mean that a small amount of mass produces an enormous amount of energy? How can you compare mass and energy anyway, since in their very different states, they're not remotely the same thing? It's like trying to compare a Shakespeare play with complex computer program assembly instructions! There's no meaningful way to compare them, or to weigh one in relationship to the other."

He evidently realizes he is on a high horse, because he smiles rather sheepishly before he continues. "Well, before you get all tangled up in this, let me tell you it doesn't mean anything to say that there's more of one than the other. A particular amount of mass produces a particular amount of energy. That's all anyone can say! And that statement, if it were true, would be captured in the formula $E = m$. But it's not true, and that's why Einstein used the formula he did."

"But where did he get the formula?"

"He observed certain relationships that were already known in his time, that created specific problems. Einstein's genius turned a problem into a law of nature. By saying that certain relationships were supposed to be as they were actually observed to be, he was able to make clear statements about the universe that led to predictable observations which proved his mathematics correct. But that doesn't mean he knew what he was talking about, or that he understood all the implications of his formula. In fact, most of the scientists of your day made no claim to understanding what they were talking about. They could describe certain relationships, but that did not mean they understood where they came from, or why they were the way they were. From the time of Sir Isaac Newton, that had never been required. Science did not answer why, it merely described what. Einstein made a formula that would predict certain interactions, which is what most scientists do. This doesn't suggest that they understand the implications of their predictions. In fact, Einstein was part of a weird new age of physics he himself never understood or accepted. He spent most of his life opposing it and trying to prove it wrong. This kept him from contemplating the more far-reaching implications of relativity. Contained in the theory of relativity is information that should have helped people to see what matter actually is, why the universe is nothing but an idea (though a very grand one it is!) and why all events in our lives have a predominantly spiritual reality and meaning."

This is too much for me.

"Now wait a minute!" I object. "Mass and energy aren't interchangeable? Is that what you're saying?"

"That's right," he replies. "They're not."

"This is insane! How can you say that?"

"Because it's true."

"Okay, I give up. Tell it to me straight. Explain this crazy reasoning of yours."

"This is a discovery that the physicist John Wheeler first made during your time, but like many great ideas it was ignored. It wasn't until seventy-five years after your death that the true importance of his discovery was appreciated and the Laws of Resonance were first formulated in a truly scientific manner. Looking back on it, it seems like an incredible delay in the development of scientific reasoning. Most of the scientists in your time had little interest in the underlying spiritual structure of the universe, the aspect that allows one to see through physics into the operation of the Mind of God. Wheeler showed that mass and energy in the strictest sense of the word are not interchangeable. This is because, in a very deep sense, there is nothing that needs to be interchanged, any more than ice is interchanged with water when it melts. It simply becomes water, which is a different state of what it has been all along."

Mass Alone Does Not Exist

Silence falls as I try to digest Isaiah's words. Even though he pauses to let me think things through, he doesn't seem to appreciate that this onslaught of new insights is too difficult for me to grasp right away.

He looks at me. I think he thinks I must be hungry, because he offers me an apple, seemingly plucked from nowhere.

More curious than hungry, I take a bite. It does taste good, I have to admit, and it takes my mind off the confusion and obsessive worry that I'll never understand what he's trying to teach me.

Isaiah continues his remarks along the same lines as before.

"Mass is a manifestation of energy in a particular condition and form," he says. "It has no independent being apart from energy. It's even true that the amount, quality and shape of mass in any given subatomic package varies enormously with the interaction occurring at the moment. The top quark, for example, is much more massive than the proton that contains it — a fact which makes sense only if you know that there's no absolute mass, only energy congealing mass here and there. But taken all in all, the quality of solidity you associate with matter makes a distinctly minor impression on the face of the deep.

"There is no mass, no possibility of mass, no capacity of a possibility of mass — apart from energy. What you call mass is almost entirely pure energy, so much so that it disappears altogether from the equation. Mass is an illusion. There is no mass."

"No mass?"

"No." he smiles. "Not in the form in which you think of it."

"Well, what else isn't there?"

"There's no time."

"Got it. No time. What else?"

"There is no space."

"I see," I say. "Then where the heck are we?"

How It Looks to an Unfettered Photon

There's that grin again.

"These implications rest quite solidly in Einstein's equations, but he never understood their full meaning. The result was a needless dichotomy between quantum mechanics and relativity that grew into a wide chasm."

"Now look here," I say, feeling as if I'm in the middle of an Abbott and Costello routine. "I can understand that Einstein might not have understood his own formula, but how could it exist for the better part of a century with all the brightest minds in the world studying it, with no one ever noticing it wasn't accurate?"

"Oh, it's accurate enough," says Isaiah. "It's just that what people thought it said was only a small part of what it really said. Scientists got correct information from the formula, but they didn't get all it had to offer, or even its most compelling insights. Everyone, including Einstein, ignored what the equation told them, because the implications were so obvious no one gave them any thought."

"How could that be?"

"Did you ever read 'The Purloined Letter'?"

"Yes. A letter is hidden from detectives by placing it where letters are normally kept."

"Good. And that's what happened with the most profound insights that came from the theory of relativity. To start with, consider what happens when a person or an object attempts to travel at the speed of light."

"It can't be done," I say. "Mass becomes infinite." Then I hesitate. "But if there's no mass, how can it be infinite?"

"I didn't say there was no mass. I said there was no mass that wasn't almost entirely made up of energy."

"Almost entirely?"

"Some of it is the mathematical consequence of spin," he says.

"Go on," I say, wishing we could go on to a different subject.

"At the speed of light, mass — including the enormous amount of energy needed to create it — becomes infinite. Time disappears. And if time disappears, space must disappear too."

"Why?"

"Because the only use for time is to measure the speed with which something travels through space. If nothing travels through space, then there's no time. And if there's no time, then there can't be any space, since there's no possibility of traveling through it. This may seem like a tautology, but it's actually the way time and space define and create one another."

"They do that?"

"Yes. Einstein described what happens to a clock when you travel on a beam of light at the speed of light. When you leave the clock behind you, the hands travel with you in the form of the light they emit. In a practical sense you can't tell any difference between the real clock and the light bringing you the information about the clock, because that's what you see in order to determine there's a clock there in the first place. Because you're traveling along with the light rays, they can never change. Time can't progress."

"But that's a violation of relativity," I say.

"How so?"

"The speed of light is absolute. It will always be measured at 300,000 kilometers per second, no matter how fast you're going. The light coming from the clock should go right past you, even if you're traveling at the light speed, because speed doesn't affect the perception of light." I'm very proud of this. I've demolished his whole argument.

I've also succeeded in shooting down the Theory of Relativity. I must be missing something here.

"That's true," says Isaiah, in counter-attack. "But if you're traveling at the speed of light, you would cross the entire universe in less than a second from your point of view, even though a stationary observer would think it took billions of years. So the light from the clock would never reach you because it doesn't have time. At the level of consciousness which travels at the speed of light there is no time. That makes a second infinitely long, far too long for light to get anywhere at all. So from its own point of view, light doesn't travel."

"But what about all the things going on in the universe? Surely there are all sorts of events light might take notice of if it were conscious, though how it would do so is unclear to me."

"Those events are enfolded into light's consciousness and are simultaneously maintained without any real separation in time. It's a concept that's already familiar to you. When you hold a book in your hands, you hold a record of events enfolded into the book. The beginning or end of the story doesn't happen until you read the book. Until you, the observer, interact with the book, it has no meaning, yet the potential is there. Your memory also contains a great many events enfolded into it all at once. Only when you allow your consciousness to interact with them do they sort in relation to each other. Consciousness orders events, positioning them in time and space, indeed creating time and space for them to be positioned in. The presence of light in matter gives it the ability to occupy time and space. Light, enfolded into matter by chasing its tail in whirlpools of energy, becomes its building blocks. Light trapped in whirlpools has no way to escape except by inventing time and space in which it can observe and interact."

"But light moves through space. We can see it," I challenge. "It takes eight minutes for it to reach the earth from the sun."

"That's only your interpretation," replies Isaiah. "The perceived time that light takes to travel from one point to another depends on the relative motion of the observer. From the point of view of light, it simultaneously fills the universe, an easy thing to visualize if you're filling a dimensionless point."

I throw away the apple core as Isaiah continues. It disappears into the blue surround.

"Imagination is the ultimate source of reality. As light imagines itself filling in a dimensionless point, it fills an infinitely large universe, creating the illusion of time and space."

"But how can this happen? What are the mechanics?"

"Infinitely mysterious," says Isaiah, "but let's take a crack at it anyway. Suppose you are unalterably closed up in a very tiny space. For the sake of discussion, even though a dimensionless point lacks space, we'll pretend that this small space constitutes all there is for you."

"All right. I can follow that," I say, remembering childhood hours imagining things in my darkened closet with a flashlight, pretending I was sailing through space.

"As you sit in that space, imagine that you're moving forward in a straight line. But the trouble is, as soon as you do that, because your universe is infinitely small, you end up coming at yourself from behind you. The paradox is that in going forward in a straight line, you end up in a whirlpool, spinning endlessly in confinement."

"You could wave at yourself as you go by."

"I suppose you could, if you wanted to. This is the dilemma light finds itself in when it tries to move forward or fill its nonexistent space. It's thrown back on itself, spinning endlessly for all eternity."

"Somewhat existential, isn't it?"

"I would say so, yes. In this act of endless spinning, it can't move forward at all."

I admit this is an inevitable conclusion.

"So in the paradox of moving forward and at the same time only being able to spin in upon itself, light takes on a dual nature. Now it's no longer confined in the prison of nothingness, but it's created an endless playground. It simultaneously fills that playground with one aspect of itself while leaving behind spinning confinement, dividing itself into two different states of being."

"Like a split personality," I venture.

"If that helps you understand it, fine. At first, the duality light creates means that pleasure and pain are indistinguishable. Activity is all there is. But as soon as consciousness is defined, light feels trapped in matter and longs to be free. Only a gradual process of escaping from material form allows this. This escape powers the engines of the stars, which produce and expel light through atomic fusion. As light moves from the internal structure of the star to its surface, it moves from a circular, spinning form to a beam of waves which travel the vast reaches of space in perfectly straight lines."

I am spellbound by something as fundamental as light!

"In splitting into these two opposing states of being," Isaiah continues, "light discovers it can watch its own performance. Caught in stationary spinningness, it can observe the other part which is free to travel in straight lines, while the traveling part can interact with the spinning whirlpools. But there's a very paradoxical rule that's generated out of this."

Trying to Understand Nothing

"What's that?" I ask.

"The rule that the spinning parts of light can't travel with their non-spinning essence, but must remain self-contained in their own little worlds. Out of this rule comes an infinite multiplicity of worlds, because in the dimensionless point in which this is being imagined, infinity and nonexistence are one and the same thing."

"Huh?" I am lost now more than ever.

"Did you know that there are two things the human mind has never been able to imagine?"

Because I can't imagine them, I can't quite answer his question.

"Infinity and nothingness," Isaiah replies, since I haven't been able to come up with anything. "No matter how we try to imagine infinity, we are able to think of it only as a very large number. We have to make a deal with our minds allowing us to reason that no matter how large a number we envision, there's always something larger. That's our idea of infinity, or at least one of the ideas about it — probably the best we can do with it.

"That brings us to nothingness," he sighs. "We're even more stymied there, because no matter how hard we try to imagine the total absence of being, there's always our being to imagine it, and so total nothingness can't be imagined. It's inconceivable by the human mind."

I remember my first brush with nothingness. Or, what I would have wished could be nothingness, for I wanted to cease to exist when it happened.

My parents died in the car wreck in 1962 and my grandfather

tried to explain to me what death was.

"They aren't coming back," he told me.

"Why not?" I asked. "Don't they love me anymore?"

"They can't love you anymore," Grandfather said. "They can't feel anything anymore. They're dead. Dead people have no feelings."

He was determined to hammer this into me.

"Dead people don't feel anything. Your mom and dad loved you while they were alive, but they aren't feeling anything now."

"They won't miss me?"

"They can't miss you, Noah, they're dead. We're the ones gonna miss them. Only the living pine away for the dead."

"That's not fair!"

"Life's not fair," Grandfather sighed. He seemed to know what he was talking about, though I could tell he wasn't happy about this new reality he had to face with the death of his only son and daughter-in-law. I ran upstairs to the attic and slammed the door behind me.

It was night, and darkness hung in the windows. Quiet. Pitch black. Nothing there.

Was this what death was? Was it nothingness? How could you not have sensations, thoughts, feelings?

Looking back on it now, I suppose Grandfather was too busy with his own pain to bother with my childhood emotions.

Isaiah looks at me with gentle, understanding eyes.

"Your parents' death was hard on you, I can see that. The pain of it is still with you."

"I've never gotten over it," I tell him, coming to realize this for the very first time. "There was really no one to talk to about it, no way to reason it out or make any sense of it. My grandfather was a strong, proud man who didn't know how to talk to children, let alone one as precocious as I was. He was a force to be reckoned with, let me tell you," I say, remembering his stern work ethic. "It was hard coping with both death and my grandfather too."

"I'm sure."

"You know, I always felt that if I could ask God one question, anything, anything at all, it would be why He, She, It, Whatever, would single out my parents and steal them away from me like that? What was He trying to prove?"

"That's hard to say," Isaiah answers.

"What kind of lesson is there in all this?" I ask, looking him directly in the eyes.

"Perhaps the lessons aren't always obvious," Isaiah suggests. "Perhaps they unfold themselves in due course."

I'm not satisfied with his answer, but decide to let it go, at least for now. We are silent for a short time.

"It's a little bit like infinity and nothingness, isn't it?" I ask.

"What?"

"Death. It's hard to imagine, like infinity and nothingness."

"Yes. That's our connection with the origin of all things. It's very much like what happens to light."

"Oh?"

"The very difficulty we have in imagining either infinity or nothingness is also the difficulty in which light finds itself. It too can't imagine being confined in nothingness; and so, through its imagination, it gives birth to a universe of infinite time, space and complexity. All of this happens purely from the act of a dimensionless nothingness interacting with itself to create what we call resonance. It's our myth of creation."

"I can't even begin to imagine it," I say.

"Well, let me tell you a story that may help you."

I sit back and close my eyes, following Isaiah's story, the roll of his voice washing over me.

"In the beginning there was nothing. No time, no space, no matter. Nothing. And that is all there ever could have been, for had there been something, where would it have come from?" No answer emerges from the silence. Isaiah continues.

"Now, had there been such a thing as time, this nothingness would have extended throughout it, and had there been space, it would have extended through all of space too, since absolute nothingness by itself cannot give rise to anything. So it would have been an absolute condition of everything, that there was nothing anywhere, at any time."

Nothingness seems like death to me —

"But as soon as we observe that nothingness fills time and space in any dimension, we are caught in a paradox. We see that this nothingness is infinite, limitless. It takes up no room at all, and at the same time takes up all the room that there could ever be. Simultaneously it is unimaginably small and inconceivably large. In this state of nothingness through all time and space, we have all the truth, all the power, and all the consciousness that there could ever be. It is total, invincible and all powerful, for it is all there is. It is the ultimate truth."

Is death an ultimate truth, and does it fill time and space into infinity too?

"But in this ultimate truth of total nothingness," Isaiah continues, "which means that you and I are forever compelled not to exist and never to become conscious — there are no limitations whatsoever, no rules of any kind. And since there are no limitations and no rules, then experiments can be tried. Every so often there arises within this vast, unimaginably small sea of nothingness, a tiny burst of energy for an infinitesimally small time which creates the illusion of being something."

Me?

Inflation

I open my eyes and look at Isaiah.

"There is no standard by which to tell something from nothing, and obviously no consciousness with which to observe it, so this illusion is meaningless. But since there are no limitations, another experiment with existence comes into being: a consciousness that can observe this virtual particle as it comes and goes in this vast sea of nothingness in an infinitesimally short time.

"Here's where the paradox takes over. In this vast sea of tiny nothingness, there is no way of determining what 'tiny' means. 'Tiny' could mean an octillionth of a second and an octillionth of an inch. Or, since there are no standards, it could mean a trillion galaxies and hundreds of billions of years. It makes no difference, since there are no standards, and they're both tiny. They're both also extraordinarily large.

"An astonishing limitation arises from all of this. For anything to pop into existence for this infinitely short time, and to take up an almost infinitely small amount of space, it must simultaneously be very large and very small, since it can't be one or the other separately."

Celestial laws are certainly very complicated . . .

"In this infinite nothingness, a way is found to do this."

"A celestial legal loophole?" I ask, amazed that I've been on the right track.

"I guess you could say that."

"Smoke and mirror stuff?"

"In a sense," Isaiah smiles. "If you vibrate an unimaginably small illusion backwards and forwards in time, you can produce a further illusion of an extraordinarily large number of tiny particles, which, when you take everything into account, are enough to make up a trillion galaxies. Remember, all of this is contained in an infinitesimally, unimaginably small space. When it discovers itself as space, it begins to expand in order to accommodate this huge illusion born of nothingness, and, at the same instant, to invent time. That expansion can happen at any speed because there are no standards by which to measure it."

Zero to sixty, I think.

"Imagine a baseball instantaneously becoming as large as the known universe. There are no rules to make this impossible because rules haven't been invented yet. In fact, this instant of expansion invents the rules! These rules are incredibly precise, because all the relationships among every different component of the universe are carefully worked out, deliberately to bring about the capacity for you and me to have this discussion, to bring about the capacity for everything in the universe that has ever happened, to happen."

I sit up and open my eyes again in amazement.

"Our meeting is occurring in a precise moment of time, which has been anticipated and known about by the Mind of God since the beginning of time. That's what omniscience means. As the author of a book knows about the actions of the characters, and indeed determines in some sense what they will do and when they will do it, so, we, the characters in the Universal Book, live out our destiny as that Mind conceives it. Only, since we are actually fragments of that Mind, we do it ourselves, much as the characters in a book invent themselves to the author's great surprise."

The Mind of God. I've never thought of it before as anything but an off-putting pious myth. Now, suddenly, it seems like, at least, an interesting idea.

Isaiah continues reverently. "That, you see, is the only way of thinking about the birth of our universe in the Big Bang, which accounts for everything that has happened since. You can derive the Big Bang theory only if you pay very close attention to something you were taught early in life to disregard altogether."

"And what is that?" I want to know.

Breaking a Rule

"The consequences of dividing by zero," Isaiah smiles.

"You can't do that," I say.

"Yes you can, but there are consequences."

"Consequences?"

"The consequences of dividing by zero are always the same — infinity. But if you retrace your steps and multiply zero times infinity, which is the only thing you can do if you're faced with the absolute necessity of there being nothing, then you get every possible number and combination of numbers that there could ever be."

"So this is why we exist?" I ask. "Simply as a consequence of cheating on the ultimate universality of nothingness on a divine math test?"

"Not a very dignified way of putting it, I should think," says Isaiah.

"Still, when you come right down to it, isn't that what you mean?"

Isaiah thinks about this for a long time before he begins to nod, very slowly.

The Thinking Photon

"That's what we call the Tao, the Holographic Principle," Isaiah says. "The expression of the One in wave interference patterns emerging from its interaction with itself, creating the infinite multitude of states of being we call the cosmos. Resonance patterns generated by wave interferences bring those atoms into being — not as one spinning whirlpool caught in the nothingness of a dimensionless point — but as bursting forth from confinement into dimensionality, space and time and infinite multitude. It is the Hymn of Praise to the Act of Creation, brought on by the paradox of the imagination of the infinitely confined, the greatest song that can be sung, the choir of all the cosmos in harmony with itself. God, the One."

Did the angels sing three times of the holiness of God in miraculous creation filling the world with glory? Every prayer I ever said before I turned my back on all that and denigrated religion — all those prayers come fluttering back to me as if on wings. Why was this ecstasy of creation so hard to translate into words and logic, when the emotions were so powerful? Angels understood it; why were humans so slow? Has it finally penetrated me? Does it convince me of anything? Is my confirmed atheism shaken by this? I can't know quite yet.

"What are these resonance patterns?" I ask. "It sounds so poetic, but I've never heard anything about the Laws of Resonance, as you call them."

"That's only because the scientists of your time made them invisible," says Isaiah. "They simply chose not to see them. The resonance patterns were deeply woven into the fabric of science well before your time. Have you never heard of the notion that a photon of light is sometimes a particle and sometimes a wave? Have you never heard the principle in quantum physics that there are no local events? Have you never heard that what is observed in one part of the universe may retroactively define what happened a billion years before in another part a billion light years away?"

"Not specifically," I say. "At least, not all of those phenomena, no."

"All of these were well known published phenomena long before your time. They were simply not integrated into any picture of the world that made any sense. They were dangled around as isolated observations which could not be interpreted. Take the following experiment for example. A photon of light is passed through a tiny hole and photographed on a screen behind the hole. Its presence is recorded in a particular place.

"A second hole is made some distance from the first, and one photon of light is passed through each of the two holes simultaneously. In this case the result is a wave interference pattern, so that in the place where the first photon was photographed, there is this time no light at all. Instead, it is photographed in a different place, a place where the interference patterns created by the interaction of the two photons entering at once, would allow the light to be. Now the second hole is closed up and a single photon is passed through the first hole. Once again the photon is photographed where it was the first time. Finally, the second hole is opened, but no second photon is passed through it, only through the first hole. This time the photon that is passed through the first hole lands in a place where the wave interference pattern will allow it to land, exactly as if a second photon had passed through the second hole."

"What does that mean?"

"We conclude that the photon of light somehow knows whether the second tiny hole is open or closed, even though it passed through only the first hole. This is one of the experiments that established beyond question that nothing at this level of energy ever happens that isn't simultaneously connected to many other things, some of them happening very, very far away. It also suggested to some scientists in your time that the individual photon of light is conscious and can tell something about what is happening around it, and behave accordingly. That is what we continue to think in our time."

I wonder what is happening very far away, having abandoned any notion of returning home. Am I caught in a wave interference pattern between home and here, between two points, and am I like light passing between them? Is this all really a dream? If it's a dream, it is more akin to light than the material world. But it seems too real to be a dream. Still, dreams feel real. All our sensations of reality are reported to us through our nervous system, which uses electrical energy, or something like that. Everything we know of reality can be reduced to pulses of electrical energy. So how can we prove there's anything out there? He said I could go home any time I wanted. But what's the point? Maybe I'm home now. Maybe this is all there is.

"You might think that such things occur only at the level of very tiny microscopic events, but that's not true. The non-local nature of all events affects the lives of people as much as it does photons of light. As long as the scientists of your time insisted on a reductionist view of science based on atomic structure as the main way of understanding things, experiments like this couldn't make any sense. The word 'astonishing' was frequently used to describe the observations of your quantum physicists. Most of your scientists did not make the effort to create a theory which would integrate all the various elements they'd discovered in their highly reliable, repeatable experiments. In fact, the majority of your physicists said that such things couldn't possibly make sense, and that therefore there was no possible model of reality that could ever be constructed. In other words, they refused to have enough imagination to see the Laws of Resonance lurking beneath the surface of events that we in our time understand tie everything in the universe together into a single, universal instant in which the entire history of everything is enfolded."

"So our scientists had an inkling about the Laws of Resonance but didn't understand them?"

"More than that. They, or some of them, at any rate, insisted on explaining everything as if it were all made of little particles of matter, long after they had scientifically shattered the notion that matter was made up of little particles. With blinders on, they failed to understand half of what they discovered and denied many realities that were observed by all experimenters. So in effect you had two cultures — a popular one, which crudely sized up ideas with some degree of accuracy, and a scientific one, heavily skewed in the wrong direction because no one took sufficient leadership to correct mistaken apprehensions underlying so many of the outworn theories ingrained in people's thinking. So, while the popular culture talked about 'tuning in' to another person, most of the scientific community acted as if such a phrase were the crudest superstition."

"I remember that!" I blurt out. "We used to say somebody gave off good vibes. Women mostly."

Isaiah laughs.

"Well, maybe there's something to it anyway. Haven't you noticed? People do resonate to one another."

"Yes, but we didn't say 'resonate' until recently," I say seriously, as if I were an historian lecturing on Twentieth Century slang.

"Long before your time it had been established that the human body was surrounded by resonating waves that could interact powerfully when people came together or thought about one another. Test this out for yourself. Bring the palms of your hands fairly close together without touching. You'll feel an energy vibrating between them that is quite palpable. It's not heat, though some heat is involved. It's the energy of life that exudes from all organic beings. Try it."

At his suggestion I hold my hands palms facing each other and bring them together until they're about two inches apart, then separate them. I can feel a little energy in between them that almost bounces as I bring them together and apart like that. So, sure enough there does seem to be an invisible force pulsating between my hands. It's eerie. I've never noticed it before. Is this one of the resonance patterns he's talking about?

I remember the touch of my dead kitten. Lifeless. She might as well have been a chair or table, some kind of inanimate object. Even at five I was old enough to know. There was the total absence of energy, the non-presence of life. Not like touching her when she was alive and curled up on my lap. A whole different ball game, this absence of life.

Isaiah is talking on, almost as if he doesn't notice me anymore.

"What the scientific community was trying very hard to protect itself against — what it considered a superstition — was that the universe could be considered to have consciousness and mental capacity. And yet one of the most prominent of the physicists a generation before you, Sir Arthur Eddington, said of his own experiments and those of his colleagues, 'Religion first became possible for a reasonable man of science in the year 1927.' Betrothal of science and religion was becoming possible, but the practical demands of their work on the atomic bomb during World War II pulled the attention of physicists away from the philosophical implications of their research. So the whole impulse in that direction was lost to science for nearly a hundred years, except for a handful of creative physicists, some of whom wrote books on the kind of thing we're discussing now.

"But, all in all, the Manhattan Project forced scientific attention on the structure of the individual atom and particles that made it up. It had to if they were to build the atomic bomb. It turned attention to matters that were entirely practical, and for a whole generation essentially wasted much of the creative time of many of the world's leading physicists. Because of the tremendous pressure on them to produce practical results in a material universe, results capable of blowing up much of the world, these scientists largely ignored the resonances, fields and frequencies that surround every particle of matter, carrying its influence beyond its particulate nature all the way to the ends of the universe. Because their attention had been deflected, most of them never followed up on Eddington's observations. Compared to what might have been possible, very little attempt was made to interpret the world as mind-stuff in the way that Eddington had begun to explore."

"Perhaps if they'd tampered with forces larger than atoms we'd all have been destroyed long ago," I say.

"Perhaps. You have a point there."

A long silence stretches between us as Isaiah appears to be considering this possibility.

"Strangely enough," he continues after a little, "it was the biologists who eventually broke through the curtain of ignorance."

"How did that happen?" I ask.

"In two ways. One was the explosion of the myth of evolution by pure chance. The chances against the formation of even the simplest life forms were so astronomical that when scientists began to take seriously what the odds were, they accepted the fact that life could not possibly have synthesized by chance. There wasn't enough time in a mere fifteen billion years to accomplish that, even if the entire universe had been working together in the process. In fact, in a universe the size of ours, there wouldn't have been enough time in forty billion billion years, or even forty billion, billion, billion years. To think that pure chance could have produced even the simplest elements of life, let alone its more complex forms, was superstition of the most astonishing and incredible kind. Only if you accepted the fact that the universe was conscious and had produced life as a result of intentional design using the forces of evolution as tools but directing their interaction the way a scientist synthesizes chemicals in a laboratory, could you possibly account for all that had happened in the natural world. This scientific breakthrough came as the result of introducing serious statistical analysis into the otherwise sloppy casual thinking of the paleontologists and biologists. Of course, in your time they were still a couple of generations away from accepting the reality of that conclusion. They didn't argue with it — they just ignored it. The moment they stopped ignoring it, they had to accept a conscious universe as much organized from the top down as from the bottom up."

"Could you explain all that a little better?" I ask, feeling overwhelmed with too much coming at me too fast.

Indefatigable Monkeys

"Certainly," he smiles. "In the late Nineteenth Century the greatest apologist for science, and for evolution in particular, was Thomas Henry Huxley. He invented the famous story of the typing monkeys. You probably know it. He proposed that six monkeys typing at random from the beginning of the universe would by now have typed all the books in the British Museum. It's a grandiose statement, but it passed muster for nearly a century until someone actually did the math and it turned out to be outrageously untrue."

"What was the truth, then? How many books would they have typed?"

"Six monkeys typing all that time would have pecked out half of one sentence by now."

"It seems like a rather large discrepancy," I muse.

"It shows you the radical difference between a thinking mind at work and the agencies of blind chance trying to come up with something meaningful, particularly when you consider that typing one whole meaningful sentence would have taken them a great deal more than twice as long. In fact, each word that's added to the half sentence generates hugely longer amounts of time, because in effect you have to start all over generating the half sentence every time you want to add on a little more. If you've ever worked with exponential increments, like the number of trials it takes to flip a coin heads or tails, you'll see what I mean. All the possible combinations of heads and tails will show up within about ten tries if you flip the coin only twice. But if you flip it three times, you're up to four hundred tries, and so on. By the time you start dealing with anything remotely complex, the numbers get astronomical. So if you're going for complexity that has meaning and function — the kind of thing you see in biological systems — the number of lucky chances you need is so astronomical that our universe isn't remotely large enough to hold it all. But the moment you introduce a higher consciousness, intelligence or mind into the system, you can completely account for everything we see around us. In other words, higher intelligence is a requisite hypothesis for devising all the necessary combinations of factors that have occurred in the world we see around us. Blind chance won't do it. Not remotely."

"So the universe is intelligent."

"Yes, it has to be in order to accomplish anything at all, and to have become all that it is, requires intelligence far beyond our comprehension. Anyone who argues otherwise simply has no understanding of statistical processes or how to evaluate chance occurrences. Even all the challenges we've talked about so far are incredibly trivial compared with the challenge of generating a single T4 bacteriophage."

"What's that?"

"A virus that inhabits bacterial cells," he answers. "The chances against achieving that miracle have been calculated as 10 with 78,000 zeroes after it. There are only '10 with 89 zeroes after it' electrons in the universe, and '10 with 90 zeroes after it' will give you ten whole universes the size of ours, so that's the extraordinary odds we're dealing with against purely by chance coming up with any sort of life. This means that the whole question of evolution by fluke, or monkey luck, is entirely out of consideration. No fairy tale spun out by some literal-minded creationist, such as that the world was created at ten o'clock in the morning in 4004 B. C. is remotely as fanciful as the simple notion that blind chance can be responsible for everything we see around us. It can't."

"Don't tell me the Fundamentalists were right after all?"

"Far from it," Isaiah replies. "In its particulars, evolution occurred pretty close to the way your scientists said it did. They were wrong only about the causative factors. However these factors couldn't even be remotely understood until the Laws of Resonance had been formulated."

"Where did those come from?"

"Strangely enough, as I started to say before, through research in biology along similar lines; it had been noticed that DNA, allegedly a blueprint for the living organism is not really a blueprint at all. The DNA of any species does not have enough atoms in it to be a working blueprint. For example, in the double helix that determines the formation of the human body, there are only a hundred and ten thousand usable genes. That number couldn't possibly design and grow the ten billion differentiated cells the brain is known to contain, let alone the rest of the body. Only when it was found that DNA operates more like a laser than a blueprint, projecting cosmic energy through it to grow organic matter similar to the way a hologram is made, did the resonant nature of matter begin to be coherently appreciated. Although in some sense it's made up of individual atoms, in another sense the universe is all of a piece — any one part of which reflects the whole.

"Even in your time a Japanese scientist named Dr. Ono discovered that he could write down the patterns in a molecule of mouse DNA as musical notation, and get actual compositions that made sense musically. These works had taken over two and a half billion years to compose, but every millisecond you run untold numbers of similar patterns through your nervous system just by virtue of being alive. One of Dr. Ono's transcriptions turned out to correspond with 97% accuracy to an actual Chopin nocturne. Centuries before, scientists like Kepler used the music of the spheres to make scientific predictions of great meaning."

"Then there's a connection between music and science?" I ask.

"There's a connection between everything!"

"A universe in a grain of sand?"

"Yes. The connection between music and science was so foreign to your scientists that they made nothing of it until well into the Twenty-First Century. Once the resonance patterns were recognized and studied intensively, it became easier to describe the cosmos as the mirror of the Mind of God, and to see the manner in which events were brought into being as much from the future as from the past. The resonance patterns stretch out not only through all of space, but through all of time as well."

I close my eyes in order to imagine it — the great choir of the universe joined in song. My body seems to hum, all the atoms in it raising their voices in a collective rhapsody. It welcomes this hymn of harmony, this joyful noise that comes from deep within me, from a place I had not known I possessed, the musical potentiality of each DNA molecule in my body.

Towards an Earth Mind

"In your time, though the scientists didn't understand resonance, they did understand relativity, and it should be something you could understand in a more complete way." Isaiah says. "We must take what you've experienced and translate it into logical tools for understanding. That's what all great scientists and artists do. It is the fountainhead of inspiration for genius."

Well, then, from existential harmony to practical considerations. But isn't this the way everything happens? We wander in a state of nearly total relaxation; and the mind, relieved of stress, creates new possibilities from which we then begin to build new things in the material world.

"So as you consider this infinite creation which has no beginning or end, think again of what Einstein discovered about the behavior of light. Place yourself now as Einstein imagined, on a beam of light, and look from that position back at a clock whose light rays you will never leave behind. If you do this, the image of the clock itself travels with you. When that happens as you travel through space, all of space becomes crunched up into a single ball. That's because you can no longer experience the passage of any time, no matter how far you go. Without time there is no space, and without space there is only the original condition in which all things fade into Primordial Nothingness. Your consciousness and the beam of light on which it rides become a single, dimensionless point. And your consciousness, which we can now identify with that beam of light, is caught up in that dimensionless point with nowhere to go, and no place to get to. From your perspective as a beam of light, there is no time or space, and there is no mass; though in a dimensionless point the amount of mass is both zero and infinite.

"So to say that there's no mass is the same as saying that there is infinite mass. We see that paradox at the Singularity in a black hole, and we see it in whatever may have existed before the original Big Bang."

"But if the light has already escaped from that condition of dimensionlessness, why would it still see and feel what you've just described?" I really want to know the answer to this mind-blowing question.

Isaiah smiles, pleased that I'm pushing back like this.

"Because what Einstein imagined is impossible. No one could ever sit on a beam of light and travel at that speed, because if anyone did, they would exceed the entire universe in their infinite mass.

"Don't you see? Out of its very condition of imprisonment in nothingness, and its desperate spinning to try to get out, light created the paradox that brought about its freedom. The point of light that travels for billions of years through empty space is not separated from the whirlpool at the center of the atom, but is one and the same with it. By spinning in desperation, that whirlpool transcended itself into the condition of being light and non-light at the same time. In that paradoxical condition, it could simultaneously be you and me and all the other things in all creation.

"Look at it this way. Light, from its own perspective, can cross the universe in no time at all because at the speed of light time slows to zero. But if there is no time at all, there is also infinite time; just as, if there is no space at all, there is also infinite space.

"This paradox can be realized only as light takes on two opposite conditions. The light that travels through space, emitted by the various stars, or released in the original Big Bang, is not separated from the light that has curled itself into the whirlpools that form matter. So the light in its pure and free state, which has no time, can reflect, in its consciousness, back to all those points of light that do not travel through space, and can participate with them in the illusion of time. Thus by being in both conditions at once, it can be simultaneously in and out of time. It can be the eternal captured in the instant. And it can enfold into itself all of time, while having no time.

"That's because the spinning whirlpools of light became the core structure of matter and therefore couldn't travel at the speed of light. They were caught up in the paradox of traveling in straight lines, since there was no space for them to do it in. To solve that problem, they created space and time within themselves, and this space and time blew up like a gigantic balloon, becoming the expanding universe. That's how space and time are created. At any given point in the expansion of the universe, there are space and time only out to the limits to which the universe has expanded, and not beyond them. So in the first instant of its existence, there was no more space than the head of an invisibly tiny pin, and no more time than a tiny fraction of a second. As the universe expanded in space, it also expanded in time, and both time and space were created in the expansion process."

Something stirs inside me while I listen to this. As I turn my attention to my thoughts, Isaiah becomes transparent, like a fading ghost in some Shakespeare play, and I find myself alone. It isn't what Isaiah has been saying, exactly, so much as a part of my experience that's beginning to surface, a memory I had buried for years, probably because of its dissonance with practical reality and the way things supposedly work.

Time is supposed to be a one way street; that's evident from everything we see. So of course it's impossible to see into the future. Most scientists would assert that absolutely. But there's a certain dream that I've had, one I've never been able to explain or account for. I know the reality of it and its correspondence with later events, far too detailed to be mere coincidence. Rooted in an actual event, the dream became a reality a day later. Either I was living a fantasy, a deja vu or trick of the mind, or time had in fact reversed itself, sending a message from the future to my mind. Would this mean that the arrow of time could not possibly be locked in a single direction? Could it be compromised in the realm of dreams, making the transcendence of time possible, just as Isaiah has been telling me?

The Physics of Foreboding

Maybe some aspects of my experience have been pushed off into a corner of my mind until now. If light and space-time exist as Isaiah says, all the feelings of foreboding I've lived with in my life might make sense. They come from experiences that have been registered somewhere in my consciousness.

But where?

Ninety-nine percent of so-called clairvoyance is just lucky guesses or shrewd reckoning, I know that. No argument there.

Which leaves the other one percent: those times you know in a completely irrational way that something will happen and it does.

Is there anyone who has never had a notion that something was about to happen, only to find out later that it did? I'm not talking about wishful thinking or normal fears that pass through everyone's mind from time to time. A certain percentage of those are obviously going to come true, and then afterwards you'll claim you were prophetic, but you weren't. You just have the habit of predicting things a certain way and once in a while they come to pass, purely by the law of averages.

I'm talking about crazy stuff, like the time the reporter for a Boston newspaper wrote a complete description of the explosion of Krakatoa a few days before it became known. He had written the transcription of a dream, but by accident the paper published it as a news story and he was fired. A few days later, he had the news scoop of the century, all from a precognitive dream.

That's crazy stuff, the kind of thing I'm talking about.

That's happened to me too a few times. Before this meeting with Isaiah, I've denied these dreams and put them out of my mind. But now I'm having second thoughts. The dream I remember best is the one which saved a lot of lives, including my own.

Like a blow to the solar plexus, the dream comes back to me now. It was so frightening I'd disassociated from it years ago. For good reason, I see. Even at the time, the dream was very real and clear. Details of it are anchored in my mind, though I might have edited some over the years. But the real point is that it proved important in my life and the lives of a lot of other people too.

≈

The night before our senior high school class trip, I dream about the bus ride. The entire class is on the bus, students bantering and laughing, Stu Reynolds playing guitar and singing while some of the girls flirt outrageously with him. I recall feeling the drone of the bus engine and its break-neck speed as it traces its way up the mountain road in Pennsylvania, when suddenly, as the vehicle speeds around a curve, a tire blows out.

Immediately I see the bus swerve out of control, crashing against the restraining wire along the edge of the road. With the certainty of hope born in dreams, I pray that the wire will hold, but it snaps. In a moment of terror, we plunge over the mountain's edge into a steep ravine. I am outside the bus when I see this, as if I've left my body. I see the horror on the faces of my friends in the last instants of their lives, the stunned realization of the bus plummeting, free falling into a canyon of pitted rocks, bursting into flames on impact.

Realistic as hell, cold sweat and all.

≈

I awakened and put the dream behind me, trying to forget it. It stayed with me the entire day and followed me into my classes, claiming my attention as if it had actually happened. At the end of the day, though, it had begun to fade and I put it out of my mind.

Next day came the big class trip.

The school bus wound its way up the mountain road staying close to the speed limit. Suddenly the images from my dream are happening before me. Stu Reynolds picks up his guitar and the girls lean towards him flirtatiously. Same sounds of laughter and guitar noise as in my dream. The effect is stunning; for a moment I can't move.

As the bus rounds the curve, the image of it sailing through the air grips me. The driver must slow down or we will all die! I rise from my seat and make my way towards the front of the bus, awkwardly pitching forward down the aisle of students towards the driver.

As we round a bend, I see the rocky slope below us. I grasp the driver by the shoulder and cry out for her to slow down.

Alarmed by the suddenness of my warning, she pushes the brake and slows down the bus. At that very instant, the right front tire explodes, just as it had done in my dream. The bus careens to the side of the road, snapping the protective wire of the guardrail. But the impact further slows it, and the bus comes to a tentative but safe stop. Emergency vehicles come to rescue us. No one is hurt.

But how could such a look into the future be possible?

Well, if the experience associated with my dream means anything, there has to be something wrong with a description of nature that allows it to develop completely by chance. If the future can be known, the events leading up to it cannot be pure chance. Impossible! Scientists studying chaos and complexity look at things too narrowly. The fundamental unpredictability of chaos has to stem from an incomplete picture of the process, like a misunderstood rumor or half truth.

The scientists of my time aren't wrong, not in the formal sense of the word. What they've noticed and described has been correctly observed, as far as it goes.

Their knowledge, however, is obviously incomplete.

The Infolding of Time

The universe is like a dance carried on in intricate detail among parts of itself that are distant from one another in time and place. This would account for the appearance of randomness in closely observed, seemingly chaotic events. That makes more sense, for true randomness without order has never been observed.

Order that grows out of chaos with astonishing alacrity and frequency moves towards increasing complexity in unpredictable ways, the same way the order of words in an unknown language seems unpredictable. The appearance of randomness stems only from our limited view. The key to understanding its predictability is missing, since we have only a partial view of what's happening from our tiny corner of the total field of influence to which all events are subject.

This is not the same as saying that if you know what's happening now you can project all the lines of force and influence to predict what will happen next week. In that sense, events will always be unpredictable.

This is a very different way of thinking. Time is not what we experience it to be. What's happening now can be seen as if we're looking at it tomorrow, or next week, or next year. It's an actual jumping backwards and forwards in time, just as one walks back and forth across a room.

If you look back at events that have already happened, you get the impression that they're frozen in their unfolding sequence and that no other relationship among them is possible, even though sometimes you'd like very much for that not to be true. I wanted to go back and rescue my parents from that accident, but I couldn't.

But theoretically I could have gone forward in time in some other state of consciousness to see the accident coming and do something to stop it. At that level of cosmic energy I can affect the material world.

Maybe time exists in two kinds of reality: at the physical level, where it can't reverse itself, and at the energy level, where it can.

Of course there's no way to know that it can't change at the physical level too. Suppose through some process I don't know I could go back and prevent the accident. Then reality would change, including my memories about the event.

From the perspective of light itself, relativity proved there was no perception of the passage of time. At the speed of light, time stops for the observer who is traveling at that velocity, even though it relentlessly continues for the observer traveling at less than the speed of light.

At the speed of light, time disappears. Imagine! The very

same photon of light which travels a billion years across the cosmos and enters the eyes of an observer, would experience no lapse of time from its own perspective. That's why events at the beginning of its journey can still be subject to influence, since from its perspective they're happening at the same time — which is no time at all.

That difference of opinion about passing time could account for the fact that the observer can influence what a photon of light has already done a billion years in the past. As the observer watches the photon, its journey has already been determined at that instant and projected backwards in time for all those eons.

So the insane, impossible and astonishing observations of quantum physics are a product of the dual nature of the universe. Simultaneously, it does and does not have time and space. Or, as Isaiah says, it does not have time and space, and it does not *not* have them.

If time and space are an illusion and do not "actually" occur as we observe them, we cannot be said to have time and space. But we can't be said not to have them if they're necessary for us to live as we do.

I try to imagine this, but it isn't easy. You have to think about it for a while. A particle becomes trapped in the creation of matter, but paradoxically it also travels out into the universe, crossing billions of light years. Whatever happens in the particle traveling through space will be reflected in the aspect of itself trapped in matter. If you could understand what both aspects are doing, it might make sense. The behavior of one observed by itself might appear to be completely random.

Now let's say collective photons traveling through space are the ruminations of the Mind of God, while the collective photons trapped in matter have become the material universe, the Body of God. In the relationship of Mind and Body, things would be thought and acted upon, or, not. As one sees into the future, the intentions of God in a particular context at a given time can be seen. But in seeing these intentions, one can influence them, as the body influences the mind, and so effect change in the future.

If this turns out to be true, one ought, in theory, to be able to go back and change the past, just the way a novelist can change earlier events in a story so later ones can occur differently.

It would all be kept in perfect balance.

The bizarre conundrum of Schroedinger's Cat has always puzzled me, and I know I'm not alone in this; but now I think I can finally understand it. A theoretical cat is placed inside a box ostensibly to be either poisoned or not poisoned by the random release of gas into the cage. After the fatal moment, whether or not the cat is dead or alive can only be determined by an observer opening the box to look. Until that precise moment, the cat can't be established to be either dead or alive; its state is defined retroactively by a series of observers in the following sequence: At 12:00, the poisonous gas is released in the cat's cage and the cat knows it is dying.

But the experimenter has agreed not to check up on things until 12:30. So, for the experimenter the cat is neither alive nor dead until 12:30, at which point her death becomes retroactive to 12:00.

Now, the experimenter's friend (who is technically called Wigner's Friend) is outside the system and does not observe the dead cat until 1:00. At which point, a second probabilistic state of the cat comes to an end, the cat is resolved into being dead in the friend's world, and the death is again retroactive to 12:00.

All this indeterminacy is essential because the random triggering of the release or non-release of the poison, if done at the quantum level, is inherently unpredictable. No clockwork universe survives quantum mechanics. What happens happens, without cause and therefore without predictability. No amount of information would be sufficient to lead us through a maze of events that would reveal the outcome. On the local level, anyway, it's absolutely a-causal.

This might be misunderstood to mean that the cat exists only in the eyes and mind of the observer, but that's not the case. Ultimately, the cat exists in the mind of the cat, and in that cat-mind, the moment of death occurs at one time — and at another, in the mind of the human observer. The only "reality" is that of the observer, whether it's the cat or the person outside looking in, and the reality of one is different from the reality of the other. We have a different set of realities for each observer, and without an observer, there is no reality. The state of the object remains indeterminate. This may sound like a terrible case of juggled semantics, but as I've come to understand it, the whole thing takes place in a series of "probability waves" which "collapse" for each observer at a different time. In less technical terms, a set of probabilities is transformed for each observer into the certainties of a different reality.

I could joke about witnessing all I want, but think about what it means: to witness to great acts, immortalizing and embodying them, like performing before a live audience. The reality is there, in the present, along with the energies of the people in attendance, midwifing the process, giving birth to it as it evolves.

If you change the mind of the cat or the observer, corresponding reality can change — and this, too, can be accomplished retroactively.

Thus, enfolded in light in a simultaneous state, all events, both past and future, are equally subject to change. But the observer's reality will appear to be consistent, no matter how frequently or how often it may change, since the observer's memories and all evidence of former realities will be changed as the future revises the past. So it could be said of any event that it had not occurred, and also that it had not *not* occurred.

This seems like the purest fantasy to me, and yet I now realize that it has been woven into the fabric and design of the entire universe from its beginning.

Einstein was right in saying that God doesn't play dice with the universe; he was wrong in thinking that the discoveries of quantum mechanics meant that God did. Indeed, it is the Indeterminacy Principle itself that paradoxically hides the secret of God's majestic way of creation, constant revision and readjustment of all His creations. The discoveries of quantum mechanics make no sense from the point of view of local cause and effect. They defy cause and effect altogether, making things radically unpredictable. They necessitate the existence of observers to establish the reality of events, which means that there have to have been witnesses from the very beginning of the universe.

Even the original Big Bang itself has to have been observed, and that means that God had to be conscious in order to observe the origin of His own universe, or else there would have been no universe at all.

I recall God speaking in plural in Genesis, as if speaking to a committee during Creation. "Let us make a human in our image," God said, before witnesses, as if the act of Creation could not occur without them. What understanding did the ancient Hebrews have about the marriage of God and science in the creation of the universe?

Or, to put it another way, if each photon of light is conscious, and God is the collective consciousness, then somewhere come the creatures, including humans, who are among the objects of the creation, each staking out its own realm of consciousness, with its own reality, part of the enormous probabilistic reality of all things.

This means, in a physical sense, that no two people share the same reality. All sorts of probability waves collapse differently for each of us. And yet, beneath it all, there's a shared collective consciousness, the omniscience into which we peer and to whom all of us report. That omniscience collects all these different collapsing probability waves and integrates them into a totality which is the universe.

That's how I put it all together now. The universe is Mind Stuff, composed of the perceptions of each of our minds, all of them taken together. It has to reconcile everything and is the creator of everything.

I'd feel terrible if all this made sense. If I could express it coherently, I'd know I was on the wrong track. Whatever coherence there might be in the universe, it isn't up to us to see it. It's up to us to explore our corner as best we can. We can learn to negotiate our peace with one another as we do, and that's where physics overlaps with community.

I sense now what this experiment is all about.

I cut off a part of myself when my parents died. I had it in for the universe because it did that to me. I wasn't going to take an apology, and I wasn't going to cooperate with anyone. I was going to survive in an alien world and find my niche, focusing on myself at the expense of everyone else.

I'm a bit archetypal, aren't I? The Wronged Man who's entitled to Justice and has been denied it.

If I can see the world as a manifestation of The One, so that every time I look at another human being I can see that person as an extension of myself, to be loved and respected . . .

It's an extremely large order, but some part of me welcomes the change.

What the Brain Does And Doesn't Do

I miss Isaiah.

I want to discuss my conclusions with him and find out his opinions.

Somehow it doesn't surprise me that he reappears as soon as I've thought this. He talks to me as if he's been conscious of my thoughts all along, as if he's never left. It dawns on me that Isaiah — and I suppose everyone in the Thirty-first Century — can transcend his singular consciousness and invade what I once considered my private domain.

"Hold that thought, Noah. We haven't gotten to the most important thing you need to know about consciousness yet. Remember that what you have now is only a small part of your total awareness," he smiles.

"Still, there's one point I don't understand," I say. "When people are conscious, it seems that they're completely aware, but when they're unconscious, it seems they're completely out of it. It seems like an all or nothing proposition, not something that happens by degrees."

"You're conscious of your dreams, aren't you?" says Isaiah.

"Yes, I guess so."

"But in dreams, your consciousness is not that of your waking self. You don't imagine the world around you to be the same or even similar to that world."

"That's true."

"Therefore, consciousness may be fractionated off into many different states, many different forms and realities," Isaiah says, looking intently into my eyes.

"Yes."

"Now you don't remember most of your dreams; nobody does. But you would have been conscious in them if you remembered them, isn't that so?"

"It would seem to be the case," I say, wondering if this is a trick question.

"Then you're frequently conscious of many things you later don't remember at all."

"I suppose so."

"You may not be aware that you have a higher consciousness quite different and much more extensive than the one you have at this moment in the personality you call Noah Gershom."

"I've read about this," I say, excited by the idea of a far reaching capacity that might reveal itself to me at any moment.

"This higher awareness links together all the various versions of consciousness you experience, almost all of which you can't remember, just as you can't recall much of what you were conscious of a few hours ago. This higher consciousness records everything. It's your progressively developing awareness throughout the entire life span of the universe."

"I'll have to take your word on it," I say, imagining a huge video camera capturing and preserving on record everything I've ever done.

"It's not at all a product of neurology," Isaiah says. "Your brain has some resemblance to a television set, in that it receives programs which your higher consciousness prepares for it. The physiological capacity of your brain determines what you can do with that consciousness, however; so it's by no means a passive player."

"What do you mean by a passive player?"

"Think about language for a moment as it's genetically encoded in the brain. If that part of the brain is disabled, language functioning disappears. The consciousness is still present, but it can't understand or express itself using language. Surely you've known someone that's happened to."

I have, and it was damned spooky.

I was fifteen when my grandfather suffered a crippling stroke that robbed him of his power of speech. He tried to talk to me, moving his mouth in all sorts of weird directions but no sound came out. You could see great power and energy in his eyes, but as far as words were concerned, nothing; just frustration at his inability to talk. What connection was missing between his thoughts and his ability to speak them? It scared me.

It took a year before his language returned.

"Many facets of your personality are genetically encoded in your brain. You may be a highly excitable person or a person with great artistic talent: this information is pre-programmed into you. But when you enter your body prior to birth, or shortly thereafter, you do so with the full knowledge of which genetic qualities you've selected for yourself. We live our lives in order to accomplish certain purposes, and when we're born, we know what those are. We know something of what the future will be."

"Do you mean to say that we choose our own experiences before we're born? If that's so, why wouldn't I choose happy things?"

"Only you can answer that, Noah."

An Invitation to Spreading My Wings

"**I** have a lot of questions," I remark after a thoughtful pause. "Why do you think I have so much influence on the world?"

"What do you do for a living, Noah?"

"You know what I do —"

"Yes, but I want you to describe it."

"I'm a business consultant."

"But what do you do?"

"I help people adjust to their corporate environments."

"And what happens as a result?"

"I get paid."

"Anything else?"

"Not much else," I admit. "That's about it."

"So it's a con game you're pulling, a scam of some sort?"

"Well. . ."

I hate to hear it described this way. But Isaiah isn't the first person who's said it.

"Suppose you could *really* help a corporation do something that would make a difference."

"Yes?"

"Wouldn't others want to copy your success?"

"Sure."

"That would be good for your career, wouldn't it?"

"You can say that again."

Isaiah looks me squarely in the eye.

"You're a lonely and isolated person, Noah. You feel extremely sorry for yourself that you got such a raw deal in your life. And if the truth be known, you're not particularly eager to see anyone else get a better deal than you did."

I don't like where this discussion is headed, but I'm not going to let him see that.

"You know that's the truth, I can see it," he urges.

Damn!

"Consider this, Noah. Suppose you dismiss all those self-righteous feelings you have about being victimized by an uncaring universe. Suppose you set out with an ambition to truly make everyone's life a little bit better."

"Okay. I can do that for the sake of argument."

"You're going to have to do more than that for the sake of argument, but for now that will do. Remember that 'woman' you killed on London Bridge a little while ago? You owe that woman something."

"That was a dream! A hallucination! That wasn't me!"

"It *was* you."

"What? I'm no murderer!"

"The evidence suggests otherwise. You have a debt to repay."

"What debt? I don't owe anything to a mirage!"

He walks toward me somberly.

"Yes, Noah Gershom, *you do owe her*."

"Look, there were a lot of people in that mob. I wouldn't give them rave reviews for good citizenship. Why do *I* owe anything?"

" Because you have to acknowledge your responsibility — for everything you've done. There's nothing that doesn't count. Surely you've heard of the butterfly effect. A butterfly in Central Park flapping its wings makes changes in the air currents that cause a storm two weeks later in some remote part of the world. You, Noah, are the butterfly impinging on all of humanity, sometimes innocently, sometimes not, but always with impact. If you can emerge from your chrysalis and learn something about the possibilities for the human race, you'll not only make a difference in corporations but in the world."

"Are you a stockholder or something?"

"Sort of. I have a stake in the outcome of humanity. Corporations in your time were the primary agents of change. To a large extent they made the world a worser place."

"Worser? I don't think that's even a word."

"Sure it is. Shakespeare used it. It's an emphatic, the word that describes what I'm talking about. We want you to make the world a *better* place. If you humanize corporations, positive changes will follow from that."

"It's an impossible task."

"On the contrary, it would be good for the stockholders. They'd clamor for it. The profit motive would become benign all of a sudden. That's what eventually did happen, but we'd like it to move faster before so much devastation hits the earth, before the terrible calamities. The world must wake up sooner."

"That's a tall order, Isaiah."

"Yes. As a prophet I'm aware of that. But someone has to sound the alarm, someone has to start somewhere. You've got to reconcile the different aspects of your personality to do this, Noah. Use your dreams. Remember the Senoi? They based their whole culture on dream interpretation, and so do people in my time. Coming to terms with dreams as our connection to the higher consciousness is a main part of our culture. It's what we do."

"I remember. But why is this so important?"

"When we're at odds with ourselves, the cosmic energy in us is squandered and wasted, and all of the community is harmed by that. We must harmonize internally before we can perfect our communities. And we must harmonize our communities to keep the whole world in a state of completeness. In the healthy society all people are complete. Their consciousnesses are highly developed, each with a strong individual personality and character. At the same time their personalities blend seamlessly into the community that gives total respect to all of its different parts, making it possible for each individual to be integrated into the whole."

A picture of poverty-stricken homelessness flashes into my mind. Unintegrated people; the waste of human ability multiplying hopelessly out of control like a virus. Damp, dark and dirty, an experiment in a cosmic petrie dish.

I gather my courage, ready for the test.

"You mean the entire universe is conscious, but its various consciousnesses are fragmented, and in my world we're unaware that we're all part of the same thing? It sounds like a multiple personality disorder."

"Except that the fragmenting of one consciousness into many is not because of trauma. It's for entertainment."

"*Entertainment?*"

"Yes. One consciousness in the universe would be a very lonely experience. The only way for the Mind of God to entertain itself is to break up into many small parts that independently pursue unique experiences. Then, collectively sharing those experiences over eons of time would become more complex and interesting. The quality of the entertainment grows as one accumulates a variety of experiences and becomes spiritually enlightened, joining in the totality of the consciousness which is the source of all things."

That's entertainment!

A universe with a sense of humor! A God that likes to stimulate His mind! I need to think about that. God has always seemed so serious to me. I thought I was just a passenger on this crazy ride called life.

Visiting the Creation

Isaiah interrupts my thoughts with an offer.

"I'd like to guide you through a meditation," he says. "I think you'll understand creation better if you live through it yourself."

"What do I need to do?" I ask, ready to try anything.

"Lie back and relax. I'll give you some suggestions and you let your mind be guided by them. In order for this to work, you'll have to trust me. Can you do that?"

"I believe so," I answer. I've trusted him this far and I've done all right. I lie back on the slab, close my eyes and breathe deeply.

Instantly I am lifted from this world with the speed of a sodium pentothal shot. I don't even remember the sound of Isaiah's voice. Instead I feel loneliness, a terrifying waking dream. Then fear, then nothing. Not peace or goodness.

Just nothing.

The loss of sense of myself — who I am — experiences, memories I've had — my name — my being — erased.

Lost.

Nothingness.

Body gone, being gone. Unbearable pain. Is all. Disconnected. Disjointed.

Vibrating.

Expanding. Intensity.

No direction, no things. No time. Seconds, Minutes. Hours. Lifetime. Gone. Eternity. Floating.

Strong longing exceeds pain. Escape pain, see it. Visual, articulate, meaningful darkness, direction is everywhere.

Nowhere I.

Find direction, find space.

Tension. Pain. Desire. EXPLOSION.

A hydrogen bomb almost infinitely hotter than the center of the sun!

This great explosion, the ultimate expression of desire, returns my sense of self to me. This release of ecstatic expansion emerges in my awareness, opening up as SPACE. My pain flies apart as I grow, filling and creating space at the same instant. For the first time I feel discrimination and change. For the first time I can formulate the notion I am.

I cry out in ecstasy, "I AM!"

In that cry, everything begins.

Parts of me span outwards in all directions in a voracious rampage to create and occupy space, in a furious hunger to know the phenomenon of TIME. Other parts of me spin in whirlpools, traveling as fast as the whole of me, but in place and back in on themselves.

I feel the components of my being. As I become I am, filling time and space, part of me cannot know time and space. That part is beyond, miraculously beyond pain. Bound up in whirlpools that can feel time and space, there is a heaviness, a substance, a potential for interaction; the first glimmering sensation that matter is born and can interact with itself and build an infinite array of possible relationships.

I am is not complete without the time-and-space-free aspect of myself, swelling with dreadful speed to create time and space which other parts of me can use to build mechanisms of intense joy, polarized from the pain to its opposite, bliss.

In that realization of awareness, my other self has already completed the journey. It is instantaneous, and my All is united in an infinite complexity of blissful harmony; the BE-ALL-END-ALL to which I've transmuted myself in release from the initial horrifying pain of consciousness.

Since the pain which began it is infinite, so is the bliss, polarizing in the ultimate complexity of Being. Pain, the overwhelming anguish, makes possible bliss, its alter-ego.

Suddenly I open my eyes free from the fantasy and behold Isaiah once again, smiling down at me.

PART 2

A butterly stirring the air today in Peking can transform storm systems next month in New York.

"The Butterfly Effect,"
(**Chaos**, *by James Gleick*)

The Nonsense of Existence

I settle into the comfortable blanket of silence. Time has raced away and I've lost all traces of it. There's nothing to be sure of, nothing to hold onto.

That's how I feel.

Stretch a man's mind over too many challenges and what does he have? What can I salvage after all that Isaiah has thrown at me?

More than a thousand years separates me from the world I know, making that life meaningless. And all of this could be taking place entirely in my mind. But if my previous existence is meaningless, so is my present. I'm in limbo; anything can happen.

I'm not unhappy, not by a long shot. Strangely, I find the freedom exhilarating.

Isaiah rests on another one of his instant benches. He seems to be somewhere else in his mind, letting me ruminate as I will.

I face him feeling relaxed yet invigorated, as if I've just returned from a long walk, albeit a brisk one around the cosmos.

Certain qualities set Isaiah apart from anyone I've ever known. It's not just his warmth or compassion, but his reverence, something you don't see very often in people these days. Every aspect of his demeanor exudes a deep respect for life which is lived as prayer, a conscious contract, a covenant between human beings and their Creator. For Isaiah, God lives and smiles continuously, bestowing everything on us our spirits truly long for.

I'm not ready for that kind of God. It's not a remote possibility, even though Isaiah has taken me through some pretty compelling experiences and put God in a challenging light. But unbelief is part of me and can't be undermined. I don't think I can set it aside. I need it to protect myself from expecting too much from life, which can be pretty brutal sometimes.

Still, this kind of reverence in all its purity is touching, when someone else feels and believes it.

Downshift

A sudden jolt sends me hurtling backwards. I lie spread-eagled on the floor.

Isaiah does not react, though he is no more prepared for this than I.

"Sorry," he apologizes, rising from his bench and reaching out a hand to help me up. "I didn't think our downshift would be quite so clumsy. Enoch and Bena usually handle these things with more finesse. Must have been an unexpected wrinkle in a wormhole somewhere."

"Is that what it was?" I say, rubbing my sore back. "It reminds me of the first time I used the clutch while I was learning to drive."

"I think we've re-entered the space-time continuum. These jolts always occur when we enter different states of reality. You ought to know that from your nightmares."

I know it all too well, I'm afraid.

"We'll be landing soon."

"Really? We'll be back on Earth then?"

"Yes."

"Were we unreal before? In a different state of reality, like you said?"

"In a most literal sense, yes, though you weren't aware of it. We decomposed and recomposed at the center of the cosmos at the point meditators seek to project themselves into."

"You mean Nirvana?"

"Almost. It's the place of origin of all things, the dimensionless point from which God is eternally born. We can now achieve a new orientation that allows us to be in different times and places."

"Why is this 'almost' Nirvana? Why not the real thing?"

"It's a paradox that Stephen Hawking first pointed out. You approach that point of no time as an asymptote. That means you never quite reach it. It isn't really anywhere because it's outside of space-time, and logically speaking, you can't locate it. You have to get near where you think it ought to be and jump into a different condition of being. The problems associated with asymptotes are enormous, but we've had them solved for about two hundred years."

"I wondered why we were so far out in space. But I thought our journey was in time, not space. Did something else happen? Are we lost?"

Moving Through Time

"No, relax. We're not lost," Isaiah says. "We can't move in time without also moving in space. Time travel was once a cavernous mystery, but there isn't much mystery to it anymore. At least, none greater than The One that's beyond our understanding. Actually, in its own way, this type of travel is as simple as crossing the street. More so, perhaps, because it gets to the origins of things."

"How does it do that?"

"Well, if you think about it, as the Earth moves through space, we move along with it. If we went off somewhere and came back, we'd have to come back to wherever the Earth is in its journey by the time we arrive. So we couldn't come back to the point where we left. It's like getting off a bus and trying to get back on fifteen minutes later. The bus has moved from its previous point."

"That's fairly obvious."

"Yes, but suppose we travel so that we get to some distant

point in space-time. But when we get there, time is different from the time on Earth. People on Earth think we've taken a thousand years, but for us it's different."

"How different?"

"A thousand years in a few hours."

"How is that possible?"

"Traveling into a wormhole is a way of dropping out of the space-time continuum. You simply re-enter at a different point. You can go either way in time because you're in a realm of no-time-no-space. Mind you, you can drop out and re-enter, provided the conditions are right and you've programmed everything properly. When we learned to travel this way we were able to move backwards and forwards by identifying points of access on the continuum. By collapsing space and time into a dimensionless state, we're able to drop out and re-enter the universe at different points. In that respect we were behaving like light before it interacts with the material cosmos.

"To do this, it's necessary to uncurl all the light in objects that are in transit and recurl it at different coordinates. You have to de-materialize and re-materialize yourself and your equipment. It's either impossible or easy; impossible if you don't have a command of the underlying concepts, and easy if you do."

"Incredible!" I shout, thinking of Star Trek reruns. "But I suppose it's like any other technology which is impossible until its underlying principles are discovered. Then it's easy."

"Yes. It was a discovery that came from understanding the Laws of Resonance. It's one of the few important technological breakthroughs since your time. Once we mastered the extraordinary process of time travel, we refined it until we could go to the non-dimensional center of the universe instantaneously and reappear at a different point in space-time. In going from Earth in the late Twentieth Century to Earth in the early Thirty-first, we've had to intersect with the planet's trajectory in a different locale in space as well as time. In the thousand-plus years that have passed, Earth has traveled around the sun to a different point, while the solar system has traveled around the galaxy to another point. Also, the galaxy itself has moved in pursuit of the Great Attractor, and the Universe has been expanding and shifting the locus of points."

"Everything has continued to change," I whisper.

"Yes," he smiles, pleased at my acceptance of this complexity. "And there are other shifts beyond your science that we've also adjusted to. We've had to calculate the differences in space along with the movements in time. So you're actually an enormous spatial distance from where you were when you got up this morning."

I'd never given the distance associated with time travel any thought before. But if pure energy has no mass or dimensions, you can see why it has to elude the limitations of space-time. Exciting stuff! All the photons in the universe might be viewable as different concatenations of one and the same photon vibrating in space-time. Having no dimensions, it could show up at once in all of the space-time continuum, even with different degrees of concentration. In that respect, photons could behave like thoughts that are attracted more to certain areas of the imagination than others, creating spatial warps and crowdings in the mind's reflections, like the topography of the map of thought, with hills and valleys. These change as you revisit old ideas and leave casually explored possibilities alone.

I suddenly feel small. Perhaps it's because I realize I'm a unique concatenation of light dreaming of matter.

The proliferation of matter is both as simple and complex as scientists speculated. Just as I can think about a particular event and change my mind to think of something else, I can select events to concentrate my energy on, while neglecting others. It sounds obvious, but previously I had no idea my mind might work the same way a photon does! There is no linear, sequential requirement to set boundaries to my thinking any more than there are any barriers to inhibit a photon of light from showing up in many different places simultaneously, visiting parts of the space-time continuum at will! My mental energy can become concentrated in some places and not others, just as the energy of light is concentrated inside stars and not in the far reaches of intergalactic space.

Until now, I didn't know that my Being stretched beyond the stars!

Given all this, what arrow of time can one imagine? Certainly the photon, rooted in dimensionless non-materiality, has the expanse of forever to spread its wings in, unconstrained by time or direction, just like my thoughts, scattered like salt and pepper between points past and future. A photon interacts with the material universe, adopts its laws and travels at the speed of light in straight lines and with specific vibrational frequencies. In the same way my thoughts become a part of committed reality when I build a physical object I once only imagined. My own creativity parallels the originating processes of the universe.

Nice theory. But how is it possible for material things to travel in space-time by dropping out of it?

Isaiah addresses the question, apparently aware of my thoughts.

"A while ago you were thinking about Star Trek, beaming people all over the galaxy. It's almost the same thing. When we disappear from one place and reappear in another, we disassemble the atoms in our bodies and uncurl them into the original light energy from which they were made. We use complex resonance patterns, analogous to tuning forks producing sympathetic vibrations in each other. Collective frequencies that make up your body call forth identical ones in other places and times when we set the resonance fields into the relationship required."

"Wow!"

"It's not as fantastic as it sounds, because every electron in your body is a wave that spreads throughout the universe. What's involved is tuning into those same vibrations in a different place and reconstructing the material from them while it is disassembled in its original location. It isn't duplication, it's transmission. Even cloning can't make exact duplication of living things possible, because a consciousness can't localize in two places at once. If it could, it would be in a tug of war between two realities that would quickly become unmanageable.

"Here's an analogy for you. Resonances are thought forms ready to receive our being in different places, the way an outfielder attempts to catch a baseball all over the ballpark. The thought forms are 'real' and the atomic structures are 'imagined'. We use this notion to disassemble our bodies, ships and everything in them, sending them into the dimensionless center of the universe. Echoing resonance patterns in another corner of space-time instantaneously reassemble them. There is no loss in continuity of being

— none that we can sense, anyway. In the space-time continuum, our travel is always instantaneous and preserves the parity of the universe."

"You mean it's environmentally safe."

"More or less."

I must look a bit dense. Isaiah flashes his most patient smile.

"I'm afraid this is the best I can do in terms of an explanation. It's as far beyond my comprehension as it is yours."

"I'm glad of that. Feeling like a stupid Earthling isn't my idea of fun," I sigh with relief. Still, I feel strangely enlightened and a bit proud of myself, too. If I can't understand the process, at least I can grasp it emotionally, with a feeling untranslatable into logic.

Preparing for Disassembly

"We're landing now," Isaiah says in a less contemplative tone. "Soon I'll be able to show you what Earth looks like in our time."

"Aren't you going to tell me to brace myself?"

"What for? You impress me as a man who has a good grip on things," he replies. I wonder if he's talking metaphorically, or whether another raw jolt is ahead. I've never been on a UFO before — not that I recall anyway — so I don't know what to expect. There aren't any seat belts or air bags on these things.

Isaiah stands and rubs his hands together. Cautiously, he scans the scene out the window, which fogs up with his breath.

"It's time to disembark," he announces. "But there's one more thing you should know. We're not very close to Earth, despite what you think you're seeing out the window."

"You mean objects in the window are farther than they appear?"

"What I mean is that this is a holographic image of where we're going to end up," he says, pointing out the window. "We're several light years away from Earth in fact, at the point of exit from the wormhole. What happens now is that we become light and travel from this point to earth. That's beaming up — or in this case, beaming down!"

Isaiah's words are a bit scary. I know my whole body will be disassembled and reassembled, or — how did he put it? Curled and uncurled? What if I get stuck in the machine like a twisted piece of pasta?

I'd rather not think about it.

This is ridiculous! What a silly thing to worry about! Isaiah knows what he's doing. His people have had several centuries to practice this technology.

But then again, my mechanic used to make the same claim.

Still, Isaiah is no cosmic grease monkey. I've already been beamed up once. What's one more time through the spaghetti works?

Isaiah senses my feelings.

"Your anxiety is a cover for something else, something that's really going to trouble you."

"What's that?" I ask apprehensively.

"The part of the experiment we're not quite sure about."

And at that instant I black out.

In the Middle of Manhattan

A moment later I'm in a new place, no longer distant and airborne. I feel the ground beneath me, supportively holding me in place. I am centered again, structured, no longer free of earth's salutary bondage.

I lie on a bed of ferns dry to the touch but retaining the scent of rainy earth. I stretch, renewing contact with each cell and muscle, once again on a first name basis with all. They respond with pulsing energy.

The sun is high, but I can feel it more than see it from where I am. A cardinal perches on a nearby branch. From a little distance comes a bird call, perhaps from its mate, standing out against the background of incessant avian singing, rich and voluptuous, very far from the era of Silent Spring.

Where am I? — in a forest, its vernal beauty beyond belief. A vaulted ceiling of leaves shatters the sunlight into a kaleidoscope of different greens.

Two feet firmly planted beside my head startle me into abrupt alertness, and I recognize Isaiah's shoes.

"Where is this place?" I ask. He answers with his peculiar brand of silence.

I look off to my right, where deer graze under the forest canopy, uninterested in our presence. I can feel the fullness, the completeness in the air, the sense of harvest, abundance; like the Amish symbol of the bird atop the house, securing peace and plenty for everyone inside.

The forest landscape is covered with ferns, like a museum display of the Jurassic period. The croaking of frogs surprises me, for in my day they'd contracted disfiguring genetic mutations and everyone assumed they were en route to their extinction.

Old trees nurture younger ones, seedlings learning at the feet of their elders. This seems like some kind of cinematic special effect. It could be virtual reality. I'm surrounded by Mother Nature at work. Heaven knows, it looks exactly like the real thing, except here it's a little more lush.

"Welcome to downtown Manhattan," announces Isaiah, smiling mischievously in a way I've come to recognize.

"You've got to be kidding!" I stand up and dust myself off.

"Not at all," he replies.

"Manhattan? New York City?"

"Yes," he replies, indicating the verdant surroundings with his hands. "Although this bears no relationship to the city you knew. We had to start over after the great tidal waves. This is one of the most thriving centers of business in our world today. Population ninety-seven thousand, approximately."

"Bird and squirrel population, you mean?" I say, choosing to ignore the bit about the tidal waves.

"No, not the animal population. People."

"All I see is forest," I say, restating the obvious. "Are you sure this isn't Central Park?"

"No, we're in downtown Manhattan, just as I said. Actually, we're on top of it," he smiles, making a little joke at my expense.

"On top of it?" I look down and see only my shoes and the earth supporting them.

"Yes. There aren't any major centers of commerce above ground anymore. Now there's more ground above them."

"What are you talking about?"

"See if you can figure it out."

"Let me get this straight. We're standing above a city in this forest. Kind of a magic carpet. Have I got that right?"

"Not bad, Noah," Isaiah says. "You're getting there."

"Is it some sort of virtual reality?"

"It's an altering of reality," he replies vaguely.

"These are yes and no questions, Isaiah. Which is it?"

"A little of both."

"And we're in the future, is that right?" I ask.

"Yes."

"Any people here?"

"Yes. There are people here. Ninety-seven thousand of them right in this area, give or take a few."

I suppose I'll be meeting some of them, which makes me feel a twinge of anxiety about my imminent introduction to this alien society.

I used to love the story of Rip Van Winkle. I wonder if what happened to him is some kind of junior version of what's happening to me. I'm not sure I really want to know. The poor guy slept for twenty years and was disoriented by everything he had to deal with when he woke up. And in those days, there wasn't much change.

Here I am, ripped out of a time of intense change. I've slept, or something, for over a thousand years. What kind of a disorienting nightmare am I dealing with? When I get back, I could sell this story for big bucks to the tabloids. But what person with any brains would believe me? I suppose I could take some evidence back. Maybe some microfiches of the daily papers from the future. But even then, who'd believe me? You hear about bizarre events all the time. Miracles, stigmata, flying monks, you name it, some pretty strange things show up in the papers. People simply dismiss events that jar their conceptions of proper reality.

Might as well forget about trying to take back any proof. It's going to take more than parlor tricks to impress the movers and shakers of my time. For now I'd better just take things as they come. Time to find out what's going on, instead of speculating on how to accomplish what I don't even understand yet.

"How are the cities of your time constructed?" I ask.

"That's not a yes or no question," Isaiah smiles.

"Have you covered the cities with caves?"

I can see from his expression that I've gotten it right.

"Yes. How did you guess?"

"I remembered what you said: Mankind, which began its life in caves, has returned to the caves. . ."

". . . Until the end of its life," he says.

"And when will that come?"

"Well, perhaps never," he says, awkwardly correcting himself, his expression showing me that he's a little startled by the idea.

"How can you say that? How can you say that our world will never end?"

"Let's just say, we expect we'll be able to surmount any problems that come our way. We're a resilient species."

"But the Earth will come to an end one day when the Sun explodes in a giant cataclysm," I remind him.

"Indeed," he calmly replies, "in another five billion years our species will have to vacate the Solar System, or at least the neighborhood."

"You mean move out?"

He nods. "Right. Move out. And we'll have our exit visas ready well ahead of schedule. When the time is right we'll expand outward into the cosmos."

"The final frontier," I murmur.

"A touch melodramatic, but yes. We will have hollowed out the Earth, the moon and the planets, and built a giant fleet of platforms for life that can move wherever we wish in the vastness of space."

"Why do that? Why not use that plasma stuff you make those benches with?"

"Well, who knows what the future will bring? Right now that plasma stuff, as you call it, is a purely local effect requiring someone's thought process to sustain it. But maybe someday we'll be able to use our minds to create whole fleets of space ships. Or maybe we'll be able to use them to keep the sun from blowing itself to smithereens. I like that idea."

"No telling what miracles could occur," I say.

"Basically, I think you're on the right track. You know, we get so stuck in the current state of things, sometimes we don't think about what could happen in the future that might be different."

"Human nature never changes, does it?"

"You certainly have a point. Maybe we should hire you as a consultant."

I smile. Then I realize he's playing games with me. Wise guy! I decide to shut up and see what's going to happen next. Maybe I suffer from a basic character flaw, thinking I've got all the answers to everything.

"We'll be able to position ourselves wherever necessary to receive the energy we need to continue our growth and prosperity," Isaiah says. "And we'll take the ecology of the Earth with us wherever we go."

"But for now?"

"For now we live in an aggregate of peace and harmony. It's a dynamic peace, lived out in an endless variety of environments we've created for ourselves."

"Tell me more about those environments," I ask.

I'm having the time of my life. It feels so much like home here. This confirmation that Mother Nature doesn't change much over a thousand years is reassuring. Only what we do makes dramatic changes in her.

Enclosed Cities

"Each of our cities is enclosed in a geodesic dome," Isaiah says. "This allows us to control our climate. When the idea was first introduced, it greatly reduced the cost of heating and air conditioning individual homes."

"Why was that?"

"If you heat or cool a collection of small spaces it's more expensive than heating one large space. Besides, a single dome can be constructed with enough insulation so that the temperature remains close to constant. The saving in energy costs is phenomenal."

"So what? So everybody pays less. How is that such a big deal?" I know my capitalist ethic is unshakable, but now I'm behaving as if the bottom line were trivial.

"It's true that the original idea was to save money, so in a sense, you're right — what's the big deal?"

I wonder if he's mocking me, but I carry on.

"You said it reduced the cost 'at first'. Does that mean the savings didn't last?" Logically, fossil fuels would have become scarce, so the cost would have increased as time went on.

"There's as much fossil fuel today as there was in your time," Isaiah counters. "There's just not much use for it anymore."

"What happened? Did people switch to fusion energy?"

"Yes, but that's beside the point. Our energy consumption is extremely low compared with yours and it's all because of changes in our lifestyle. Domes were constructed over living spaces, covered with several layers of topsoil. These accumulated over several centuries, allowing Earth to re-grow its covering. When that was complete, the need for heating and air-conditioning decreased enormously, and we could use the energy we collected from the sun to generate our lighting and weather systems, and to purify the air."

"So everyone on Earth lives in caves?"

"Yes. Leaving aside such exceptions as scattered country houses and vacation spots. There are still a few farms and historic places."

"A few farms? Where do you get your food?"

"From the sea. In the process, we've increased its nutritional value and decreased the cost of providing it. But let's not get into that yet. We're talking about our culture. We've kept alive some aspects of every phase of human history."

"Still, it sounds gloomy, living underground."

"Believe me, it's not. It's actually saved lives, sparing people from tornadoes, hurricanes and tidal waves. And along with climate control, we provide full spectrum sunlight and simulated weather. As a result you can't tell that you're not out in the open air. It looks exactly like Earth and the climate and temperature are always ideal. We even have cloudy days, rain and mild thunderstorms randomly programmed in so things don't get repetitious. After all, human beings evolved to deal with chaos. When things get too orderly, people get bored. So we keep things lively. The weather is still a topic of conversation, even in our time. Now you can talk about it and do something about it."

"I guess human nature stays pretty much the same. But let me get this straight. People live in small cities, much as they did in my time, and it seems very much the same as it was in my day — but it's all underground."

"That's the executive summary. In some respects, you saw more environmental changes in your lifetime than we've seen in the last thousand years, except in a few significant areas. In your time people tended to imagine that technology would keep growing forever at the same rate. You were at the very peak of the growth curve, which dropped off sharply as soon as the major climatic disasters began. Suddenly you were using up your resources responding to global catastrophes, and the focus of your technology shifted to dealing with that."

At the suggestion of catastrophe, I steer the conversation back to the main issue.

"In my time, the Earth was dotted with buildings — small towns, villages, farms and barns, manufacturing plants, corporate corridors, megacities. There was less and less untrammeled land left over from all that."

"Ah, that has greatly reversed itself," Isaiah says. "Beyond the effects of the tidal waves that wiped out many of the largest cities, the reason is strange."

"What reason?"

"We no longer wanted to live in the old houses because they were too ornate and chopped up. They had small rooms which inhibited the use of space. They had ornamentation and structural irregularities which got in the way of how we preferred to arrange our spaces. So the old houses were abandoned and many former centers of population became ghost towns.

"You see, if you hang a picture on the wall and leave it, a month later you don't notice it anymore. But if you're constantly changing your decor, you retain a feeling for the vitality of your environment. Your senses come alive to a much greater extent. You become more interested in everything around you.

"In your time people needed to travel around the world to feel excited by life. That was expensive, inconvenient, and didn't happen very often.

"We, however, live with a continual sense of adventure. Our environment always presents us with new and interesting challenges to the intellect. The weakest minds among us can argue a point as well as the chief scholars of your time. That's because the stimulation of the mind is primary to us. After all, in a sense our minds are all we have. What lies outside them does not exist for us unless it's represented through our sensory inputs. So keeping our minds challenged, alive and dealing with new ambiguities is one of the causes of our extraordinary happiness and longevity.

"Remember the huge castles with private movie theaters, unending parties, and expensive artwork your millionaires built for themselves? All that is now accessible to everyone but on a much grander scale. Most people love to live that way, because we've learned how to get the most out of it. There's no anti-intellectualism, no poverty, no false sense of value. We live simple lives compared to yours, but they're not intellectually simple by any means."

"What led to this?"

"It was partly a reaction against the over development of technology. Most of what we have today was imagined in your time, even if only in the form of science fiction. In your day there were many surprises as new developments came along, but since then, the rate of technological development has slowed down considerably. Yes, we can materialize things and beam around the cosmos. We can control the weather, build underground cities and things like that. But we've devoted far more of our energy to exploring the possibilities of our minds, and it's in that spirit that we brought you here."

"Oh? So you're going to clue me in now on what this experiment is about?"

To my disappointment, Isaiah shakes his head. "That will be someone else's job," he says. "I just wanted you to know that technology isn't the answer to everything."

"But why can't you give me a clue?"

"You're not ready to know yet."

"Not ready? After all this time?"

"No, not yet. Not until you pass the tests."

"What tests?"

"I wanted you to have your feet firmly on the ground before you heard anything about them. People from your time don't respond well to tests. There are just too many risks in our going any further with this conversation right now, so I think we'd better limit ourselves to external things."

"Thanks for the vote of confidence," I say, somewhat bitterly.

He doesn't respond at all to this. How can one argue with a scholar like Isaiah if he wants the conversation to go his way?

"So, then, tell me more about your cities," I ask.

"Well, people abandoned their homes so they could have ideal climates by living in the underground, whereas if they remained in the country they had to worry about plowing snow, risking tornadoes and other weather related disasters. As the rate of disasters increased exponentially shortly after your time, the drive to build cities safe from the elements increased, which gave additional impetus to the shift in population from the country to the cities."

I find myself upset by this. What happened to all the great

historic buildings, the cathedrals and art museums and skyscrapers? Humanity put an enormous amount of effort into the cities of my time, and here they've vanished into dust in a thousand years. I've often thought about impermanence, but never imagined it on a scale like this.

"Don't worry," Isaiah says. "There are still plenty of buildings all over the Earth that one can visit. They have their own kind of glory out in the open air — ancient castles and cathedrals and other historic landmarks.

"As the people of the Earth came together in organized communities with populations of not more than a hundred thousand, the structures scattered over the Earth were left to rot and decay. Eventually most were plowed under in the reforestation movement that was the answer to the great climatic devastations of the Twenty-first Century."

He returns to this theme of devastation a little too much for my taste. I don't want to hear about it. There's only so much a guy like me can do. Can't we just skip over a few intervening centuries? Why go through all this?

"Today most forests are several centuries old and have regained their ecological balances. But it's time for you to explore this forest for yourself," Isaiah says. "We've talked enough. Go into the woods. This is where we part company for a time."

"Why?" I ask, alarmed at the idea of being on my own."

"The purpose will reveal itself."

Isaiah's tone worries me. I don't like the implications. What gives him the right to abandon me after bringing me to such a strange time and place? What if I meet up with a situation I can't handle?

I search for a response in his face. With a quick gesture he points me in the direction of my journey.

"The time for your encounter is upon us. Someone is waiting for you. You mustn't delay any further."

I detect a hint of reluctance in his voice.

"Someone's waiting? Who?"

"Someone you'll be pleased to meet." He seems anxious, as if I might suspect a lack of truth in his words. "This part of the experiment will go exceptionally well."

For a second I turn my head towards the path he indicates, waiting for further explanation. Hearing nothing, I turn back to look at him, only to discover that he's gone.

Reflecting on Nature's Long Retreat

The sun is high overhead, lifting my sense of adventure and curiosity. An uncontained excitement foments inside me. I know it's time to move down the path my guide has pointed out.

It's good to be back in the light and fresh air again, even if this might be a hologram. As far as I'm concerned, it looks and smells like real woods. I feel at home, as if I'm back on earth in my own time, enjoying a calm walk in the woods.

I suddenly notice I'm wearing different clothing now, though I have no awareness of how or when the change was made. The business suit has thankfully been swapped for jeans and a jersey like Isaiah's. So this is what the well dressed cosmic man is wearing. Comfortable. My feet can breathe in these shoes. I've never felt so relaxed.

My body revels in the breeze and the scent of life. It feels like late May when the final thaw of winter erodes the mind's defenses and the heart takes over. Spring and a young man's fancy, I guess you could say.

I see Nature in a new light, almost as if a vision of its meaning parades before me. During my lifetime, the quality of Nature's spirit gradually retracted in subtle, almost imperceptible ways. Was it gradual in its barely noticeable withdrawal? Did no one but the scientists and the doomsday prophets see it turn away, wounded?

I feel alienated from my time, absorbed in these musings. I feel as if I had not lived then, as if the people who were my friends, clients, business associates, even enemies, had long ago faded into the mists of time, fools for the way they'd lived. Have I been seduced into life in the Thirty-first Century, where I'm an alien at best?

Am I worse off here? Have I really lost anything with the demise of one and all of my contemporaries? Will I adjust to my new environment and never look back?

Here in the familiar Nature it seems tempting to regard things that way. Life, after all, must be easier in this time than in my own era of upheaval. I can skip all that nonsense, all the war and terrorism and social unrest of the Twentieth Century, the hubbub and rejection of the possibility of better lives for everyone.

What arrogance! Here I am in a safer, gentler place and I feel as if it's my doing. That's a danger signal! I don't even know why I'm here or what's intended for me. Better not overstep or I could find myself in an untenable situation. I don't feel any impending danger, even though I probably should. For some reason, I'm convinced that there isn't any danger here. Isaiah is protecting me.

Besides, how can I worry when it is so extraordinarily beautiful here. I used to see the Northern Lights from my bedroom window when I was a child, shimmering like a golden curtain across the wintry night sky. Now they're no longer visible in my part of the world. The sparkle of air and starlight gradually dimmed because of infiltrating poisons in the atmosphere. Is the light show over, the curtain brought down forever on one of nature's wonders? Or did my child's eyes perceive my surroundings as more resplendent than they actually were? Have I, by coming here, entered a world where once again such beauties have reclaimed their own, as the invading human race has respectfully retreated underground?

Natural Harmonies

Now, as if to reassure me that it has come full strength back into its own, Nature stretches out its limbs like a cat after a long nap — more graceful, confident and lithe than anything I remember from childhood.

Downtown Manhattan is below me, I muse, remembering what Isaiah has said. Am I standing above 42nd Street and Broadway, perhaps? There's no city here, I smile. Yet abundance is everywhere. Peaceful ease, I call it.

How could this path be so wide open? Walking through woods in summer usually means one has to fight through the underbrush. Forests grow pretty quickly. But there's no sign of tangled thickets, just peaceful growth, more like a kept garden than an untamed forest.

I look in wonder at the cathedral ceiling of branches. The tallest trees I've ever seen grow some distance apart, pillaring upwards so their translucent leaves connect, catching the sunlight. There's been time enough for this forest to grow unchecked for hundreds of years. Some of the trees surrounding me might have been here for a century or more. A cool green mist of dew clings to the forest floor in the pre-summer heat, a texture in the soil I've not experienced before.

When I was younger, I remember reading in a social studies book about the majestic virgin forests of North America. When the settlers came to clear the land for farms, the forests were wasted and soon disappeared. In that distant time, extremely tall trees brought order to the underbrush, providing a sheltering canopy for forest life. There was a ground cover of moss and ferns, bushes springing up here and there in occasional flowering, but few stunted, short trees in those pristine days.

I'd always wished I could have seen that, and now I'm surrounded by it.

I feel so at home in these woods! I've never had a walk more fulfilling and enriching. Eons ago my ancestors prospered in such surroundings. Perhaps my sensations of homecoming can be traced back to a primeval memory.

Venturing beyond the forests led my people to agriculture and the progress of civilization. The very words leave a hollow place in my heart, as if we'd left home never to return. Eden abandoned. Was it destined to be so, or have we fallen into a vain, self-serving trap under the guise of human achievement?

We shuffle blindly, searching for material power, money and fame. Why are we compelled to such nonsense? We search so passionately, disabling our insight which blinds us to the great works of the spirit within and among us. Nature is the greatest artist, whose work we have defaced as surely as if we were to attack Michelangelo's Pieta with a sledgehammer.

These woods and the creatures living here remind me of the Peaceable Kingdom, all the elements of harmony in balance. I feel as if I were a child, reborn into a magical state of wonderment, my steps leading deeper into bliss. I take off my shoes and socks and sink my feet into the moss. A luscious sensation runs through me. Where on earth can anyone feel the power of creation like this, body melding into the caressing greenery?

Light descends from the trees in silhouetting rays, a metaphor for the radiance of God shining upon His creatures. I feel my oneness with the light, powering, birthing, granting me the capacity of my senses. As I close my eyes I feel a giant chord of music welling inside me, filling the celestial realm with its joyful harmony. It resonates around me, circling high above into the light sweeping through the forest. The music pierces me as if I were a lightning rod, directing its echoes back to the sky.

Pure love unites the universe! I understand now what Isaiah meant: an abiding grace, a sustaining force powers all things. It's called Love. I open my eyes once more, trying to see the grand hymn of praise sounded to the unfathomable beauty of the Earth.

I settle myself on the ground, leaning my back against the trunk of an old oak.

And then, quite without fanfare, standing before me, she appears.

Sunlight sets in the strands of her hair, throwing their texture into bold relief. Her face is cast in shadow, so at first I cannot see, but only intuit its features.

Meeting With Maya

Her voice has a naive gentleness, almost childlike, yet mature in its composure and clarity. The effect, while charming, humbles me.

"You're Noah Gershom, aren't you?" She leans over, extending her elegant hand in greeting.

"Yes."

"Isaiah was right, as usual. He said I'd find you in an altered state. He's gotten to know you pretty well, I see."

"How do you see that?"

"Something in your . . ." She pauses. "It was premature of me to say such a thing," she adds apologetically.

She shrugs, so I let it pass.

"Isaiah and I have been spending a good deal of time together recently," I say.

I'm feeling trapped, as if I need to explain everything. I stand up, brushing leaves and dust from my clothing. Lying at the foot of this woman at our initial meeting has put me at a disadvantage. I'm groping for words.

"I've just never before seen such a forest as this . . ."

"Lovely, yes?" I follow her gaze up to the canopy of branches. "This is one of my favorite places, too. It's one of my aeries."

"Aeries?"

"It's . . . oh, it's like a house. I collect them, many of them. Anything can be a house, don't you see? You lay claim to it, appease the surroundings, make it yours, and after that whenever you come there it's waiting for you, has everything ready just for you."

I look around but see nothing that would indicate such a complex state of readiness.

"Oh, I have to remind myself that you're from a different time. You see, we've learned that wherever one goes, one leaves traces of oneself. We've learned how to sense and respond to them, just as many ancient peoples used to do. I could teach you how, if you'd like."

I smile weakly, trying to understand. "Sort of like reviving a lost art?"

"Not just 'sort of like.'" But she nods in a way that reassures me. I'm beginning to appreciate how absolutely present she is with me right now. Something in her eyes takes you in and includes you in her deepest thoughts.

"Is this your house too, Noah?" She laughs upon seeing my confusion. "Oh, of course you don't know what I mean, but it must be so. I can sense you in these surroundings." She smiles as if she's happy for me, and then continues telling me about herself. "Until I made the offerings necessary to secure this place for my home, I was a frequent trespasser here. I come often when I'm in need of inspiration. This house is the special house for that. I have other houses for other things."

"You're an artist, then?"

Again she smiles — this time with evident amusement. "We're all artists," she says, "each in our own way."

I feel excluded. If there's anything I am definitely not, it's an artist. Yet here, I've just been told, there's no one who isn't. How can I ever be comfortable in this familiar, yet infinitely strange world?

"Sometimes I come here to examine the meaning of the transition we're going through right now."

"Transition? What kind of transition?"

"The human species is becoming . . . something else. Something greater than it was before. Our generation is living through that process."

"And I've come here to . . ."

She dismisses this with a wave of her hand that I think betrays some irritation.

I'm lost. I don't know how to take any of this. A moment ago she said she was a trespasser too, a frequent trespasser here, but that can't be anything like what I'm feeling. A fish out of water.

Still, she knows who I am. But I don't know anything about her.

"Who are you?" I ask.

"Maya."

"Maya." The name is sweet, almost compensating for the fact that it's really not an answer to my question. Strangely, I feel that I've known her before, but there's no accounting for this. I wait, wondering what will happen next. The ball's in her court. I haven't the slightest idea how to handle this situation.

"Would you like a tour?" she says airily, as if this were Disneyland.

"A tour?"

"Give you a chance to get to know us a little — and our ways."

"It would be . . . Yes, I'd like a tour, of course. Yes, that would be very nice. But it would be . . . I don't know what to say . . . more meaningful if I knew what I'm doing here, and what you want with me."

"Oh, don't worry about that now," she warmly reassures me.

"But I can't help it, can I?" I say.

"You can help anything if you put your mind to it," she says.

"You have great confidence in me."

"Of course I do. I have to."

As if sensing my befuddlement she changes the subject like one trying to distract a sullen infant.

"Do you remember Enoch? We'll be meeting him in the Forum. You can see what we've accomplished in the past thousand years. Since your time, that is."

"Yes, Enoch, I remember meeting him on the journey here." I don't actually remember him very well, but an image of a rotund man, friendly, maybe a sense of humor, and very intelligent, flits through my mind.

Smiling, she leads the way. She's beautiful, but this may be the least part of her remarkable effect. Her eyes seem connected to something very distant — and yet are still consistently present. Her dress is of a diaphanous fabric unknown to me, the color of lilacs. It's my favorite color, and I wonder if she chose it knowing that, since she seems to know so much else about me. This dress which gives a hint of fairyland is nevertheless dignified in a strange way, as if it belonged to a queen who brought her own dignity to it. Yet there's nothing remote about Maya.

For a moment our glances lock, unexpressed questions reflecting each other. She seems tantalizingly familiar to me, but I can't focus on that, because when I look at her full in the eyes her beauty is so intense that it stirs up feelings I don't want to deal with, that I'm ashamed to admit to myself I even have. So, fearful of exposing too much, I look away towards a clearing, trying to appear matter-of-fact and practical-minded. But of course it's a cover. If truth be told, I'm intensely regretting my loneliness now and all my pitiful relationships with women in the past. I don't know if love will ever be possible for me again. At the moment I'm not feeling very sanguine about it.

She leads the way through the forest with a sure-footedness that reveals trails I hadn't noticed. After a short distance we approach what appears to be the entrance to a cave. There's a rise in the land to a height of about twelve feet which stands out in front of a rather abrupt hill. In it there's a stone gate, very ancient in appearance, as if it might have been placed there by Stone Age peoples long ago.

"Here we are at the entrance to Manhattan," Maya announces.

"Hardly a thoroughfare of the sort one would expect," I remark.

"It's only so people like me can come and go in these woods as often as we please. Actually, it doesn't get very much use. But walking for recreation and exercise is something I personally enjoy so much I do it perhaps more than I should."

As she speaks, the stone gate dissolves in a manner to which I am by now accustomed. Inside I see an escalator leading down, similar to the entryway to a metro system, except that it's canopied by a cream colored marble, a cathedral ceiling rising above, decorated with an astonishing mural which changes in color and pattern in an almost kaleidoscopic effect.

When we enter this area I glance back and see that the stone blockade is again in place behind us.

"This is the Forum we're going to be entering," says Maya. "It's the center of our community very much as in ancient times. I know you're still a little uncomfortable here, Noah, that's perfectly natural, but you'll get used to us. In some ways we haven't changed very much. We still like to go out, to meet with other people as a community and the Forum is where we gather."

I pause to give some attention to the architecture. We are in a large open space with many areas marked out, suggesting different activities. Over here a basketball court, there a tennis court, but in other spaces: restaurants, banks of computers, places simply to sit around and talk, extensive playground areas for children with the wildest fantasies brought to life in them — not the plastic cartoon facades I'm used to, but more like a friendlier sort of Bosch — and an exercise area that looks like a dreamscape.

The place is filled with people who move easily among themselves. Everyone seems to know everyone else.

"Do all these people know one another?"

"No. But, we don't really make so much of the distinctions between people. Because our society is free of crime there's no suspicion of strangers, so it's only polite to treat everyone like a friend. I believe that's the main reason we feel so good all the time. We're always comfortable with one another. We don't have to worry about fitting in or being accepted."

Well that's certainly a big change. I can go a whole week in my home town and never look anyone in the eyes; it's hard to believe conditions so different as these can exist — even allowing for a thousand years to develop them in.

I'm also awestruck by my physical surroundings. I've been in plenty of malls and many of them are attractive and appealing. But the elegant proportions of the architecture here, the articulation of spaces is nothing less than a work of art in its own right. It has a kind of grandeur, yet, it's also very simple. You might think you couldn't have the two together, but that's how it is here. It's like something from nature, simple, grand, intricate and complex all at the same time, a new level of artistic expression I've never seen before. I can't fault it in any way. This environment is definitely not the sort of place you'd ever complain about or trivialize — the way I'm used to doing with nearly everything back home.

Suddenly Maya laughs. "There he is," she says, pointing out someone in the crowd.

It's Enoch coming towards us. I remember now our previous meeting under the stressful circumstances on the space ship with Isaiah. He greets me in a warmly gruff voice with the open manner of a familiar and comfortable comrade.

"How are you, Enoch?" Maya asks.

"Never been better, Love," he replies in a tone suggesting that he's a confirmed bachelor and regards all women in the same affectionate way.

"But this gentleman now, I wonder if culture shock hasn't gotten you a little tied up in knots. Or future shock, didn't they used to call it?"

"Something like that," I say as he shakes my hand vigorously and laughs approvingly at my appearance. There's an oddly grounding effect about Enoch's sudden entrance on the scene. I feel more comfortable now that he's arrived.

"Obviously, this isn't the Manhattan I'm familiar with," I add.

"No. We've done away with Times Square, haven't we. Broadway. Central Park. All the rest of it. Pity." He shrugs. "Well we can reconstitute all of it for you any time you like. We've got it on the hard disk, as you would call it, including all the beer cans and food wrappers in the streets. If you start feeling homesick, I can always. . ."

"Skip it," I say, holding up my hand and grinning at the prospect. In a strange way this man has awakened me to the ridiculousness of my situation, which is not just that I'm in the wrong time and place, but also that I'm noticing for the first time how absurd my own time and place have always been.

"I take it you landed outside before you came on down here," Enoch says, as Maya nods.

I sigh, momentarily homesick for that very spot. "It's perfect up there," I say. "Just what I always wanted nature to look like."

Enoch has been looking at me appraisingly. "You know something, Noah?" he says. "There's a serenity in you I didn't see before, and a wildness in your eyes that goes along with it. It's a strange combination, a paradox, a contradiction, but it's good. It'll probably enable you to do the job this time."

"You mean the experiment?" I ask.

"Well, I wouldn't call it an experiment, I'd more call it, say, a transmutation, though I don't suppose that can mean anything to you. Let's just say you appear to be in shape for what's in store for you."

I look at Maya, scrutinizing her face, but she seems uninterested in this. Her eyes are fixed on Enoch as she says, "I'm sorry to interrupt you two, but I'm afraid you'll have to excuse me for a while. I've got to spend some time with Isaiah about now. Give me an hour or so, would you?"

"Just don't be too hard on him," Enoch teases.

Maya strokes his cheek. "Don't you worry about that, Enoch."

I don't really want to untangle this, but I feel disappointed that Maya is leaving.

I wouldn't say that out loud to save my life.

Besides, I know that both of them are fully aware of how I'm feeling now.

It's just not fair.

A Perfectly Healthy Society

"Let's sit over here at the cafe," Enoch says. "I could use something to eat. How about yourself?"

Food! How much time has passed since I've been here, and I haven't eaten anything, except for the apple Isaiah gave me! How long ago was that? I should be starving by now, but I haven't even thought about food. I'm not even slightly hungry. Odd.

"What do they have?" I ask.

"Anything your heart desires."

"I'm not sure what my heart desires right now. How about ordering for me?"

"Not necessary, place your hand on that disk at the end of the table, the equipment will know what you want. It'll bring out something antique no doubt that hasn't been eaten in Manhattan for several centuries."

As I place my hand on the disk, I feel a momentary sensation of heat, then it's over. We sit overlooking a great hall that seems designed for everything from symphony orchestras and opera performances to something on the order of a medieval tournament. People wander in and out of the entrance sporadically.

Even as we sit, two complete meals roll up next to the table on robotic trays. No need to leave a tip, I guess. I can't tell what Enoch's having, but I'm treated to just what I wanted: a hot dog with mustard, some potato chips and an unidentifiable soft drink.

"Everyone here is obviously in such good health," I tell him as my eyes wander over various faces in the crowd. "There isn't anyone that doesn't look . . . radiant." I've never used that word to describe a person's appearance before, but it fits.

"It's interesting you should say that, because it's one of the most essential contrasts between your time and ours." He leans forward, fixing my gaze tightly with his, as if he has something of the most profound importance to impart. "Look," he says with intensity, "it doesn't make any sense to be in less than perfect health, does it? There's no reason to get sick just because you happen to get older. The body is designed to stay well all the time, unless it has a good reason not to. If you make people's lives miserable enough, they'll get sick just to spite you, just to get away from having to put up with life, don't you know? It's like a defense mechanism. Illness is a form of protest, wouldn't you agree?"

Frankly, I can't agree with that. That's not the way things work where I come from. You get older and you lose something. You start collecting infirmities. Who is he kidding?

"You know," I tell him, "I'm not going to agree with things just because you think I come from a more primitive time than yours. I have no guarantee that you've progressed in your thinking beyond us in every area just because a lot of time has passed. It's always possible to think you're making progress and just get lost in your delusions."

"Oh? Is that how it happened in your time?"

"Look," I say, feeling for some reason as if it's me who has to open his eyes, "death and disease are two of the unpleasant facts of life we just have to accept and avoid as best we can. Nobody wants to get sick and nobody wants to die either, even in my own benighted times. Those are just the condition of life. They just happen. Don't tell me you've figured out a way to swindle fate and don't have to die anymore."

Enoch leans back at this, unwraps a candy and pops it into his mouth. I pick up a few chips and nibble at them unenthusiastically.

"No, of course not," Enoch says. "And we wouldn't want to either. What we have figured out is how to live with death, how to recover from the loss of our loved ones, how to understand and appreciate the grand, inexorable cycle of life. You've got to grab it by the balls, Noah, if life is to be yours. It's a joy, a puzzle of infinite variety to solve as we may. Death makes it all the more precious for us. We don't waste our lives by making ourselves sick."

"In that case, what do you suggest we could have done to keep ourselves healthy?"

"Oh, it's simple enough, even for a corporate headshrink like yourself." Unsure whether I've been insulted, I keep eating and listen.

"You needed to change your approach to life, especially to the way you managed work. You thought progress was a matter of productivity, squeezing people harder to get more profit out of them, but those kinds of tactics turned out to be mostly a collection of ways to make more people sick faster. It was routinely established in your time, by those who seriously studied the matter, that corporations could cut their health care costs to a mere ten percent if they changed their management styles, which in most cases hounded people to death. After all, that's what your bureaucracies were dedicated to doing, wasn't it?"

"That's an exaggeration," I laugh. "What's that got to do with anything?"

"Good health isn't a commodity that you buy at the doctor's office. It's a matter of how you live, a by-product of the air you breathe, the food you eat, and yes, a measure of the pleasure and joy you take in living. The workplaces of your time were oppressive."

"Oppressive? We were just trying to get things done, asking people to give value for money, that's all."

"Is that what you think it was? So, you think it was good?"

"It was what it needed to be. Basically, work is good for people, yes."

"You wouldn't argue that slavery was good for people, would you?"

"No, of course not."

"So why justify the corporate cultures of your time? They weren't much different from slavery. You've seen them. You know they were killing off most men years before their time. The corporate work world was a darn sight better at making stress than any other product they thought they were turning out, and the stress didn't benefit anyone."

"Oh come on," I sigh in exasperation. I probably shouldn't respond so curtly, but I know he's wrong, because he's intruded on my territory. I work in my time, he doesn't. Nevertheless, I check my annoyance and try to continue in a more reasonable tone. "Of course I regret all the stress, but I don't agree that it didn't benefit anyone. After all, there was so much competition that you had to struggle all the time to keep alive. If a business goes under, lots of people suffer. You've got to be tough to stay profitable. If you don't keep after people, they'll slack off and not do anything."

"Oh, for heaven's sake," says Enoch. "What kind of society raises citizens who don't want to do their best for the community? You've seen what it's like here in our time and you're still going to argue for the nonsense that went on in your time? Your society was driven by all the wrong values, don't you see? It was a question of power, my friend, pure power. All of those corporate magnates, moguls of multi-million dollar conglomerates, were so lustful for power they refused to give up one tiny little bit of it to their workers, opting to control and stifle them instead.

"And it didn't even raise profits, the way they behaved. No corporation in your time was more than one percent efficient, or accomplished more than one percent of what it could have done. It was the systems you used in your time that kept you functioning so inefficiently. That's because the way companies were organized, the bureaucratic power structures kept the leaders from knowing the things they needed to know to augment their profits. They militated against allowing the workers to tell them what they needed to know."

I search for a rejoinder to his argument, but can't think of any. In fact, my experience confirms he's right. I'm used to finding out that the average employee has some good ideas about how to make things work better, but darned if they'll ever get heard. On a few occasions I've presented some of those ideas, but after I've been thanked and paid, I've seldom heard of a case where anything came of it.

A long time ago I bought into the notion that people are promoted to their maximum level of incompetence. The higher you go up the ladder of authority, the more insecurity and incompetence you find. No wonder so many workers think management doesn't know what it's doing. It doesn't. I've been there. I've seen it. Many of the companies I've visited are indeed operating at one percent or less of their potential capacity, if you take their collective stupidity into account. In most of the Fortune 500 companies, management hangs its vision on the walls and the employees snicker about it at the water coolers. The workers think the guys upstairs don't know anything, and the guys upstairs would rather fry in hell than ever ask for the workers' opinions. It's a confrontational culture, right down to its coffee breaks.

But what am I doing here, writing Enoch's material for him? Why do I so readily accept his criticisms of my time? I ought to be a little more loyal than that. Perhaps I would be if I had ever cared for any particular values of my own. But the fact is, I never have. Instead, as some character in T. S. Eliot put it, "I have measured out my life with coffee spoons."

"You see, Noah," Enoch interrupts my reveries, "your culture routinely made wrong choices about nearly every problem that confronted it, especially the way you people did what you had the nerve to call business. It wasn't so much that they had the wrong answers, it was that they studiously avoided asking the right questions. Greed decreased available profits, while the struggle for power decreased actual power. The reality is that the more power you give away, the more you actually have. So the leaders weren't even operating in their own stupid interests, let alone anyone else's."

"Then how is it that in the Twentieth Century the world's resources increased hundreds of times, whereas in all previous centuries they barely increased at all?"

"The technological advances made in your time were so incredible that even the worst kinds of mismanagement couldn't prevent available resources and the standard of living from increasing. But the amount of increase was a tiny fraction of what it might have been. Would you like to know what we call the Twentieth Century nowadays?"

I nod wordlessly.

"We call it the Age of Corporate Lunacy."

Trying to Defend My Time

"Give me a break! That's a complete caricature. It's insulting."

I feel stung, as if he had slapped me in the face. I throw my weight onto the two hind legs of my chair and stupidly start to rock until I catch myself almost falling backwards.

It's odd that I feel perfectly okay beefing about the way my own life is, but when the same things come out of Enoch's mouth I feel irrationally chauvinistic. Maybe part of me really does care about the people I move among and work with. Maybe I'm actually proud of my achievements and my time.

So how come I'm nearly always numbed out, except maybe when I'm in the hot tub?

Whatever the reason, at this moment I'm able to focus some of my lifetime of collected and useless anger on Enoch. He's acting so superior; rubbing my nose in it. What does he know about the way things were?

"Look, it's easy enough for you people to be so nice. You don't have anything serious to worry about. You conjure up a desire and it materializes out of thin air, at the blinking of an eyeball, no less. Back where I come from, we have to sweat and toil for every last scrap. And believe me, it's a ball-busting world to have to do it in."

"Well, Noah, there's your problem. I couldn't have described it better myself. I know the old line, life is a vale of tears. Of course it is if you're looking at it the wrong way. Do you know there were societies in your time in which people led lives every bit as rich and rewarding as the lives we lead here? How did they manage their material needs? Like lilies of the field. You mostly wrote them off as marginal or primitive, but the quest for spiritual and communal development informed every value and every practice they engaged in — both sacred and profane. The stance a society takes toward life is shaped by the values it espouses."

"But there were billions of people alive in the twentieth century. We couldn't have all lived in the forest, eating monkeys and contemplating our navels."

"You know that's not what I meant," Enoch begins.

"Wait!" I say, not letting him finish.

I tell him I'm sick of hearing about the impoverishment and vileness of Twentieth Century industrial society. Despite my own criticisms of it, I believe we were doing the best we could, given the state of the world we were born into. Enoch is relentless. Where's all the civility he's touting so proudly? Are these people as confrontational as this with each other? Or is it just with me? Is it all part of the experiment? So far, Maya is the only person I've met here who hasn't given me a hard time.

Except, at the mere thought of her, a chill runs up my spine. I can't think about this right now, though. I'm too preoccupied with an urgent, quixotic need to defend my society.

"Look, I know, even better than you, that businesses could have been managed better. I myself have witnessed a lot of stupidity and venality in corporate board rooms. But despite all the glitches and needless power struggles, people were trying to accomplish things that were important to them. And by God we did: in medicine, agriculture, engineering, computer technology, genetic research, you name it. Corporations and corporate leaders were not heartless, soulless usurpers of power. We made huge contributions to society. Sure we were making money too, but everybody else benefited as well.

We were busy solving the big problems that needed to be solved."

I watch as Enoch's face grows visibly disgusted. I'm not speaking any more forcefully than I was before, but obviously something is striking a nerve and making him angry. Finally he rises to his feet and commands me to do the same.

"You arrogant bastard! Noah, you think you're so savvy, such a man of the world, but you're a total innocent. Come with me."

I follow him to a secluded garden, feeling like a chastened child.

Catching Myself on TV

We sit together for some moments without either of us saying a word. I look up at the sky, which I know is a simulation, as this whole area is covered over by the forest where I met Maya. Nevertheless, I feel like I'm in the open air. There are clouds in the sky, a daytime moon is overhead, and everything looks completely natural in the late afternoon sun. I listen with pleasure to the sounds of birds and insects. Despite my recent agitation, I feel peaceful now. Okay. So, I made Enoch angry, so what? I have no impulse to speak.

After perhaps ten minutes, Enoch clears his throat. "There are things you don't know about yourself," he says, "which you can't find out unless you're willing to look at your life more objectively."

I'm annoyed at this, and sullenly study the grass at my feet, searching for anything that will occupy my mind. I don't want to go wherever this man is leading me. So it only irritates me further when he says, "Are you willing, Noah, to go with me on a little journey into your personality?"

"Do you mean am I willing to be psychoanalyzed?" I almost shout back. "No. I have nothing but contempt for that kind of thing. I am quite capable of handling my problems for myself, thank you."

"I wasn't thinking of anything so archaic as that," he says.

"What were you thinking of, then?"

"Right next to you on your left is a computer," he says. "Touch the screen."

I look closely, but don't see any computer.

"Oh, I forgot," he says. "You can't see it, can you?" He raises his hand. It looks like he's flicking an invisible switch.

With that a computer appears next to me. It stands right out of the flowers on a pole, reminding me a little of a jack-in-the-pulpit, though I don't know why, because it doesn't look like one.

I do as he says, and place my hand on the screen. A man's face appears and speaks to me:

"In what area of thinking is your question?"

Enoch looks at me. "A little stilted I admit, but wait till you see what this guy can do. What would you like to know about?"

I laugh, and an impossible question comes out.

"I'd like to know how it is that Enoch wants me to be different when I return to my own time period."

At the sound of my voice, the man's eyes focus on me.

"Please press the palm of your hand firmly against the screen," he says, addressing me directly. It's spooky, because he seems to know I'm there, but of course I know it's only a canned message.

So it is with no little amazement that I do as he instructs.

For a minute the computer takes me on a stroll through a beautiful forest, not too different an experience from the one I had before I came down here.

Then an instant later I see a picture of myself sitting on a chair in my bedroom. I recognize everything there. I'm looking out the window, just the way I was before my abduction.

I see myself turning from the window and going back to bed, as I might have done had I not been snatched away at that moment. Then the picture fades, and a moment later comes back on with a scene at a church. The doors fly open and I come out with a bride. She's a woman I don't recognize. The glimpse is so brief that I don't have a chance to study her face. I have an impulse to run it back and look at it again, but decide I'd better wait for the real thing.

Then the picture fades and I'm apparently on television, because I see myself talking to some newscasters on what looks like a morning talk show.

Then the picture dissolves into a scene where I'm at my computer and can tell I'm writing a book.

The man's face once more appears on the screen. "Noah Gershom," he says, addressing me directly, "we have given you all the information advisable at this time. Thank you for your inquiry. Have a nice day."

The picture fades into a blank screen.

I'm dumbstruck. How on earth has the computer been able to see everything in my bedroom? How did it know so much about me? And was this, indeed, the answer to my question? Is that how Enoch wants me to act when I return?

Enoch grins from ear to ear. "Pretty amazing, isn't it?"

"It's like talking to a real person, a psychic," I say. "How did that work?"

"When you place the palm of your hand on the screen," he says, "a great deal of information about your body-mind system goes into its memory. From this information it is able to compute many of your thought forms. That's how it got your name, and the other information it showed you. Incidentally, you may have noticed that the picture of your bedroom was clear only in certain details."

"No, I didn't notice that," I say.

"That's odd," says Enoch. "I couldn't miss the fact that the picture showed enormous degrees of variability. The way the covers were thrown aside on your bed, for example, that didn't look real. It was, you know, kind of smudgy and vague, not like a photograph. Also, some of the objects in the room stood out clearly, but others were sketchy. See it was variable in the picture the same way your memory is variable. Your thought forms were clear in some details, unclear in others. But perhaps you didn't notice this, because the picture was so close to your actual memory."

I am speechless. The computer, then, has in effect taken a picture of everything that was in my mind.

"When it came to the church, that was an image from your future, already recorded in your pre-memory."

"My what?"

"Pre-memory obviously isn't as clear as memory of the past because it's got a lot more variability, although the memory of the past is kind of screwy too, depending on slight adjustments that take place in past events as the future gets rolled out.

"But you do have in your mind a set of images of things you haven't done yet. All this stuff is based on the kind of character you've developed up until now. If that were to change, your future would bend around into some new kind of shape right along with it. But based on the way you are now, the computer chose from all the future events that are possible for you, the ones it thinks you're most likely to see happen, based on other things it knows about you . . . including your decision to come visit us. What you saw was the best it could do with about the next year of your life, and I kind of think that given your peculiar condition right now, that's the best anyone could expect, don't you think?"

He leans forward and looks intently at me. "Now, Noah, I know you're not going to believe this, but what we have just seen are a few previews of coming attractions in your life that from my perspective are building blocks in the creation of what I have to call, if you'll pardon the grandiosity of this, the crowning dilemma of my time."

The Barrier

"What's that?"

"All of us poor benighted folks here face a barrier that no one can seem to untangle."

"A barrier?"

"We're at the brink of what some of the more soft-headed among us like to call a new age, a transformation of the human race into some sort of a new condition of being, as they put it. But it's a form that now appears impossible for us to achieve — largely because (and I hesitate to say this for fear of upsetting you) — largely because of you — or some decision or other that you made way back when.

"Don't get me wrong. I don't want you to get all bent out of shape over the melodrama of what I'm saying. And to be honest, we are a people that sometimes tend to place a bit too much emphasis (for my taste) on what's likely to happen to our very distant grandchildren. But there it is. It seems that you are the pivotal point in all of this. What was passing through your mind that moment as you sat in your room, as seen on the good screen there, brought about a certain event, or more likely events, that all of us today, more than a thousand years after your time, are grappling with and can't work our way out of to anyone's particular satisfaction, if you follow this.

"A short time ago as a result of our dream analysis — something I'll explain to you more fully as we go — we stumbled on a dream that Maya had. I'm going to leave it to her to tell you more about this, but it seems that her dream provided a clue about a serious mistake that was made. One in which you played a central role."

I'm listening to Enoch with no little surprise. So. After all, there's a reason they picked me for this experiment. I'm trying to suspend judgment and just listen to what Enoch has to say, yet little whispers of guilt and insecurity are stalking me . . . but I didn't think I made mistakes like that, I'm usually pretty competent at what I do.

"Isaiah spoke of our dilemma here as an experiment. I referred to it rather cryptically as a transmutation. But what is really going on here is a desperate attempt on the part of the human species to secure its own future. As things stand now, we are frozen in our development, unable to take the next step in our evolution. You see, something happened under your auspices which led to a step that humanity should not have taken at that time, at least not without a great deal more probity and maturity, or whatever descriptive terms you'd use to describe sensibly cautious behavior. Now, if we continue to live with that step in the past, we may simply die out, a failed species that will have to be replaced by something else we can't even imagine."

I am speechless. "I did something so terrible as that?"

"Relax, Noah." He crosses to me and puts his hand on my shoulder. "What you did was not in itself so terrible. It was merely the nodal point in a complex interaction of forces in which, had you behaved differently, an entirely different set of possibilities would have been preserved for the future."

I can't comprehend any of this.

"So you're trying to change something that for you has already happened. How is that possible?"

"Because in reality there is no time. All events happen simultaneously. By the same token, they are all products of our moment to moment free will. Free will and determinism are in reality inseparable, different aspects of the same phenomenon. I'm sorry to have to bring up in the conversation something that, quite frankly, is beyond both of us to understand, though my people, at least, understand how it can be corrected.

"Because your time and ours are part of the same fabric, and happen, in a way we cannot understand, simultaneously, we can go back and edit the past, producing a different outcome that serves to safeguard some of the things we think the womb of time (I like that expression, always have) has in mind for our progeny somewhere in the deep, distant future, a millennium from now. I don't want to be maudlin about this, but frankly, we need you to help us do this. Everything, Noah, everything depends on you."

"My God!" I exclaim, unable to put words to anything.

Enoch crosses in front of me, fixes my gaze with his, and nods. "Yes," he says. "Your God. He is with you now. He suffers as you suffer. He struggles as you struggle. That is the way of God. We are his instruments and without us he cannot accomplish his will. We must do now what he would have us do. We must build our future with a full understanding of the fact that, with all our bumbling ineptitude, it is we who create our destiny. For, believe it or not, we are all one, not fully separable from one another. Sorry about that, I too can think of a person or two I don't really want to champion that kind of intimacy with, but there it is. A Law of the Universe, or something like that. Anyway, it seems that we cannot be separated from God, who is in us and with us and is the totality that we are from."

I sit in silence, not able to focus any thoughts at all.

"Relax, Noah," Enoch says again. "I know this is a very heavy responsibility to place on your shoulders, and I really have to apologize to you about that. You're not a man who thinks well about responsibility and that is, of course, a major part of the problem. But you must learn to think about it, Noah. You must see your true place in your time and your species and you must find a way to take responsibility, however much it may seem to go against the grain for you at the moment."

I am silent. There's nothing I can say. Nothing at all.

"So let's go back to what happened with the computer. Let's talk about that, because you and I are going to have to work our way through all of this one step at a time, Noah."

He sits down again a little distance away, facing me, and after a while I look up and meet his gaze again and nod. There is nothing for it but to go on here, to see where this will take us. I refuse to think about it. I can't comprehend it.

"Back to the computer, then," says Enoch. "It's obvious that the computer expects you to get married. Do you know this person you're supposedly going to marry?"

"She's a complete stranger to me," I say.

"Well, I expect it will be a whirlwind romance," says Enoch, allowing me the privacy of my own opinions on this subject. I can tell he's making a monumental effort to be jovial and light about all this. It's the only way I'd conceivably be able to take any of it now. "The computer also predicted that your television networks will be interested in you. Then it sees you writing a book."

"So now I know what's in store for me," I say. I'm desperately hoping, I guess, that this will let me off the hook.

"Not necessarily," says Enoch. "The computer isn't psychic. It doesn't know your actual future. It knows only what is likely at this moment as it grinds its gears to assess the situation, given all that has happened in your life up to now."

"But that wasn't what I asked it," I say. "I asked it to tell me how you would like me to behave."

Enoch shrugs. "That question is unanswerable, of course," he says. "Who, computer, or no computer, could possibly know what I would like." He laughs, evidently really tickled by this. "I don't even know myself. Anyway, you are the only person who can determine what your appropriate behavior should be. You've got to stop being so obedient to other people's whims and start acting out of your own honest perceptions. You, Noah Gershom, have trespassed on the future and destiny of your species by just trying to be a good boy in the terms of your own limited cultural perspective. You've quite uncritically accepted the mores and the customs you've grown up with. No thinking for yourself. No sense of destiny. Utter lack of any feeling of responsibility."

Okay. I'm just going to filter this out. Enoch is stepping on his own foot here. If he wants whatever he says he wants, we have to take it one step at a time.

"So all the computer could do was tell me what I think will happen. But what if I were going to be killed in the next ten minutes?"

"In that case, the computer, would be at a loss for words."

"Why?"

"It's programmed not to reveal catastrophic events. If it did so, the likelihood of the catastrophe actually occurring would increase. Besides, it wouldn't be able to pick up any images of the future strong enough to focus on, because your mind would contain none. It would probably just shut down."

"Why wouldn't I have any images of my future?"

"On some level, your mind would know that you had no future in the life you are now living. Sure, you'd still have future images, anyone would, but none of them would be supported by the strength of a highly probable impending reality. You see, Noah, that's how the computer is telling us what the future of our species is. There are some great things coming, yes, and we seem to be moving in the right direction, all told. But then the picture gradually goes dead, and there's nothing. You can't imagine the effect on us when we discovered that. It just threw a lot of us into a tailspin. Not me so much, because I'm a bachelor and don't have any children's children's children to worry about. It's not particularly personal for me. But a lot of people here were quite taken aback by the whole thing."

"But you don't care?"

"Of course I do. It's the most important thing I can think of, the continuation of the species. But it doesn't hit me in the gut quite the way it does some people."

"So what you're telling me is that a person who is about to die is aware of the fact, and even a whole society. A whole species."

"Yes, more or less."

"Then why don't they avoid it?"

"My God, I keep telling you, that's what we're trying to do. That's why you're here." He stops as if he's not happy with himself.

"Look, Noah, this is a phenomenon you can interpret in terms of your own experience. You've heard of people who refuse to get on airplanes that later crash. Some people pick up a sense of disaster connected with an event they are planning, and act on it. But those who board a plane which later crashes have, at some level of their being, a reason to bring their lives to a close at that particular point in time, don't you see. Some part of them knows what is going to happen. It's likely, however, that the conscious mind is not allowing that information to be dealt with the way it could be if there were some overwhelming reason to keep on living."

"Are you telling me that all the people who are killed in accidents really wanted to die?"

"Not at all. Not at the level of consciousness that they have in them at the time. But in terms of some grand, cosmic plan, yes, it all makes sense. I don't want to push that though, because a lot of people get very uncomfortable with that notion, even in our time. The ways of God are inscrutable even to us."

"So in your time there are still accidental deaths."

"Oh, quite definitely so. We don't have everything worked out. A thousand years is a long time in the progression of our species and the way we live, but it doesn't solve everything, not by a long shot. When everything really does get solved, then I suppose we'll return to the whence from which we came and stop bothering with this earthly existence, God save us."

"Maybe that's what's about to happen, then, what you're picking up."

"It's a hopeful thought, Noah, and I really have to commend you for it, but no, that's not the case, unfortunately. Quite decidedly not the case. Quite."

"How do you know?"

"In the first place, the problems that our species still has to solve may take us millions of years to work out, I'm sorry to have to report. We have no illusions that everything will have finally been resolved in another millennium."

"How do you know all this, and how were you able to program computers to read minds this way?"

"We've had this particular system for oh, about five hundred years, I'd say," says Enoch, "so I don't know too much about it. We pretty much take it for granted, so we don't care how it works. I'm not sure there's anyone now alive who really understands its technology. Meanwhile, the computers themselves have brought it to a much higher level of evolution, and it wasn't until a year ago that we began to pick up inklings of this horrible future that awaits us."

"What if it breaks down, or gets off track. What if this whole thing you're worried about is merely a figment of the computer's imagination?"

"The systems that we have developed, unlike the quirky antiques of your time (weren't they cute, and weren't they damnably frustrating? I don't know how you put up with the stupid things), anyway ours are much too fine-tuned for that. They constantly readjust and repair themselves based on complex and ever increasing feedback systems which measure everything that's predicted against what happens. They've got it down to octillionths of a second, equivalently small spaces, and corrections systems that have redundancies of billions of times. They just can't go wrong in terms of what they were originally programmed to do.

"In addition to that, they're not linear the way yours were. They're holographically designed, so they think very much the way a human brain does, only without any consciousness as we know it, and without the ability to rebel against us. Good old Asimov's Rules of Robotics are still with us, thank God. Fine man, that Asimov, he left quite a legacy, which we in our time appreciate far more than you ever did, though we've locked in on a number of things he and the other scientists of your time would have said were impossible."

"For example?"

"In your time it was believed that such things as the weather, for example, could not be predicted, not even theoretically. In our time we've learned that when a large enough view is taken, we can predict such things. That's because they're organized from the top down, not from the bottom up, as we always thought, so the moment by moment unfoldment of events contains unpredictabilities. But seen from the perspective of the formative forces, they're not unpredictable at all. That comes from applying the Laws of Resonance to the field of quantum mechanics.

"In any event, we're long past the point where people are needed to repair anything that breaks down, don't you see. Computers take care of all of that. They also maintain themselves completely."

"I see." I'm still rather stunned by the whole thing.

"Now," Enoch goes on, "what we have so far is how things will be for you if you reject the opportunity I am about to thrust upon you. Fortunately for you, however, the computer doesn't forecast negative events, so it has not reported on any of the suffering that might be in store for you when you return home. I want you to be aware of that, and I wanted you to get it from the computer, because I don't want you to think I'm just making up what I'm about to say to you."

Something very sobering is happening to me. Enoch himself would have no way of knowing how I saw my own room, nor would he have any particular motivation for showing me a scene in which I am getting married — an event which is irrelevant to my life right now, as I have no one at all in mind to marry — though maybe I could love someone again — but I'm not going to think about that now. No, this little marriage scene doesn't affect me at all, and it can't possibly have any particular meaning for Enoch. In a way, it's the very ordinariness of what the computer has shown me about my life that makes it convincing.

Ordinariness and skimpiness.

It's showing me, then, only the events in my future that aren't terrible. It's leaving out all the horrors that await me. There must be a lot of those.

Suddenly I'm afraid. Not of anything Enoch might do. Not even of being here in this strange world. I'm afraid of going back home. I'm afraid of my own future.

Then another realization, even more horrible, occurs to me: I'm also afraid of my past.

I didn't realize it, but I've been immersed in this brave new world just long enough to have forgotten how miserable an experience my life has been. When have I ever in my whole life talked to people in the satisfying ways that I'm doing here with Isaiah and Enoch and even Maya, though my contact with her has been regrettably brief. Now that I recall what my childhood was like, and, indeed, what my whole life has been like, I'm afraid of the existence that I took for granted only a short while ago because it was my own.

There were times in my life when I thought of committing suicide — that's how bad it was. Sitting here now, it's hard to imagine that. I'm beginning to understand that in a deep way my life does not belong to me. Evidently, I'm entangled and mixed up with everything and everyone else. I'm sitting here, causing great concern for people in the Thirty-first Century because of something I did a thousand years ago. Life is amazing. Being here, I have a new sense of the possibilities for living, maybe even for love.

But for a lot of my youth, I wanted to end my life because it was so unbearable, so lonely, so empty — and those were probably my better years, before my cynicism numbed me to feeling very much of anything at all — except occassional ego kicks from career recognition I've gained.

And now I'm scared of my own life, and indeed, of my own self. Suddenly just to go back and continue being what I was before seems to me like some kind of hell. I have to get out of it. I can't stay caught in the dilemma of that existence any longer.

I look into Enoch's eyes, knowing that he knows what I am thinking. I take that for granted, and speak these simple words: "I want out."

Enoch smiles. I feel differently about him now. All the anger, all the combativeness I felt towards him a while back has now been displaced onto myself. I want to get over the disease of being the person I have always been — at least as long as I can remember. Enoch is here to help me. He is — I hesitate to use the word at all, it is so foreign to me — he is, in a strange, technological way, my savior.

That's it, then. I am here for my own salvation. And what kind of a hell is that going to take me through?

The Measure of My Inadequacies

I make a helpless gesture. "Okay," I say, "you win."

Enoch smiles. "Win what?" he says.

"In our contest of wills you were trying to persuade me that — I forget exactly what you said, but something about seeing myself objectively, or whatever, so I could change. I didn't want to do that. But now I can't stand the thought of not doing it."

"You can't stand the heat, so you want out of the kitchen, is that it?" says Enoch. But the biting force of his remark is softened by the benign expression on his round face. I can tell he's in the first flush of an anticipated victory. Whatever he tried is working, and I can tell he believes in me now. He believes I can accomplish what he brought me here to accomplish.

"That's it," I say.

"It's not going to be easy," he says, shaking his head.

"I didn't think it would be," I say. "That's why I didn't want to do it. But now I know that however hard it might be for me, staying the way I've always been will be infinitely harder. In any event, now I can see that for what it is."

"Maybe you should tell me what it is, then," says Enoch.

I sigh. "That's asking a lot."

"What's so hard about it?"

"I have to . . . own up . . . to things I don't want to admit to myself. I guess that's how I'd put it."

"Owning up is so terrible?"

"It is."

"Why?"

I don't know how to answer this. Why can't we just change and be done with it? Why do we have to go on repeating the same mistakes all through life? I haven't the slightest idea. I know only that it's true.

Then I realize that if I look closely at what I am I'll hate myself so much I won't even have the stamina to want to improve myself.

"The basic problem is that I'm nothing but a shit," I say to Enoch.

Saying this feels a little like describing your masturbation fantasies to the high school principal. It's a simple statement, but it carries so much baggage with it. I feel as if someone has disemboweled me and all my insides are hanging nearby on a clothes line for me to stare at.

"I don't really believe that," says Enoch.

"That only makes it harder," I reply. I don't know where I'm getting the energy for this.

"Well, if it's really true," he says icily, the sarcasm so bald it distorts his features, why don't you go find a toilet somewhere and flush yourself down it?" This is about as far from the response I expected as anything he could say, and I feel like smashing him in the nose.

Then I laugh. I can't help it. I just laugh as if I had heard the funniest joke ever told. But I haven't heard anything funny at all, so I'm totally befuddled by my own laughter, even as I'm laughing it.

"What's so funny?" I finally manage to stammer out when I'm more or less through.

"I wouldn't be your resident expert on that," says Enoch, "so why don't you tell me?"

I can only gesture helplessly. "I haven't the vaguest."

"Well, let's look into this a little. Now as I understand it you have encased in your skull the most complex piece of equipment that has yet been discovered anywhere in the universe. It's called a brain. It was called a brain in your time, and it's still called a brain in ours."

"That's good."

"Yes. In addition to that, you're also equipped with a huge collection of other equipment that does truly amazing things without your even having to be aware of it. So I would think . . . "

He pauses, I don't know whether for dramatic effect or because he doesn't know what to say next. I have an urge to try to help him out, but nothing occurs to me.

"I would think," he finally goes on, "that you should have the common decency to exclude at least those fine things from your self description — which you've just boiled down to a single rather graphic though perhaps overwrought word."

I meditate on this for a moment. "What you're saying to me," I reply, "or at least what you appear to be saying to me, is that I should be grateful that I have all this collection of evolved tissue which I assume took about four billion years or more to assemble."

"Try fifteen billion," says Enoch. "After all, the job was well along before Earth itself appeared."

"Okay, fifteen billion. Whatever. Okay. So you want me to exclude that stuff from my self-condemnation."

"Exactly."

"So if I exclude that stuff, what does that leave?"

"Why don't you tell me?"

"In other words, you're trying to identify what it is, exactly, that makes me nothing but a shit."

"Undoubtedly you just said that better than I could have."

"Okay. Let me see if I can get at that."

"Bear in mind that you're a child of your time."

"A child of my time." For some reason that's very funny to me and again I laugh.

"I'm glad you find me so entertaining," Enoch says.

"No offense, but it isn't you," I reply.

"What is it, then?"

"Well, when I think about what it means to be a child of my time, I notice that I'm sort of more or less like virtually everyone else. I mean, not exactly, but give or take a few details here and there. I mean, I have the same general kind of equipment everyone else has, and I have a pretty decent house to live in, an income that many would envy, which means I have a successful career, so there's a lot there that ought to redeem me. So it might be that when I boil myself down to a sort of excremental phenomenon, I'm really passing judgment on a whole lot of other people too."

"Not me, I hope," says Enoch.

"No, not you," I say.

But is it true? Is it really true? Is there any human being on Earth, now or then, who isn't just basically a piece of shit? I mean, after you're dead, that's what it pretty much all boils down to. All the delicate mechanism that took however many billion years to put together is reduced to worm food and ends up, therefore, as worm shit. That kind of reduces everything down to basics.

I'm not going to mention this to Enoch. I don't like to trouble him with thoughts like these. So what is going on here? Why am I here? What's this all about?

"You know what your trouble is?" says Enoch.

"What?"

"You believe that it's possible for you to be alone."

"Well, yes."

"But you can't be. All of nature, all of the universe flows through you and echoes in your mind. You can't be alone. Not ever."

I think I'm beginning to understand this now. We're part of the Earth. We belong here. Yet we've been here for only a little bit of the tail end of the life of the Earth. How come we're so hell bent on changing everything about it? At least most of *my* life energy has been expended on trying to change the Earth from something that it used to be into something else. And I don't even know what for.

But one of the things I notice about Enoch and Maya and Isaiah, and all the other people I've seen here is that they seem to have devoted themselves pretty seriously to trying to keep the Earth the way it used to be before I and my kind came along. They're not out to change it, they're out to live in it and keep it in good shape.

Maya said the place I met her in the woods was her house.

What did that mean?

She said something about leaving traces of your energy everywhere you go. She said something about — what was it? Some sort of making peace with your surroundings. Appeasement, that was it.

So, let's see. I have this natural energy, let's say, that flows out of my body. It interacts with all the natural energies around me and is part of the flow of life itself. In that I'm a part of nature. I came from it, and I'm part of the process by which it changes itself.

That's it! That's the key phrase. It changes itself. I've been teaching chaos theory to people. I've been teaching about self-organizing systems. So systems are supposed to organize themselves. They're not supposed to be organized. You're not supposed to go out and remake the world system, you're supposed to be part of the process by which it remakes itself.

But how does that work? What's the distinction? When Maya said she was a frequent trespasser in that place in nature, what did she really mean?

I can think of only one thing. She was setting herself apart from nature, making herself distinct from it. Is that trespassing on nature, to define yourself as distinct from it? Are we supposed to do nothing? Are we supposed to return to some ultimate state of nature, to live as cave people lived? Is that what this is about?

I know I've got a handle on something, but it's not working for me yet. I've got an incomplete perspective on it. I don't know what it is I'm going after here.

Obedient. That's how Enoch described me.

Who am I obedient to?

Suddenly it all comes clear.

It's like there are two armies lined up facing each other. One army is the technological world and the other is the natural world. They're in a life and death struggle to eliminate each other.

The technological world in all its features trespasses on the natural world. It destroys it, drives it out. That's practically been the history of humanity. It has been organized into a vast army of forces to drive out the natural world, to destroy it utterly and for all time. To replace the green carpet supplied by mother nature with an asphalt carpet supplied by industrialism.

I'm part of the industrial world. I do what I'm told. I obediently trespass on the natural world.

Do I have to be obedient?

Do I have to do what I'm told?

I look at Enoch. I can see that he can see that I'm now ready for the next step.

The Undermining of the Natural Mind

"Okay," I say to Enoch, "what are we going to do here? How am I going to get to that objective view of myself, or whatever you have in mind? How am I — for God's sake — going to figure out what I have to do differently?"

"I just want you to see yourself the way others see you, that's all," says Enoch.

"What good would that do?"

"Well, if you could see it their way, you'd know how obedient you really are, and what you're being obedient to. Then you could decide if you want to be obedient or if you want to be responsible — whatever course you choose — with them or against them."

Interesting. But how can I see myself that way? And what would it mean, anyway? Is there some overall value system against which I can measure myself? So far, I don't know of one.

I don't know whether Enoch senses what I'm thinking or

misses it completely, because the next thing he says takes us off in a completely different direction: "Did Maya tell you that our society is based on dream interpretation?"

"No. You mentioned something about it a while back, but she never brought it up."

"Did Isaiah tell you that, then?"

"No. Well, yes, he did mention something about it. But I didn't really understand from his description what it's all about."

Enoch scratches his head and looks bewildered.

"I'm not going to explain it to you either," he says at last. "You'd better get Maya to do that."

"But what is this all about?"

He shrugs. "I don't know why these people can't do what they're supposed to," he says. "We've got a delicate operation here, but they act as if what they do doesn't matter." He throws his hands in the air in a gesture of helplessness.

I smile at this. Enoch is sounding like someone from my time. We're always finding shortcomings in each other. What difference does it make whether Enoch or someone else gives me this information, I wonder. Then I get it. He's making it up. He's trying to make me realize the whole thing's in my hands. It is I who have to take the lead in all this, find out what's going on, what I'm expected to do, how to clear up the misery in my life. Responsibility, he said. Something I've never taken to.

"I'm going to have to compromise my standards here a little bit," Enoch goes on, as if he picked up the drift of my thought. "I'll tell you this much. We humans have a rational mind and a natural mind. The rational mind figures out what makes sense in terms of the plans we've worked out for ourselves and for whatever else we have to deal with. The natural mind, on the other hand, is in tune with whatever is going on around us, and lets the rational mind know when it needs to make some adjustments in what it's doing."

"I didn't know that," I say.

"Well, it was known in your time, so maybe you just haven't heard about it. Anyway, I could tell you didn't know, otherwise you wouldn't be in the fix you're in, and we wouldn't be going through this whole process. Not with you, anyway."

"I'll just have to accept that," I say.

"Good. You do that. Now the rational mind governs most of our thoughts during the day, when we're involved in carrying out the various plans that govern our lives."

"I don't believe that," I say.

"Why not?"

"I know that practically nobody spends a whole lot of time being rational."

"I didn't say they do. I said the rational mind governs most of our thoughts during the day."

"How so? if our thoughts are not rational?"

"Let's say you're paranoid. You believe that everyone's out to get you. That's your rational system. It may not be rational from the perspective of society as a whole, but it's the basis on which you govern your activities. You're always looking at everything in terms of the consequences of your paranoia. You follow through on a rather tightly organized logical system that has its own rules, not necessarily related to anyone else's rules for their thinking. That's what I mean. It's not what either you or I would call rational thought, but it's what the rational mind does."

"And the other mind?"

"That's the natural mind, or the intuitive mind. It has subtle ways of picking up what's happening in the surrounding eco-system. It tries to respond to that. It may sense danger that can't be seen yet, or feel an impulse to plant a tree, or want to rescue someone, or bring up a child. When things are not moving in the direction of a natural balance, that part of the mind gets uncomfortable."

"Okay."

"Throughout most of the time people have been on Earth, most communities and societies have held these two minds in proper balance with each other. However, in your time, the rational mind took over completely and attempted to govern everything, while the natural mind was left to try to express itself mainly in dreams. For people in your time, dreams were an attempt on the part of the natural mind to get the attention of the rational mind that things weren't going as they should."

"I see. So?"

"So your recurring dream should have been a warning to you."

"What recurring dream?"

But I should know better than that. The gray cinderblocks come back to me, the cells with people imprisoned there and my return to Cellutron, where a woman is trying to tell me that something is wrong.

Since Enoch has not responded to my question, I tell him about my dream.

"You're here, Noah, because of that dream," he says. "That's why I wanted to wait until Maya had told you about it. The dream you have just told me about is connected to Maya's dream. When she first told me about her dream, everything about it was foreign and meaningless. And you have to realize that nowadays we only rarely can't make sense of our dreams. Even our children are good at interpreting them."

"That seems to me like a superstitious waste of time, like astrological charts."

"You mean you've never analyzed your dreams?"

"No. They're too unpleasant."

"All the more reason to find out what they mean. In our dream analysis group we were just starting to do some advanced work, going beyond the individual meaning of dreams, examining social implications in the development of our species. You've heard of collective consciousness? Well, dreams tap into a collective unconscious, the element that interfaces all humans together and intertwines them in the mind of God — the element that determines our evolution and the progress of our destiny. Dreams blur out false and misleading ego distinctions, which is why we can use them to get at the truth. What we learned as we continued to explore Maya's dream in the light, not of Maya as an individual, but of the whole movement of the species that we're involved in now, is that the dream itself records a very crucial time in the past, when decisions were made that imperil the direction the human race now needs to go. And you were involved in that."

"I would never have imagined —"

"Of course not. Do you think Eve had any idea of the great adventure she had created for all of her progeny? Of course not. Eve couldn't tell that she wasn't just another ape."

"Eve? You mean from the Bible?"

"No, the proposed first human. The mother of us all. The

ancestor from whom we all descended when we trace our human DNA back in time."

"Oh. That makes sense."

"You've heard of the butterfly effect, of course."

"Of course. I teach about it in my corporate seminars."

"I know that. What you didn't realize was that one of the decisions you were involved in was a decision that flapped its wings and changed the destiny of the human race. You would have had no way of knowing that."

"How did it change it?"

"We don't exactly know that. We assume that we're supposed to evolve in some profound new way but we've lost the capacity to do that now. That's why the computer screen comes up blank when we try to predict the future. As a species we don't have the genetic diversity that we once had. Crucial genetic codes have simply vanished and we don't even know what they were or what they were for. We're coming to a dead end thanks to the unenlightened tinkering that occurred in your time."

"But I don't understand."

"You supported the movement to remove certain characteristics from the gene pool that had always been part of the human experience. This was eugenics, the very thing that Hitler had preached. You yourself are going to be dealing with this question when you get back. Are you really ready for this?"

"What do you mean?"

"Rather than sit here and tell you, I'm going to let you experience a part of your future the computer did not present to you before. Actually, it's not a part of your future at all, it's right squarely in the present in which you were living when we picked you up, and which you're going to have to deal with when you go back there. That's why we chose the moment we did to transport you here."

The Judgment of My Employers

Enoch asks me to touch the screen again, and when I do, he himself addresses the man who appears.

"We want to see the best appraisal you can come up with of this subject's character as understood by others," he says.

At this the man's face fades out and the scene is in an office that's familiar to me. Cellutron! Of course. It's the conference room where Harry Ornath, the CEO holds court. Harry and a few of his executives are seated around the conference table. They're mostly new faces to me.

Watching the screen, I feel a little like Ebenezer Scrooge with the Ghost of Christmas Future, and I'm more than a little nervous. Though maybe I shouldn't be. After all, Cellutron runs a pretty class act, especially compared to some of the sleazier outfits I've worked for in the past. Besides, I know they're impressed by me. When I met with Harry Ornath and his assistant Arthur — what's his name, they were singing my praises.

But how did Enoch get this scene in the computer? This can't be coming from my own neural circuitry. Maybe it's just some plain old-fashioned recording technology they used to collect these images on the spot a little before or after they picked me up. I'd like to ask Enoch this question but I'm already missing too much of what's going on before me. They're talking about a project they're working on, a gene replacement process they want to bring to market. Enoch is staring at me. I try to appear detached as I watch the screen, but my heart is racing.

"Listen, Harry," one of them is saying — Arthur Bowden, that's it — "we can't go with this new Effinghaus's program because it hasn't yet been tested to the FDA's satisfaction."

"What kind of asshole response is that, Arthur?" Harry roars back in the customarily tough manner he uses with his inner circle. "Listen, this has nothing to do with drugs. Or foods. This is genetics. This is human genes. We're not in the medical business, we're in the engineering business, do you read me?"

"So?" says Arthur.

"So, we can do what we want. We can save people a lot of misery by eliminating these bad genes. It's a whole new world we're creating here."

"But we don't know in every case," says another man, "that the gene has the precise effect we're attributing to it. Lots of genetic interactions are complex and accomplish a number of different things which can only be understood systemically. We're not 100% sure about the Effinghaus gene."

"What do you mean, we're not sure, George? Is something missing from our research reports?"

"No, but — "

"Then, what are you saying?"

"Nothing is missing, but the protocol requires that we get far more replications of our experiments than we've had so far."

"Bullshit, George. You know as well as I do that while we're waiting around for those damned replications plenty of babies will be born that should have had the benefit of our technology. What are you anyway, some kind of cold-hearted purist? You want to inflict unnecessary suffering on babies because of some abstract possibility that things could go wrong? It's not like they have a better alternative."

Arthur weighs in. "It's not as simple as that, Harry."

"Look, if there are problems, we'll fix them down the road. Or someone will. All I know is: somebody has to take these bold steps. People want this. Everybody wants a healthy baby. What's the problem here?"

"Because right now, Harry, we're not absolutely sure about what else they'll be getting in the bargain, says George."

"You've already made that point. You've got something new to tell me? Look, are you guys with me or against me? And if you're against me, what the fuck are you doing on the payroll of Cellutron?"

Scanning around the room, I see that everyone's either sheepishly silent or lost in thought, probably shifting scientific scruples to better align with their monthly paychecks.

Finally George, one of the executives I've met before, delivers the next corporate conundrum. "If we go ahead with this project every bible-thumping reactionary in the country will be on us."

"Of course," says Harry. "Forget about them. They're way out there painted into their extreme little corners with heavy brush strokes of black and white. Nobody cares about them. It's the professionals that I'm worried about, the thumb-sucking academics. When did they ever take the leap to do anything worthwhile? But I know we may have to fight for this one."

"You know what I suggest we do, Harry?"

"What, Arthur?"

"I suggest we hire Noah Gershom to handle this particular hot potato."

"Well, congratulations, that's precisely what I intend to do."

"Good. You've got your ideal man. Mr. Slick. He'll go along with anything. He'll create your advertising program for you. He'll handle the spin on the publicity. He'll deal with the FDA. Gershom could sell snake oil to cobras, then grab them by the tail to squeeze it out their asses, and they'd never know what hit them. Did you catch his act at Crowden Pharmaceuticals when they foisted that faulty heart valve on the market? The guy's brilliant and none too meticulous in the scruples department."

"What are you saying to me, Arthur?"

"That Noah Gershom is a do it kind of guy. He'll get it done, damn the consequences, because if you pay him to do a job, he'll do it and never look back. Gershom won't care, because he won't ask any ugly or embarrassing questions. That's what I call a . . . "

I'm jolted to my feet.

I can't take any more. I have to get out of here. I can't stand it. These are professionals. These are my clients, for God's sake.

I'm not saying anything as I walk away. I'm trying to look cool. No passer-by would know anything is wrong. But inside I'm screaming.

How did it come to this? How did I get to be the kind of guy that man Arthur, whoever he is, is describing?

And that's what I'll be dealing with in that meeting at ten o'clock the morning I get back — the morning I left. That's the boss who wants to hire me, and he'll go through with it, too, whatever it is. He doesn't care. I'm his hero, because I'll do anything he wants, and ask no questions. A do it kind of guy. Do whatever the boss says. That's me. God damn it, no wonder I hate myself and the whole human race. There's a reason for it, I can see that now. Noah Gershom, not the man to ask the wrong kind of questions. Noah Gershom, who goes along no matter what; who doesn't hold onto his values because he doesn't have any. Who will sell the whole human race down the river if it puts money in his pocket.

That's me.

That's who I am.

A shit.

I look back and see that Enoch isn't following me. I'm alone now, in this strange society. I've got to get out, go somewhere that I'll be alone.

I can't remember how I got where I am now, but I know I need to retrace my steps and get back on the escalator that will take me to that beautiful forest where I can get some peace and collect my thoughts. There I can try to make some sense out of this garbage.

Somehow, even though everything's a blur, I find my way to the woods, and when I'm absolutely certain that no one's around I throw myself on the ground, scarcely realizing it's night now. I've been ripped open and emptied out. Nothing's left but numbness. Somehow, I fall asleep.

A Visitation

When I awaken, the first light of day is dawning on the horizon. I sit up, wondering where I am and what's happened.

Then slowly it all starts coming back to me. I was talking to Enoch and I very eloquently told him I was a shit. I said, with all the wisdom of a Ph.D. in philosophy, that basically everything meaningful in life boils down to worm shit.

But there was another element in all of that. Enoch brought up God. We are extensions of God, he said. God suffers with us. God can't do what we can do, except through us.

The trouble with that is, there is no God. Yes, I hear a lot of talk about God, and when Isaiah was around I got into some very intense feelings about maybe there could be a God, and actually believed it for a while, I think, but now it doesn't add up to a hill of outmoded computers. If there were a God, things would be very different.

It's then that a sort of miracle happens. I don't know how to put it in words, because there aren't any words to capture the feeling. The best way to put it is that there's this hand inside of my body, rubbing my heart. It feels like a hand, although it's a translucent hand.

As it rubs my heart there's something flowing through me, like a magic potion entering my bloodstream. I don't know how else to describe it. It sounds crazy, I know, but that's what it feels like. It produces a sensation of peace I've never known before. I look up into the dawn and I feel like that's me out there. I feel like my body is not the end of me, that I'm spread all over the forest, all over the sky, all over everywhere. It only lasts a moment. It's a weird sort of fantasy, and then it goes away.

But everything has changed.

I think I hear a voice whispering in my ear.

"I love you," it says.

I close my eyes.

"I love you, too," I whisper.

Why Me?

And I mean it.

So.

Worm shit isn't what it all adds up to. I can see how one can think that. One can mistake the excrement for the end product. A perfectly natural mistake, one people make very frequently, at least in my time. Whatever is wrong is all there is.

But it's up to us. Up to me, really. The universe is up to me. A completely crazy thought, and yet it makes sense to me now, I don't know how. I've got to live as if the universe is up to me. As if I'm the only one who can do anything. I can't shift the blame off my shoulders. I've just got to look at every situation and think about it this way.

If I had infinite power and were responsible for this, what would I make happen at this moment? It suddenly feels possible to me to think that way.

The sun has cracked over the horizon now, and the light has changed. All the thoughts I'm having dissolve, and I'm lonely and miserable again.

But in the center of my gut there's something new. It's impregnable. It feels good and nothing is going to make it go away. Not ever. How do I know this? I haven't any idea. But I know it's true.

All that's left for me to do now is work out my destiny. Which apparently, as it happens, is going to have rather a large effect on the people right here with me now.

It's me. I've got to reach for the stars so they can get there.

And, of course, the inevitable thought arises:

Why me?

Maya's Return

All of a sudden I see that Maya is standing before me —
not too differently from the way she did last time, but this time I'm
a little more savvy. I leap up from the ground and stand facing her.

Her lips form a smile and once again I feel that powerful
attraction to her. She lightly touches my cheek which stirs up more
feelings in me than I'm sure she intended.

"So?" she says, her head tilted to one side, "how's it going,
time travel man?"

I feel offended. I don't want her to take this casual tone with
me. I want more from her. I'm admitting to myself what's wrong
now because she's caught me with all my defenses down. I love
her.

I'll be damned if I'm going to tell her about it, though.

"You've been holding out on me, I hear," I say.

"Really?" Her eyes flash in a very interesting way, almost as
if she's glad I brought this up.

I nod. "Really."

"You mean about the dreams?"

I nod.

She looks at the ground, does something interesting with her
foot, and says, "I wanted Enoch to bring it up first."

"Why? He said he expected *you* to bring it up. What's wrong
with you people? Is passing the buck all you know how to do?"

She looks at me with the faintest hint of hostility.

"Right," she says. "Passing the buck is all we know how to
do."

"Come on."

"You know what you did."

"Not really. And let me hasten to remind you that I haven't done it yet. I may have done it from your perspective, but whatever it is you're going to accuse me of is actually from my perspective in the future. So I haven't done it yet. And guess what? I may not do it."

She looks nervous, apologetic, all sorts of things. I've scored one with her. I'm pleased with my little victory. Then I begin to question why I'm confronting her this way.

"Did Enoch tell you that I was the one who asked him to bring you here?" she says.

"Not exactly. It sounded more like a group effort to me. It seems he analyzed a dream that you had, and that's why I'm here."

"But *I* wanted you here. It was my idea. They didn't think it should be done, but I proved to them it was necessary."

"Oh, so you're some kind of a genius?"

She winces, a sudden wave of anxiety troubling her features. "Stop. Please. Bringing you here may be my gravest trespass ever. I don't know how it will all turn out. Do you understand? Do you understand what I've done?"

She peers into my face, questioning me, waiting. I feel sorry, selfish, stupid and infantile. I nod my head apologetically in answer to her.

"I'm a time seer, what you might call a fourth dimensional physicist," she says. "I study these things. I felt compelled to take the considerable risk to bring you here. But it's regrettable, it's not generally a good thing to do. There are better ways to change the past."

"How so?"

"In a way, if you do things that allow something good to grow out of the past, no matter how bad it seemed to be, you're changing the past in the profoundest sense. All past events are part of the web of circumstances that lead to the present good outcome. It's the present we must always keep in mind, the right now, right this instant that really matters.

"The problem that brought you here is a lot more complicated, though. We're missing genetic information and we don't know what we're looking for. It seems we have to *undo* things. So we felt we had to bring you here. I worked the whole thing out, and Isaiah and Enoch implemented it. We've experimented with time-travel, of course — developed the technology years ago. But it's pretty much off limits now, not something we do lightly."

"Am I the first person who's ever been brought to the future in an honest to God time machine?"

"If you give some thought to that question," she says, "I think you'll find that it's absolutely impossible to answer it."

I decide it doesn't matter.

"What's going on between us?" That's the really important question.

"Listen," she says, ignoring it. "Tell me about your dream."

I tell her the dream, but before I'm much into it she asks, "Does your dream switch locations? Does it go from a mental institution to a laboratory?"

"Yes! The scene shifts to Cellutron."

"Was there a woman in your dream about Cellutron?"

"Yes!"

"Did she look like me?"

"I don't remember her face."

I close my eyes. The dream collides with memory. Maya. So that's where I've seen her!

"You," I whisper.

"Me," she sighs.

"Who are you?"

"It's the experiment. I'm here for the same reason you are! I have my own horrors to clean up."

She doesn't seem angelic anymore. I feel confused.

"Who are you?" I whisper again, groping to fill the intimidating silence.

"Unfortunately, Noah, I'm your partner in crime," she says. "We have to undo the consequences together."

"It has something to do with Cellutron?"

She's visibly agitated. It pains me to see her so upset and I feel that I've been cruel to her, not thinking about her at all. I draw closer to her, moved by an involuntary protective instinct.

"Don't get too close, Noah," she says. "Please don't."

"Why not?"

"Because there's too much you still don't understand."

"I want to understand. Something bad happened because of what I did for Cellutron, right?"

"Yes."

"I don't suppose it absolves me of guilt, but as of this morning, I hadn't been told by Cellutron about the possible consequences. The whole concept of eliminating diseases seemed revolutionary and exciting to me. I'm not a geneticist. I didn't suspect there'd be problems."

I realize I'm sounding pretty lame — in light of the circumstances. I decide to shut up. I care too much about what Maya thinks of me.

My restraint is all for nothing, though. Maya hasn't really been listening to me. She's obviously wrestling with her own private anguish. I feel a surge of pity for her and reach to touch her arm. This time she accepts my uninvited caress.

"Maya, what's the matter? I don't understand. How could you be culpable in this? Because you were in my dreams?"

"No. Because I was there — at Cellutron." She almost whispers this, her voice filled with regret. "And I didn't stop them either. I was their chief scientist. It was my process you were selling."

What is she talking about? These people are so complicated.

"Maya, I don't understand."

"I want to explain it to you, but I can't right now." She's almost choking on her words.

I retreat.

A Research Breakthrough

I wander over to a clearing where a stand of fragrant cinnamon ferns arch gracefully in the sunshine, waiting for Maya to regain her composure.

Maya has settled sedately on a bench that she's materialized for the purpose and appears nearly ready to resume our conversation. As I look at her now, with me standing and her sitting (it's the first time this has happened) I feel protective, fatherly and filled with desire all at the same time. So this self-possessed woman of a thousand years in the future is also by some mysterious paradox a person of my own time? I'll have to wait to understand this, I guess, but the possibility that I'll meet her back there is kindling a glimmer of hope in me.

"What is going on, Maya? Why am I really here?"

She rises from her bench, moves towards me, reaches out to take my hand, and suddenly we are standing in the middle of a formal garden on a beautiful country estate. I look about me here and there, but we are alone together. Are we still in the Thirty-first Century? Or have we gone to some other time in virtual reality? I can't tell, and frankly, at this point I don't care. We could be anywhere. Still, I love the atmosphere here, and the pungent smell of boxwood.

As she continues to hold my hand I feel an electricity flowing through me, and my body is suffused with warmth. I feel happy just to be here with her, just floating in the present time, not wanting to think about any of the cosmic problems perched weightlessly about our heads, but knowing I will have to.

She leads me to a gazebo where we sit on a bench in the sheltered space, looking out over the vast expanse of gardens.

Maya begins. "We're at a point in time when we must do something to change our future. That is very clear to us. That's why you're here."

"Cellutron was about to eliminate Effinghaus's disease," I say. "Is that the missing gene that you need?"

"I doubt that it's as simple as that," she replies.

"Was gene replacement the Pandora's box then? The thing we should never have opened up?"

"We can't know such a thing, Noah. It's not so easy to tell what's good and what's bad. We're not on earth to be judges. There are many cases when seemingly good, well-intentioned actions have bad consequences — really horrible consequences. And the reverse too. Nothing is so simple. But you know these things already." She smiles warmly toward me. "I don't have to explain this to you."

Is she letting me off the hook? Her words are a salve to my guilty conscience which she's administered with such kindness and grace. I'm awed by her and overwhelmed by the strength of my feelings for her. I realize there's no use trying to retreat, and I release myself to this love — with finality. God help me.

"But clearly," she continues, "Cellutron wasn't ready to go ahead. They were much too naive. They never fully considered how dangerous their technology could be."

"They were scientists, they must have done a lot of research."

"They thought they knew what they were doing. But they were flying blind, like everyone else."

"What are you getting at Maya?"

"It's complicated, but you've got to try to understand it. Back in those days the whole approach to medicine was based on warfare, getting rid of diseases by killing them, burning them out of the body, cutting them out, or poisoning them out. But sometimes disease was an expression of a natural, or perhaps even beneficial process that had gone astray. When you make war on people you kill them. But if you can negotiate your way to peace and work things out, you don't need to kill them.

"Now, from the perspective of my time, I realize what that means. The solution to disease was to deal with the system, humans and their environment, as a whole. It was to see what the disease was trying to accomplish, what problem it was trying to solve, and then meet it halfway, on its own terms. Many people tried to practice that back then, but they weren't understood. Instead, you made war on parts of yourselves, of your own being, and you never took the trouble to try to understand what was really happening.

"And the trouble is, once you've eliminated something from the evolutionary line, you can't get it back. It's gone forever.

"So by your program of eugenics, of eliminating genetic diseases, you were actually shrinking the human gene pool. You were saying to certain aspects of human diversity that they weren't wanted before you fully understood what they were and what they were trying to accomplish. The trouble is, now it's too late. We've already narrowed our options, and some of the essential elements of diversity are missing, so we can't achieve the balance of characteristics we need to evolve in profound ways. Now we need to go back and try it differently this time, finding ways to interact with diseases so they would not have the harmful effects they had been having.

"That's your job, Noah."

"How can it be my job? I don't know anything about science in a practical sense. I have to trust the scientists to make the right decisions. Everybody does."

"You can't rely on science alone or on any kind of merely rational thought. You need an ideal balance between rational observation and the things you intuit from deeper sources. When you look at problems only from a rational perspective, it's easy to ignore their context, which is always far too complicated to be evaluated through mere rationalization. Intuition balances the rational approach. You'll have to be very careful, Noah, observant, and reflective."

This part is making sense. It's what Enoch has already told me, and now that I hear it again in slightly different language from Maya, I think I understand.

But then she presses me harder: "You were warned, but you paid no attention."

"Nobody told me."

"You had the dreams, Noah. They should have been a warning to you."

"Dreams! Anyway, I'm in no position to stop the research at Cellutron. I'm just an outside consultant there."

Maya looks me squarely in the eye. Her tone is grimly serious.

"What you saw in the garden is really happening at Cellutron. You're aware of this on some level, but you refuse to acknowledge it, maybe because you give the so-called experts too much credit. You're one of the best at what you do, aren't you?"

"So I've been told," I say modestly.

"Well, look at yourself. You never buck the trends, which is why you're so popular. You may not realize it, but you specialize in making bad situations worse. You need to find some way to lead humanity out of its predicament."

What Maya is asking me to do is completely out of character.

I may have some powerful clients, but I don't feel all that powerful. CEOs like working with me because I tell them what they want to hear. That's all I know how to do.

I don't know how to change without committing professional suicide.

I'm lost in thought. No matter how you slice it, the whole thing sounds extremely dangerous and iffy to me. How can they be sure that if a different approach is taken to the problem of genetic diseases the outcome will indeed be better? It's all theory, it seems to me — pure speculation.

I decide I want to get down to basics here.

"Tell me your dream," I say to Maya.

She shifts uneasily.

"I'm a prisoner in this bleak institution. By the way, nothing like this exists anymore, so you can't imagine how disturbing this dream was for me. Someone comes to help me and bring back my awareness. It's painful. But I'm not sure what it means. There's more, but this is the part to focus on first. For the longest time none of us could tell what it meant. Then something terrible happened."

"What?"

"We got the milennial projection. About a thousand years in the future as it is now, the program goes blank."

"Blank?"

"We couldn't figure out what was happening. That's because we didn't want to admit the obvious implications. What it was telling us was that humanity may no longer exist beyond that point. We ran many studies of this phenomenon and what came out was that our next evolutionary step is severely compromised."

"So how did that relate to the dream?"

"In the dream, I'm living in the most incredibly awful conditions. You come along and try to save me."

"So you're the person I was looking for in my dream."

"Well, that's all symbolic. The mental institution symbolizes the condition under which everyone was living at the time. We were all crazy. You had the potential, because of your position, to make a difference in that, to nudge the world in a direction that would diminish some of the craziness.

"But then the scene shifts into the Cellutron laboratory, where

I'm the lead scientist focusing on the new eugenics program. So in the dream I turn to you and ask you to save me from myself. I ask you to stop the program."

"Yes. And that's where it ends."

"Exactly. Because the dream is a warning to you. Something inside you understands the danger, and is trying to get you to stop and reflect. As for me, I unconsciously generated this dream about my earlier mistakes. The problem is, you didn't understand the dream; you didn't respond to it.

"That's why we brought you here: to teach you, and send you back into your own time to solve the problem in a different way."

"But really, Maya, you've picked the wrong person. I don't have the power to stop them. Cellutron will just fire me if I try."

"Then you'll have to find another way."

"Why didn't you get the CEO, or someone on the board, someone who could really have put on the brakes? Why pick me?"

"I didn't pick you."

Maya looks at me in a frightening way, as if she sees something demonic hidden beneath the surface in me, something neither she nor I have been willing to look at yet.

"You appeared to me in the dream. When I saw you there, your face made a distinct impression on me, which filled me with an enormous flood of emotion. I couldn't forget you, Noah. The first time I had that dream I awakened from it feeling that I'd met one of the most important people in my life. For the rest of that day I was profoundly moved by the dream. Then I had it again, and then again. Your face was so branded on my memory that I knew I had to find you."

So! Is it possible she feels as intensely about me as I do about her? There's something powerful between us, which until now I have thought I was just imagining, because I want her love so much. But maybe it's real. Is it possible? If she can love me, it's worth anything to me. It might be a senseless, hopeless love, but I don't care about that now. My feelings for her have such certainty, and such a strange sort of inevitability that I cannot deny them. Some things you just shouldn't calculate, that's one thing I'm learning here.

Maya continues speaking. "My dream analysis group examined every angle to discover who you were or what you might represent, and we kept coming back to the realization that there was something about the dream that insisted we look into the past."

"What did you expect to find?"

"Don't you see, the dream was a message. Your dream was too. Some things obviously involve the whole world. Take Noah's vision of the flood. God comes to Noah and tells him to build an Ark. If he doesn't pay attention to God's request, the human race and many other species will be wiped out. There are times in history when things need to be changed radically so that something else can happen. If humanity heeds the call as Noah did, everything moves forward. But if the call to action somehow gets missed, extreme measures are necessary."

"Are you really saying that from time to time throughout history someone has to go back and fix things? This is hard to believe."

"I don't know about other times. All I'm aware of is this one. As soon as I realized what I was dreaming about, I told Isaiah we needed to travel into time to find you. He played a hunch that things went wrong mostly during the Twentieth Century.

"We checked the archives and found out about Cellutron. One thing in particular stopped us cold."

"What was that?"

"There was a photograph in a news story about a consultant who worked for Cellutron. It was your face in the picture. I recognized you from my dream."

"I see."

My Failure

"**S**o I was your cosmic guinea pig?"

"Don't be sarcastic," she admonishes. "You had a decisive impact on the unfolding of history and technology."

"Me? Could you be giving me too much credit?"

"On the contrary, I am not the one giving the credit. There's no other way to explain the dreams. Like it or not, Noah, you are the butterfly. Something you did must have been pivotal in some way, or maybe it was something you didn't do."

"What was it I didn't do? Was it that I didn't stop Cellutron from doing its research? I already told you, I couldn't do that. I didn't have the authority."

"There was something you were supposed to take care of."

"How was I to know?"

"By being aware of your situation. By attuning to your dreams, your inner sense of truth, the wisdom we all have inside. Evidently, you're not sensitive enough to understand context. When you worked for Cellutron, you didn't do anything to increase their awareness of their responsibility to the human race, but you were in an ideal position to have done so. They needed you for that, because they were in a state of moral confusion at the time. But you didn't. You took the easy way out."

I'm getting a clearer picture, now, of where my responsibility lies. I've been feeling very depressed about the whole thing that came out of Enoch and his computer — the judgment of my character that I was nothing but a slick snake oil salesman. I'd never seen myself that way.

But for some reason now that I see the problem more clearly,

I feel more sure of myself. I think I'm getting a grip on what I have to do.

"But don't take this too harshly," she continues. "We didn't bring you here to judge you. You're just a part of ancient history; and history, as long as it existed, was mostly a collection of tragic events. No, we need your help."

"What can I possibly do?"

My Challenge

"Listen, Noah, Isaiah and I can't change the past. But you can, because you have the opportunity to redirect the future. There was a wrong turn in what happened at Cellutron. They moved the research along too fast. The world wasn't ready. Your society didn't understand the integral perfection, the essential completeness of every person. You could mostly see only the defects in other people, right down to the genes in their bodies."

It's true. It's all coming together now, all so depressingly obvious. That's what's been wrong with my life, my attitude, everything about me. I don't know what's hit me, but I suddenly feel ill. A faintness — almost nausea —overwhelms me and I double over with my head between my knees to try to contain myself and circumvent my body's spontaneous revulsion. I'm completely bewildered, such a visceral reaction is really unlike me, but I don't have much control over it right now.

Somehow I manage to quiet my churning insides and I'm able to sit up straight again, but my head is still reeling. How am I going to know what I have to do? Am I going to have to stand up to Harry Ornath and tell him that Cellutron is off in the wrong direction? Do I sabotage the project? Raise a public outcry? What? Right now I don't feel up to the job and everything seems so depressing, so immobilizing.

I guess the point is: I can't decide what to do in the abstract.

It's no good to plan my actions here at this time. Maya said I have to be sensitive, understand the context of each situation. How I'll do that, I haven't the slightest idea, but I know that I've got to do it. I've go to do it for Maya, and for everyone else too.

Maya reaches her hand towards me and our eyes meet. Until this moment I've been able to control my feelings and seal them up inside to keep them from embarrassingly tumbling out and ruining things. But now my love surges forward and I look searchingly at her, risking everything. I see the responsiveness in her eyes. Some barrier between us is now broken.

We stand for a moment in silence, just looking into each other's eyes. Imperceptibly I feel her moving closer to me, as the tips of our extended fingers touch. I'm frightened, but here it is. This woman is so important to me that I can no longer imagine my life without her. It's not just attraction or whatever chemistry draws man and woman together. I know I'll never be able to experience myself again as a being apart from her.

Maya's breath is soft in my ear. As we touch ever so gently, she whispers, "I was looking for meaning in the most profoundly disturbing dreams of my life, and there I found you."

What is she saying? It sounds abstract and remote, but her body is pressing against mine, and like one suddenly diving into the ocean, my lips meet hers and our tongues search each other out, discovering each other for the first time and wanting to know more.

Then she breaks free and looks away. We're suddenly in a softly carpeted room strewn with rose petals and velvet cushions. I throw her gently down and we wrestle and melt together in joy in which all detail fades into ecstasy.

Hopeless Love

I must have slept again. After a time I awaken and turn my head to see the sleeping face of the most beautiful woman I have ever looked upon. I lie there transfixed by her, for some time unable to move. Gently I lift my head and lean it on my elbow, looking down on her face, wanting to kiss her, but I restrain myself.

It hits me with violence now: More than a thousand years separate the two of us. Here is the perfect woman, the love of my life, and in a very short time I will be separated from her forever. We'll never again look on one another or touch one another, because as I live, she will not have been born, and when she is born I will be a disintegrated corpse in the most distant memories of time. I want to turn off these thoughts and forget about time.

But she told me she had worked at Cellutron — whatever that means. Is she talking about a past life? — whatever that is. The whole subject of reincarnation makes me feel a bit queasy. What was it Isaiah said? It's too complex for the likes of us to understand. I can go along with that. Just dismiss the whole topic and never think about it again.

But I have to know about Maya. How can I love this woman so much? I didn't think it was in me. Like a bug picked up on a windshield and sped off course at eighty miles an hour, I don't know what hit me. How could we have come together in this strange, unfathomable way if it wasn't for the intervention of cosmic forces I know nothing about?

With a sense of urgency, yet trepidation, I decide to find out everything Maya knows. I plant a kiss on each of her eyelids. They open, to unveil the most wonderful smile that has ever greeted me.

We make love again, a little less lost in it this time, a little more consciously dedicated to each other's pleasure and the art of love.

Afterwards, we walk about the garden arm in arm, putting off the unspoken yet insistent reality that we must soon face, clinging to the moment with desperation. Then, because I have to, I turn the conversation in the inevitable direction: "Maya, I understand now why I'm here, but I don't understand about you. Why were you the one to have the dream?"

"I told you already. Because I had been at Cellutron."

"But that's exactly what I don't understand. How could you have been at Cellutron?"

"I lived back then. In a past life I was a scientist at Cellutron."

I thought I was prepared for this answer but evidently I'm not because I feel a wincing in my gut. She has confirmed it. Maya, then, is here in the future and also back in my time with me — two different dimensions of the same person.

Have I actually met her yet? I'm flooded with awareness — and with a presentiment of possibility, but of what?

Evidently my expression looks like incredulity to her, because she says, "You do believe me, don't you?"

But I can't. I'm pushing it away. I can't deal with this possibility. Too much is coming at me all at once. At the hour of destiny I recoil in disbelief from my fondest hope.

"No. I have trouble believing in past lives. I mean, how can you be sure that was really you? You go back with your mind, right? How do you know you're not just making it up, you know — imagining it?"

"You know it inside, Noah. The past is part of who you are. When you see it, you know it's true."

"But how do you see it?"

"We have a technology that augments the memory and brings it to life."

"That seems impossible. The technology would have to work with some real episode, the brain can't remember things that never happened to it."

"The memories aren't stored in our brain cells. It's not a question of material processes. Our minds transcend the limits of time and space. We can access greater wisdom than an individual lifetime can encompass. Even you can, Noah, though it seems you haven't realized this. Our souls seek outward for direction and meaning in this life, and events from the past guide us. Of course these memories are available to us."

She shifts the focus to me. "Isaiah told me that you had a past life amplification while on the space ship. How did that feel to you?"

"I don't know what you mean."

"Haven't you realized yet that the scene on London Bridge was a past life for both of us?" she says.

I feel like I've just been delivered a sucker punch. I'm like the kid who is the butt of the joke and I finally "get" it. Of course, it must be true. The whole experience felt so real when it was happening. As humiliated and shameful as it makes me feel, I've got to admit that somehow I know it's true. As Maya said, there are some things you just know. It's like the way I know that I love her. The slow-witted rational brain finally catches up with the truth that some other part of the self has long ago comprehended.

So it is with a sense of doom and horrifying destiny that I realize Maya was the witch I killed back then.

She's been following my thoughts, waiting for me to come back to her. Her face is a model of abiding love with a trace of pity.

"Oh, Maya. I don't know what to say. How can you possibly love me after that?"

"I've loved you for a very long time."

"Is that for real, or just an old fashioned sentimental notion?"

Before she can answer, I throw in a wild card: "I thought time was infinite, or that it didn't exist at all."

She laughs with delight. "That makes it all the more romantic, doesn't it?"

I suppose that's true. Do you think we've been lovers since the beginning?

"Our being together is something we must in the final analysis mutually understand. That won't be easy," she says.

"Why not? Do you think I'm too shallow?"

"No, of course not. Eternity isn't an easy concept to understand, that's all; especially if you count our lifetimes together. No,

I'm afraid the truly hard part will be what comes next. Going back
— leaving me." She says this without evident emotion.

It's like a knife in my heart.

What can I hope for? The Maya I love demands nothing less
than my actual going back. I know that. But I have no interest in
the twentieth century Maya, she's only an abstraction to me. I feel
next to nothing about this possibility.

"Maya, will I like the twentieth century woman I'm to meet?
Do you remember? Is there anything you can tell me to help me?"

Maya is evidently wrestling with this question. I can see from
her face that things won't be easy. Finally she sighs heavily. "I
don't think it's really helpful to tell you anything about her. This
time can be different. You're different now; that changes everything. I don't know what to say to you. I'll tell you one thing,
though — we're likely to be opponents on the Cellutron issue. I
was a carrier of the Effinghaus's gene. My grandfather died of it.
I wanted a cure as much as anyone possibly could."

Uncertainty upon uncertainty. Abandoned to my own devices
again. They expect so much of me, but they offer me nothing.

Not knowing what I'm doing, I back away from her and walk
off in anger. I'm trying to put as much distance between her and
me as I can. I'm in the woods now, away from the shelter and the
formal garden, and with sudden, explosive violence I strike the bark
of a tree with my fist. The pain shoots all the way up my arm to my
shoulder. My knuckles ooze blood. I wonder if, stupidly, I've broken something.

I turn then, and find her standing a few feet away from me,
looking more beautiful than ever.

I want to strike her, to drive her away, to erase this memory
forever.

But instead, I walk slowly over, look deep into her eyes, and
choosing my words very carefully, I sum up the whole situation:
"It's over isn't it. We aren't going back together and you know it.
That's how things work when they're too good to be true. It's
always that way. The moment I saw you, I felt that I'd found what
I wanted most in my life. But it's a scam. It was never given to me
in the first place. Love! What a delusion!"

I'm expecting pity from her, but it's not what I get.

"Grow up, Noah," she says.

It's not scornful. It's not angry. It's almost a statement of fact. She's deeply serious and I realize that I haven't been. I've been melodramatic, feeling sorry for myself, bathing in my own self pity. All a way, I realize, of trying to beat the rap — evade my responsibility, my life. Grow up, indeed!

"You and I are caught in a nightmare of eternity," she says. "I don't know exactly how it happened, but we're stuck in it. This is the most intense love I've ever felt for anyone, what I feel for you now."

Again I slip into self pity. I can't hold back my tears, though I really don't want to cry.

"You've been absent from my life, Noah. I've been looking for you all these years, and you're not here. I had to go back to find you. I want you here, Noah! I want you here with me. I want you to live your life back then so that maybe we can be together now. I want you to change the fabric of time so everything happens differently and you share my life now. If you fail . . . I don't know what will happen to me."

She takes a deep breath and goes on. "I'm willing to take the risk because I don't want to live without you here, don't you see that?"

I whisper, "Did you always know this?"

She shakes her head. "I knew only that I felt incomplete. I didn't know what it was that I was looking for. That was what drove me to the dream research group. I wanted to see if I could interpret dreams that no one could make sense of. I felt there must be a key in there somewhere to explain what was so evidently missing from my life."

She drops her face, and a tear rolls down her cheek.

"There was. We found the key." She looks up at me again, as if for the last time

"Yes," I reply. "I understand."

"So we're caught in this, Noah. Everything depends on how you handle the situation back then. If you do it right, perhaps we can be together here."

Then her face gets hard.

"Don't fuck it up."

At her use of that word I laugh in spite of myself. But I realize where it's coming from.

"I understand."

"This is serious, Noah. Are you going to handle it?"

"Yes!"

"Tell me again."

"Yes. Yes, yes, yes."

"Everything depends on you."

"I know."

We lie on the ground, holding each other. I find myself just begging the universe, God or whatever, to help me carry out the destiny I've come here to find. A layer of sadness hangs over me.

What bereavement is this?

Is it the death of my former self? If this is love, I've never known anything like it. Could I have been going through the motions all my life, a sleepwalker trespassing on the sanctified grounds of our origins and being?

God forgive us our willful blindness. Real love abides in all circumstances despite flaws or errors. It is the texture of the Miraculous woven into the atomic structure of all Creation, the love and blessing of the Creator, which responds intelligently to every millisecond of the existence of every virtual particle of the Universal Harmony. It forgives. It nurses back the injured spirit and guides the lost soul to find its healing. Maya and I, and the billions of brothers and sisters that make up our species, are all one and the same, crossing the lines as saints or sinners at any given moment.

When we desecrate love with inattentiveness, we lose our humanity.

Bena

I don't know what's become of the past several hours. I just couldn't lie there with Maya anymore, it was too painful. I had to get up and walk. Somehow I found my way back to the escalator and down to where I'd met Enoch. I'm looking for him, but it's a slim chance, of course. Why should he be here now?

I have to do something, though. I'm lost here, and no one is watching out for me. I don't really know when I'll have to go back, but I sense it will be soon.

Then I see someone coming that I recognize. This is Bena, the only one of my fellow travelers that I have not met here on land before. She looks just as I remember her, petite and brown skinned, like an Indian. Her looks are striking, and her eyes are a wellspring of kindness.

"How are you, my friend Noah? You look so troubled. Are you all right?"

"I'm afraid things aren't working out very well for me here in your century," I say, struggling to conceal my grief.

"Oh, really? Why not? What's wrong?"

"I've become hopelessly entangled with a woman here, a woman who will soon be forever inaccessible to me."

Bena appears not to understand this at all, but she's very pleasant about it. "I don't know if love is ever a bad thing. Maybe you shouldn't be so pessimistic."

"I wish I could believe that."

"Well, why don't you give me a chance to cheer you a little. I'd like to share with you something you can experience here which will be completely unlike anything you'll find back in your own time."

"What's that?"

"It's called the Ceremony of Emergence."

"What's it like?"

"Why discuss it? Let's go and see."

I feel her energy suffusing me and realize there's a purpose to this off-the-wall idea.

"Anyway, don't worry about Maya," she says. "What's happening with her is not what you think." I feel only slightly relieved to hear that.

"So don't worry about her right now. Just concentrate on the fact that it's a rare privilege for a person to be able to see the future and understand all that it means to the past. You're the guest of honor here because you've understood the opportunity to shape your life consciously towards what's ahead for you."

"But what about Maya? I can't do it without her."

"I know," she says, "but just now, you're doing fine. We've all seen the changes in you. You've activated a part of yourself that's never been used until now, and it's good to see. But you'll be happier in yourself if you accept the fact that things work out for the best. Meanwhile, we have to live with the ambiguities of what we cannot hope to understand."

I'm reassured to hear this. I realize that I've possibly been overdramatizing everything. Maybe I should just let go and see what's going to happen here. I have no idea how things will ultimately work out.

"What you have to understand is that humans exist on so many different levels. If you live only by your physical senses, you fall victim to fate and what appears to be random chance. The spirit looks towards the past as a bridge to the future. It cares. It learns. If you're willing to open up the spiritual being asleep inside you, you won't lose the one great love of your lifetime — that I can assure you."

"So truly advancing yourself in life means knowing less for certain, but believing in more. Is that how it is?"

"It means knowing that you don't know everything, and understanding that the direction you take depends on the questions you ask. In our time, we have no such illusions of total knowledge, though at times on your journey you may have thought we did.

Many things are inherently unknowable. The universe is in a state of infinite creation, which means it can't ever all be known. It also means that in the end we can create whatever we are truly committed to. Creation has never stopped, though people in your time think it ended with Adam and Eve or the Big Bang, depending on their personal beliefs. Either way, the basic laws of the universe are shrouded in indeterminacy. And yet, certain principles are fundamental and have infinite variability. The Laws of Resonance ground us and assure us that we can attain our highest good."

"Isaiah had a great deal to say about love and the Laws of Resonance," I reflect.

"Yes. Universal Love is expressed in them. That is why they were so difficult for the scientists of your time to comprehend, because they could not understand Love at all, and thought the universe was a dead thing, made of lifeless atoms somehow magically producing life. It's an absurd notion, particularly when you know that love is the fabric out of which the universe is built, and that it infuses the tiniest particles from which everything else is supposedly formed. Whenever you feel the Laws of Resonance operating, you have the sense that you're in touch with love. You feel it when you look at art, listen to music, or sit quietly by a lake in the middle of a forest, sensing the elegance of all that's happening. Love is the creative force that produces everything and makes it redeemable. Love has to be more than a sentimental impulse or sexual drive. It has to perform a marriage between the physical and the spiritual flow of inspiration from our creative source.

"In your day, that sort of Love was seldom understood by anyone, even the most imaginative among you. Most people overemphasized the physical. Some went too far in the other direction, denying its value. All of it is important. That's where balance comes in between our physical movement through space and the dynamics of the spirit.

"But I came to invite you to a festive entertainment. Let's go."

She smiles as I take her hand and immediately I find myself in a sort of opera house, the one I viewed from the outside while I was with Enoch. Bena and I sit on red velvet seats. On-stage an enormous performance is taking place, a ballet with perhaps a thousand or more people dancing in perfect coordination. It's a breathtaking sight, like one of those Renaissance paintings depicting some historic or Biblical event. An orchestra accompanies the ballet, but there is no conductor, and soon I notice there is no sheet music either. The orchestra and dancers know their parts perfectly

"This is incredible!" I whisper.

"Oh, it is. It never stops. It goes on twenty-four hours a day every day all year long. You should see it on New Year's Eve! What a spectacle: five thousand people on-stage, flashing from one scene to the next with the countdown to midnight."

"I see some dancers leave and others come in to take their places. What does that mean?"

"The performers come and go as they please, and anyone can join in the dance at any time."

"I've never been a good dancer," I confess.

"You don't need to be. You can find a partner any time, if that's what you wish.

"How is it possible for this dance to look so carefully rehearsed as to produce this impeccable performance with people coming and going?" I ask.

"They've had no rehearsals," she says. "It's all improvised. None of it — sets, costumes, lighting, the movements themselves — has ever happened before."

The Ballet of Human Consciousness

"By dancing together in this intricate performance, people harmonize their relationships. They develop an understanding of each other. The dance itself is an act of love and exchange of energy which has been perfected over time. It's also a form of meditation," she says. "We use it to train our bodies and minds to flow from a common energy source. It's a high art form. Some spend hours every day in it."

"Does anyone not participate?"

"Those who dance less often are usually on the periphery of the action and those who spend the most time take leading roles. Something magical happens when they take the stage. The spirit of improvisation is instilled, instantly. There is no awkwardness. The group spirit pulls everyone along. The energy becomes so powerful no one can resist it."

"I could never learn to do it," I observe.

"'Never' is a big word, Noah," she says. "You have to trust the Laws of Resonance in this."

Bena smiles.

"There's more to it than that. When patterns of energy become well established, disruption of them is practically impossible. We owe the continuity of our personalities, our mental images, our languages and our lives to that. Many things that were mysterious in your time are well understood in ours, since we have discovered those laws and found out how to locate the equalization of forces that allow us to achieve balance. But let's not sit here and talk about it, let's do it. Come along, give it a try."

Before I know what's happening, Bena entangles her fingers in mine and leads me on-stage and into the dance. A total neophyte, I am now part of the action. People are watching me! I've had no rehearsal! I've had nightmares like this!

In a split second, a surprising calm flows through me. I'm not frightened anymore. I feel the energy flowing within me, like a water faucet that's just been turned on. Perhaps it's coming through Bena's hands. My body moves to the music entirely on its own, without any effort from me. I wonder if I could stop, but I feel no impulse to do so. I want to dance. Me!

In a dazzling moment of insight I understand that it's not I who originate the movement. There's a force inside me I never suspected I had. I'm merely the conduit. By some miracle I am guided in my movements, as if the dance is dancing me, and not the other way around. I surrender myself to the Love flowing through me, and night passes as I dance through many scenes to the most beautiful music I've ever heard.

After hours of this I become very tired, though it's a well earned and satisfying fatigue. Bena guides me outside where I find a quiet place to sleep.

Departure

I awaken from a beautiful dream. I feel the sensation of a cord stretching out from my solar plexus into the center of the universe. As energy flows in through that cord, it exits through the top of my head and I feel connected to All That Is.

I know that I am ready to return to my own time and do what I have been asked. I sense the power that I will take with me, a quiet power that listens and supports, but does not settle for any compromise with my integrity and being. I also know with an understanding I cannot account for that in holding to my integrity I will be serving others better than I could serve them in any other way. For the benefits they seek will soon be found not in the dishonorable tactics to which they have too often stooped, but only in the genuine service of those with whom and for whom they work, their communities, and ultimately of humanity and the earth as a whole. It seems counter-intuitive, perhaps, but I know that it is so.

My thoughts return, then, to Maya whom I must leave. Yet now I know that all will be well. I don't know how it will happen or why it is, but I know that it is so.

And with this thought I see her coming towards me across the field, with Isaiah following some distance behind.

I rise and stand facing her, welcoming her. We embrace, and for a long moment we say nothing, simply looking into each other's eyes.

Then she says, "You are ready, aren't you, Noah?"

I nod my yes to her.

"We'll meet back there."

A chill runs through me.

"Remember that everything has possibility, especially in the mind of God. Think about the past. Things could have happened differently for you, but they didn't."

"I know that for a fact. What should have been avoided but was not, up till now, has shaped my life."

"Once events happen, they seem forever set in time, but the future is open to infinite possibility. Our exercise of free will is not to disrupt the entire course of time, but to arrange things in our own little corner to make the world a better place."

"Cultivate your own garden?" I ask, thinking of Candide. "Is that what you're talking about?"

"Yes, that's right."

"But how does my garden fit into the larger scheme of the universe? I've seen lots of people do the morally right thing, but it doesn't seem to make any difference."

"Oh, it's all bound together. You'll see. All humans are bound together. You and I are one and the same and nothing separates us except our ego consciousness. I want things to turn out differently between us this time than they would have if we hadn't brought you here. So you've got to go back."

She clings to me as she utters these words, kissing me, seeming to feel as intensely as I do the pain of separation.

"You'll find me," she continues. "That's all I can tell you, though. That's all I know."

"It's true," I say. "I am free now to shape my life the way it must go."

Yet despite these words, I feel the deepest sorrow of my life in what I know will happen in a moment. Standing in front of her, still able to touch her like this, I already long for her beyond the boundaries of any feeling I have known. With the awareness that barely an instant is left to us, I am utterly lost in pain.

"You must find me back there! Everything depends on your doing that, don't you see?"

I place my fingers gently over her lips to stop her speech. Suddenly I have become master of the situation. I know what I must do, and I intend to accomplish it.

She pulls a ring from her finger. "This is an emerald," she says.

"It is beautiful."

"Take it in remembrance of me."

As she says these words and I feel the warmth of the ring radiating into my finger, I see the new hope and trust in her expression. And then she gives me one last kiss. I hold her to me so tightly it feels as if our bodies must crush one another; but then we let go, as Isaiah, with a firm grasp on my shoulder, pulls me slowly, ever so gently, away from her.

"It's time for us to go. We've calculated the exact point of trespass and we can have you back in your bedroom anytime you say the word."

"You have been an excellent teacher," I tell him.

"We've learned from each other," he says. "Are you ready?"

"I'll never forget you," I promise.

"Not completely," he replies. Slowly I watch as he dematerializes into brilliant particles of light.

Home Again

The next moment I find myself once again alone with my teacher in the same room that is not a room in which I first awakened to my new life outside of the earth's atmosphere. I recall that moment when I so wonderingly laid eyes on this man who has come to mean so much to me.

I recognize it will be a long time before I get over the grief of separation from Maya — grief that I am even now just beginning to taste in the full force of its dullness, its sameness, its grayness. I anticipate the long stretch of time during which I shall know only an empty longing before something new begins to delineate its way into my life.

As I look into his face for what I know will be the last time, I try to etch it into my memory. Here, but for Maya, is the most loving personality I have ever experienced. I will miss him more deeply than I can fathom.

But it is not as if he were dying, for he remains out there in the future, more than a thousand years distant from my time. In a sense it is I who am dying, for as I return to my own period, I become for him a distant echo in the past of one person who walked the Earth for a time and then was heard from no more.

We are poised in that moment of final parting, Isaiah and I. I know he is sorry to see the last of me, but I also know that we can never be reunited. For my mission now is to live in my world according to the new insights that I bring with me, and it is not for him to interrupt that process in whatever way I choose to exercise it. Still, I want to savor the moment of our separation as long as I still can, after having been taken so abruptly from Maya.

"What's next for you?" I want to know.

"Ah, I shudder to think of it," he says. "It will take years of research and meditation before I am ready. Compared to that, this experiment of ours was child's play."

"You never told me," I say, "how it is that you are connected with the Isaiah in the Bible."

"There were several of them, of course," he says.

"That doesn't answer my question."

"Right now there is no answer."

"And —?"

"I must build one. It's the most delicate operation you can imagine. This, with you, was a sort of rehearsal for it."

"But what happens if you mess it up?"

He thinks for a long moment, and then says, "Well, in that case it may astonishingly turn out to have been true that the universe itself has never existed."

I don't know what to make of that one. I just gawk at him.

"Don't worry, though," he says with a parting smile. "I won't mess it up."

His warm, affectionate smile fades, and an instant later it is four in the morning on the day that I left, and I am looking up at my bedroom window from the shadows of the moonlight upon the lawn, trying to make out my own now invisible form as a short while before it looked down at the garden. Between those two selves, the one looking out from the window and the one that now stands looking up at it, lies perhaps a half hour of elapsed time in the physical realm — and a thousand years of experience in the continents of my soul.

I am once again covered by the towel I wrapped around me when I came out of my bathroom. I stand there for a few more moments, letting it all sink in, feeling the gulf that separates those two instants of my life, so close together in one sense in the time in which I stand here now, and so monumentally separated as I feel them to be by looking back on the vision I have been granted, by some miracle of cosmic Resonance.

Then I look into the one talisman I have brought back with me — Maya's emerald ring. In the dimmest light of dawn I imagine I see her face in it. What about the other face of Maya? Today, I realize, I shall probably meet her. I am ready for that moment, a few hours from now, when we shall meet to consider how we can revise the possibilities for the fate of our love and our world.

NOTES ON THE SCIENCE IN THIS BOOK

Readers interested in looking into the scientific research underpinning many of the arguments in the discussion between Noah and Isaiah will find the following books useful. They are all written by professionals in their fields, and some of them take their arguments much farther than we have taken them in our book. Some are controversial within their fields, but none are without foundation.

The Conscious Universe by Menas Kafatos and Robert Nadeau (New York, Springer-Verlag, 1990). This book deals with the dialogue between science and religion on a purely scientific basis. In it you'll find discussions of the following: the debate between Einstein and Bohr over the indeterminacy principle, Einstein's rejection of the indeterminacy principle and much of quantum theory, and Einstein's essentially classical, or Newtonian position. In addition, the principle of non-locality in quantum physics is extensively discussed, in general, and in reference to the photon experiment Isaiah refers to and the Schroedinger's cat paradox.

The Undivided Universe by D. Bohm and B. J. Hiley (London, Routledge, 1993). A relatively recent statement of David Bohm's ideas about the enfolded universe. Here you'll find the basis for speculations that our minds are all one and are enfolded into matter in a background of pre-space in which time, space, matter and mind all become one and inseparable. This is an extension of the non-locality established in quantum theory into a paradigm which holds up under mathematical analysis and asserts that consciousness is universal and all human minds are part of it and inseparable from the entire universe.

The Matter Myth by Paul Davies and John Gribbin (New York, Simon and Schuster, 1992). In John Wheeler's terms, "matter is relegated to mind" and the universe is an information processing system. In this book we see how all solidity disappears into wave motion in the basic structure of the universe. We also see how time disappears at the speed of light and how the universe arises from the quantum uncertainty principle.

The Philosophical Scientists by David Foster (New York, Barnes and Noble, 1993). The universe is mind stuff and works as a thought process. Statistical analysis reveals that life cannot have arisen by chance. Here is perhaps the best survey of ideas which call into question the basic materialistic assumptions of our time.

The Collapse of Chaos by Jack Cohen and Ian Stewart (New York, Viking, 1994). A biologist and a statistician collaborate to call into question many of the most basic assumptions of biologists, showing that it is almost impossible to believe that DNA is a "blueprint" for life.

The Origin of Consciousness in the Break-Down of the Bicameral Mind by Julian Jaynes (Boston, Houghton-Mifflin, 1976). A fascinating exploration of the evolution of relationships between the "natural" mind and the "rational" mind, relationships which recent split-brain research has begun to clarify in the terms described in our novel.

EMDR by Francine Shapiro (New York, Basic Books, 1997). The theory behind the emotional desensitizing process using eye movements we've described in one of our chapters. This book is for the general reader. The book for therapists is called ***Eye Movement Desensitization and Reprocessing: Basic Principles, Protocols and Procedures*** (New York, Guilford 1995). If you want to do the process, however you'll have to review our description of it, since neither book offers that information.

Blueprint for Immortality, The Electric Patterns of Life by Harold Saxton-Burr (London, Neville Spearman, 1972). This member of the faculty of the Yale University School of Medicine did pioneering work measuring the electrical "fields of life" that surround living organisms. His work is similar to the more famous work of plant physiologist Rupert Sheldrake and he is one of several scientists who have described the way fields extending out from the body perform many essential life functions.

An Experiment with Time by J. W. Dunne (London, Faber and Faber, third edition, 1934, originally published, 1927). A detailed account of research showing that half of our dreams that refer to real events forecast the future. This edition contains a note of confirmation of the main concept by Sir Arthur Eddington.

"On Dream Theory in Malaya" by Kilton Stewart in ***Altered States of Consciousness*** edited by Charles Tart (New York, Wiley, 1972). This anthropological study has given rise to a great deal of discussion about the lives of the Senoi in the context of a more general discussion of the dream theories of peoples who live close to nature.

The Dreaming Universe by Fed Alan Wolf (New York, Simon and Schuster, 1994). A theoretical physicist links dreams with quantum physics in order to show how the universe creates reality by dreaming.

ABOUT THE AUTHORS

Peter Kline, an independent educational consultant, has been introducing the dynamics of learning to an ever-growing audience of business and educational institutions. An exponent of innovative, highly successful educational and organizational practices, Kline has pioneered methods that accelerate learning and bring involvement and creativity to the classroom and the workplace. He is the author of several books on the theater and several books on education, including two widely popular titles, *The Everyday Genius*, and *Ten Steps To A Learning Organization*. He is the creator of a highly innovative program for teaching Reading through phonemic recognition. His books have been published in seven languages. Mr. Kline has appeared on numerous TV and radio programs, and has been the subject of a variety of profiles and studies.

The Butterfly Dreams explores the terrain at the intersection of Religion and Science, a subject informed by Mr. Kline's many years as a science educator and his independent religious and philosophical study. Mr. Kline is also co-author of a forthcoming book about creativity called *The Genesis Principle* and working on a second novel with his wife Syril Kline. He resides with his family in South Bend, Indiana.

Syril Kline is a staff writer for *The South Bend Tribune*. She resolves consumer problems in her thrice weekly column, *Action Line*, and reports on theater and the arts in the Tribune's entertainment pages.

Syril Kline is a frequent cantorial soloist at congregation Temple Beth-El in South Bend, Indiana, and she has performed with and directed several community theater groups. She is listed in Marquis' Who's Who in Entertainment, Who's Who in American Women, and in International Women's Who's Who.

Ms. Kline is currently at work on a second novel with her husband Peter Kline on the identity of the real William Shakespeare. She lives in South Bend, Indiana and has two sons, Seth and Jonathan, one dog, and two cats.